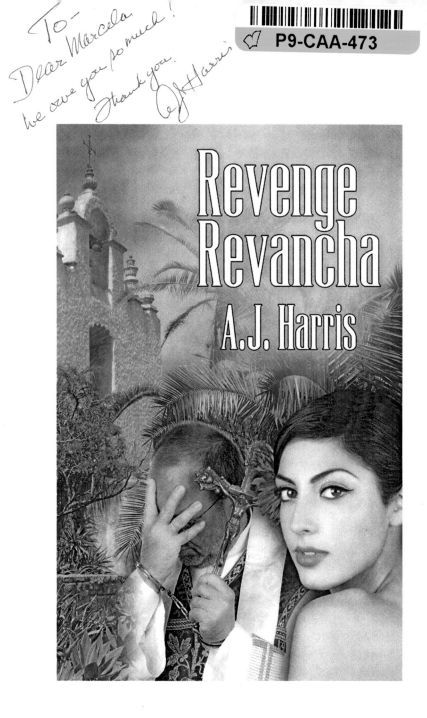

Revenge
Revancha

A.J. Harris

ISBN   978-0-9847825-4-3 (paperback)
         978-0-9847825-5-0 (ebook)

Published by Murder Mystery Press
www.murdermysterypress.com
Murder Mystery Press
Santa Barbara, California

Author: A.J. Harris, M.D.
Book Shepherd: Mark E. Anderson, www.aquazebra.com
Editor: Geoff Aggeler
Author photo: Mark Davidson
www.markdavidsonphotography.com
Cover/interior design:
Mark E. Anderson, www.aquazebra.com

AquaZebra™
Web, Book & Print Design

Library of Congress Control Number: 2014950461

Disclaimer

The novel tells of events following World War II where historical facts have been interwoven into fictitious situations. Any similarities to living characters are strictly coincidental and unintentional. Information gained from bona fide sources has been interpreted by the author and any errors are his alone.

Printed in the United States of America

Acknowledgments

The author is grateful to the following people who have given their expertise to the manuscript: Dr. Robert Baum, Dr. Helen Gordon, Dr.Ted Delotta, Pastor Harry Dutt, Felice Karmen, Joan Marks, Muriel Schloss, Laura Smith, Rita Weinberg , Dr. Johanna Yinger, Lois Allison and Lee Buckmaster. Special thanks are due the Santa Barbara Sheriff's Department. Their cooperation and kindness exceeded my expectations. My gratitude goes to Deputy Greg Sorenson for his personal interest. Michael Redmon, Director of Research of the Santa Barbara Historical Museum was an incredible source of background material.

To my editor, Dr. Geoff Aggeler, I'm deeply indebted for his many criticisms and suggestions. My gratitude to Mark Anderson, my book shepherd, can hardly be measured for his accomplishment in arranging the form, appearance and chapters into a neat and tidy volume and for the tantalizing cover.

Lastly, but most importantly, to my devoted wife, Yetta, who has continued giving encouragement, criticisms and suggestions.

Dedication

Dedicated to freedom fighters everywhere and their never-ending battle against tyranny.

Chapter 1

Señora Juanita Castillo Montenegro sat in a peignoir admiring her image in a vanity with three mirrors. She moved the side mirrors to get a better view of her long black silky hair as she brushed with caressing strokes.

She leaned inward and adjusted the side lamp to study her complexion. The pores seemed larger and the lines around her mouth deeper—those crow's feet were becoming more noticeable. The fine hairs of a mustache needed more frequent attention. She sighed and thought those changes annoying but permissible in a fifty-year-old woman who as an urchin had clawed her way out of the dung heaps outside Barcelona.

Staring into the mirror, she thought, *I'm still quite attractive.* Opening her peignoir to expose her breasts, she cupped and pushed them upward and inward to produce a deeper cleavage. She smiled knowing she could get that effect with her bra.

Leaning further into the mirror, she applied a black mascara dot to her right cheek creating a beauty mark. *Ah, so chic. If my lover could see me now, would he appreciate me? I think so.*

As she applied lipstick, her peripheral vision caught a movement.

She called out, "Is that you...?" A brilliant flash of light, a deafening report... silence and eternity claimed the mortal soul of Señora Juanita Castillo Montenegro as she slumped forward.

Chapter 2

At 8:08 a.m. the following morning, Sergeant Fernando Raul Amado, known as Fred or Freddie to his fellow officers, sat next to Deputy Bill Connors who drove the sheriff department's new unmarked 1951 Ford sedan. The driver, recently assigned to homicide, glanced at Amado. "What's your take on this murder, Amado?"

Before the sergeant could respond, the deputy continued, "Man, this is front page stuff. I can see the headlines now." He brought his hand across the width of the windshield. *Wealthy Widow Gunned Down In Montecito Estate.* With mounting enthusiasm, he went on: *Police Hot On Killer's Trail.* He jabbed at the steering wheel. "Damn! Think they'll mention our names? My little sweetheart would be impressed...maybe reward me with an extra trick or two." He elbowed Amado and winked.

Amado wound down his window and reached for a cigarette in his jacket pocket. "Careful what you wish for, Billy Boy. That kind of publicity doesn't do any damn good. If you're stupid enough to say the killer will be caught soon, they'll hold you to it. When you don't have the sonofabitch behind bars in twenty-four hours, they'll think you screwed up. Happens every time."

The deputy nodded. "I suppose you're right. How do you handle reporters?"

"Best to avoid them. When I can't, I give them some cock'n bull story. Makes no difference most of the time. They'll print what they want, anyway."

They turned onto East Valley Road, then onto a narrow meandering two-lane road bordered by native brush. Large estates were partially or totally obscured by tall plantings or high concrete walls and often occupied several acres. Fred Amado checked the address on his pocket-sized memo pad and signaled the deputy to turn into the next driveway on the right. "Here it is, Casa del Caudillo."

"Who discovered the body?" Connors asked.

"The maid. Dispatcher said she screamed into the phone... had trouble understanding her at first."

Connors looked at the street sign, *Montenegro Court*. "Nice touch having your name on a city street sign. How does one rate that?"

"Señora Montenegro is, or was, a philanthropic dueña, a land owner who donated a large tract of land. City turned it into a park for kids."

"How do you know all that?"

"Listen, I'm a pure seventh generation Latino in this county. My family tree is straight Spanish except for an Anglo grandmother and a mestizo father. I know all about important residents of Spanish and Mexican origin around here. So happens, my uncle was Leo Carrillo's side-kick and stunt man in those Hollywood westerns, and when Carrillo was Pancho on *The Cisco Kid*."

"Holy shit! Leo Carrillo? Boy, that's something."

Connors turned into a serpentine driveway leading to the estate. At an acute turn bordered by a wall of bushes about eight feet high, Amado noted damage at the bases of several plants with torn foliage strewn on the ground.

"Someone missed the turn here...probably in a hurry to get to or out of this place," Amado said. Suddenly, looming before them, was a sprawling two-story Moorish-style building with arches outlined with colorful tile accents. The early morning sun reflected off the white-washed walls that seemed to glitter.

"This is some spread," Connors said, emerging from the vehicle. "Look at all the iron work around the windows, even on the second floor. Jeez, that ought to discourage any break ins."

"Or break outs. Those fancy iron bars are *rejas*. You see them on old Spanish villas." Maybe because he was there to investigate a murder, Amado was struck by an air of menace emanating from the mansion. In spite of the early morning sun on the surrounding walls, it was gloomy, like the brooding fortress of some cruel tyrant, its thick adobe walls and ironwork fashioned to repel intruders with no hint of welcoming. The grounds were impeccably maintained but laid out so as to discourage casual strolling. Amado noted that everything about the place was threating. A sign on the gate with a silhouette of a lunging German shepherd read, *I can make it to the fence in five seconds. Can you?*

"This place is creepy. It looks like one big mausoleum. I swear I can smell death around here," Connors said.

A red-brick clearing before a six-car garage revealed two sheriff's cars and two civilian-type sedans. "Jeez, the driveway's loaded with cars. We're probably the last ones to be notified," Connors said. "There's the deputy coroner getting out of his car. Kinda unusual for him to be coming to the murder scene, isn't it?"

"It's a high profile case...good for public relations. The newsmen will quote him in the evening edition. Let's follow him in," Amado said.

A deputy stationed at the entrance acknowledged the coroner and the two detectives. Amado confronted him. "Who in the hell is in there?"

"Three deputies, besides me, and a couple newspaper men..."

"Newspapermen? Goddamit! Why didn't they just sell admission tickets and let the whole damn town in?" Amado snarled at the cowed deputy. "Don't you allow anyone else in here."

"Wasn't my decision, Sarge."

Another deputy standing at the foot of a circular staircase, at the far end of the living room, directed the men to the bedroom suite upstairs. Taking two stairs at a time, Amado raced upward, Connors followed. Framed in the doorway, Amado stopped and placed his hands on his hips. Red-faced, he growled, at the news and camera men. "All right, everyone not involved with this case get the hell out of here. You know damned well you're not supposed to be here." The newsmen grumbled but gathered their paraphernalia and left.

A woman holding a lacy handkerchief to her teary red eyes approached Amado. "Did you want me to leave also? I would prefer to stay. May I?"

Still seething, Amado said, "Who are you?"

"I'm Isabella Chavez, the deceased Señora's secretary and confidante." Amado guessed that she was in her twenties, thought she was somewhat attractive, and caught the hint of an accent, probably Spanish, like her name. "Forgive me. I cannot believe this has happened to my dear, dear, Señora."

Amado's gruffness subsided. "I'm sorry about that." He paused. "You can stay, but don't touch anything. After I talk with the coroner, I'd like a few words with you."

James Peters, the coroner, leaned over the murdered woman and with gloved hands separated the blood-sticky hairs covering the entry wound in the right occipital area.

Amado in a near whisper into the coroner's ear, said, "Jim, what're you thinking? How long has she been dead?"

The coroner bent forward to view the victim's face. "No rigor mortis. Slight facial lividity. I'd say at least eight to twelve hours." He looked around the immediate area. "I don't see any other bullet holes. Looks like a well-placed single bullet. Shooter was nearby. Small missile. Maybe a .22 or .25 caliber." Turning the victim's head to examine the face more completely, he said, "Bullet found its way near the back of the left eye, pushed it partially out of the optic foramen… not pretty."

After edging toward the body, the secretary craned her

neck to look, then gasped at the sight of the grotesquely deformed face. "Oh, my God!" She crossed herself, brought her hands to her face and left the room hurriedly.

The coroner's men arrived with a gurney. The coroner covered the body with a sheet. Amado stopped him. "Wait, there's something in her pocket." He removed a folded slip of paper.

"What's on it, Fred?" Connors asked.

"A couple phone numbers." He put the paper in his pocket, then signaled the coroner's men to remove the corpse.

"I'll be doing an autopsy," the coroner said, "even though the cause of death is obvious." Amado nodded then waved the coroner's men off.

Amado pushed the lid of his fedora up with his fore-finger then plunged his hands into his pockets and looked around the spacious room. Leaning over the three-mirrored vanity dresser, he sniffed the perfume atomizer and exam-ined the round open Coty powder box. On the upholstered dresser bench several drops of blood had coagulated.

Connors asked, "What're you thinking, Fred?"

"How in the hell does someone get off a shot so close to the back of the head without an apparent struggle?"

"Could have been a struggle, we just don't know. Whoever it was, might have snuck up, pulled the trigger. Simple as that," Connors said.

"Yeah, maybe. How about a person familiar to the victim, standing behind her talking, helping her to adjust her hair..."

"You mean like a hairdresser, a maid, maybe a ..." Connors didn't finish, letting Amado complete his thoughts. He knew Amado became taciturn when processing informa-tion. Occasionally Amado jotted something in his notebook. Connors watched as Fred Amado walked toward the bedroom door, then turned and walked back to the vanity dresser.

He said, "Bill, sit at the vanity and look straight into the mirror as though you're applying makeup. Don't laugh, I'm serious. Stare at the pimple on your nose. I'm going to come through the bedroom door and walk toward you. Tell me at what point you realize I'm behind you."

Connors sat at the vanity bench, careful to avoid the blood spots, leaned forward stared into the mirror. As Amado approached within two to three feet, Connors shouted, "Now!"

"Yeah, that's what I thought. Someone could have been practically on top of her before she knew it."

Both men left the bedroom and walked down the curved staircase. At the foot of the stairs, Miss Chavez and three members of the household staff waited for some word from the detectives. Fred Amado spoke to Miss Chavez while the anxious household staff looked on. "We'd like to talk to you, alone. Can we go somewhere where we won't be disturbed?"

"Now?" She asked, visibly annoyed.

"Now."

Miss Chavez sighed and shook her head. "Detective, I'd like to accommodate you, but quite frankly I'm too upset to answer questions and there is so much I must attend to..."

Amado, unaccustomed to being dismissed by persons he was questioning, was about to insist but remembered his chief's advice: 'be discreet and respectful when dealing with people in this affluent community who expect to be treated with deference.' So he responded politely. "I understand, ma'am. Would you answer just one or two questions?"

Before she could respond, he moved her away from the others and in a near-whisper asked, "Do you know if Mrs. Montenegro felt threatened by anyone? Can you think of anyone who might have wanted to kill her?"

She shook her head, walked away, then turned around to face the detective. "Of course not. Please, no more questions now." She ordered the house staff members to return to their duties.

"Don't let anyone in the room where the murder occurred," Amado said. "That's an order." He intended to sound officious after that rebuke by Miss Chavez whose tone seemed to diminish the importance of the law's presence.

Amado cleared his throat and walked after her. "Pardon me Miss, this is my card. Please make time to answer a few questions tomorrow in my office at the sheriff's station in Santa Barbara at 10:00 a.m."

Miss Chavez, irritated, looked at the card and then at him. "I really can't. I have..."

He interrupted. "Listen, Miss, if I get a court order and have a couple deputies escort you to a patrol wagon..." He had no authority to do that since he was not charging her with murder, but the threat had the desired effect.

She raised her head defiantly. "That won't be necessary." Turning her back to him, she walked to the front door and held it open. "Is there anything else, detective? If not, please excuse me, I have too many things to do."

"I'd like the names of the house staff, their addresses and phone numbers tomorrow."

Miss Chavez said nothing more and held the entry door open signaling the detectives to leave.

"The crime scene techs will be coming in soon, they'll be dusting for fingerprints and taking pictures," Amado said.

Detective Connors walked out, but Amado remained behind, moving deliberately until he stopped to look around. He scanned the enormous living room then focused on a life-sized portrait above the Steinway grand. General Francisco Franco in full military regalia stood next to a poised and attractive young woman who sat with a kind of enigmatic smile.

Miss Chavez, impatient said, "Detective, is there something else?"

"Yeah." He pointed to the painting. "That woman with the general—is that...?"

"That was my blessed Señora."

"I see. I won't take more of your time. Tomorrow morning at 10:00."

"Yes, yes. Now goodbye."

Chapter 3

Santa Barbara, like other southern California cities, benefited from its salutary climate and grew during the post-war period. However, old established public buildings and government facilities did not change as did those of their counterparts in San Francisco to the north and Los Angeles to the south. Streets shaded by trees, buildings of old Spanish-colonial architecture, and well-maintained lawns with flowers and fountains gave the city its charm. Residents with unwavering loyalty defended and promoted its centuries old traditions and customs and fiercely resisted any development that would alter its character.

The elegant 1931 Hispano-Suissa limousine stopped at the Santa Barbara sheriff's station at Figueroa and Anacapa. The chauffeur hurried to open the rear door and offered his hand to assist Miss Chavez.

She looked at her pendant watch. "I shouldn't be detained more than thirty minutes. Be here at 10:30."

The chauffeur tipped the visor of his hat. "Yes, ma'am."

Whether it was the stately automobile with the uniformed chauffeur or the arresting appearance of a smartly-attired woman, several pedestrians stopped to stare. Even in this town of affluence and old money, her arrival warranted a second glance.

A young deputy escorted Miss Chavez along the long broad marble hallway to the office of Sergeant Fred Amado. The staccato clicking of her heels reverberated in the cavernous hall. The deputy knocked once, then opened the door. As Miss Chavez entered, Amado stood. He had been prepared for a confrontational meeting, but his stern expression turned to an easy smile as she lifted her black veil, smiled and extended a gloved hand.

A remarkable transition had occurred in the appearance of this woman in the last twenty-four hours. When Amado saw her last, she appeared mournful, teary-eyed, and resentful. Now she was composed and pleasant.

Her beauty startled Amado, who stood with drop-jaw disbelief. Every one of her features was tantalizingly perfect. Her topaz-colored eyes enhanced by eye shadow, her full and sensuous lips and smile of pearly teeth immobilized him. He stammered, "I...that is..."

Chavez, accustomed to this type of reaction by men greeting her for the first time, spoke softly with a cultured voice that hinted of continental origins. "Detective, I owe you my sincerest apology. I was rude and disrespectful yesterday. My grief then, and even now, is overwhelming. However, the initial shock has subsided somewhat, and I am better able to reconcile my loss. You do understand, I'm sure."

"Yes, yes, of course," fumbling for words, Amado, attempted to sound contrite and almost apologetic for inconveniencing her. "Is there anything I can get for you? Water? Coffee? A soft drink perhaps?"

"Thank you, nothing."

"Just a few questions, Miss Chavez. I asked you yesterday if Mrs. Montenegro had any enemies. Do you know if she was involved in any business transactions where she or her estate demanded money? Did anyone owe her large sums?"

She reflected for a moment, then shook her head. "Not that I am aware."

Amado continued, "Forgive my bluntness, but had she been

seeing anyone? Anyone who might have been a jealous lover?"

Again, Miss Chavez shook her head.

"To your knowledge, Miss Chavez..." Before completing his question Fred Amado walked around his desk and stood next to her as she sat with her legs crossed exposing well-shaped knees and legs. He breathed in the delicate fragrance of her perfume. She eyed him curiously as he continued, "Are there relatives who will inherit the estate? We're obviously talking *mucho dinero* here." He smiled thinking the comment clever.

Miss Chavez looked up at him. "She had relatives in Los Angeles, a nephew and a niece at UCLA. No one else that I know."

"Could you give me their names, addresses and phone numbers? Were they close to their aunt? Did they visit often? Were they her relatives or her husband's?"

She sighed. "Detective, so many questions. I've forgotten some already."

"Sorry. I'll go slower." He walked behind her and looked at her neatly coiffed brunette hair, a pageboy that reached shoulder length.

"The house staff—anyone there have a reason to murder...?"

"No, of course not," she snapped, obviously irritated by the question.

"Would you give me their names and addresses?"

"Not off the top of my head, Detective, all that takes time. I can't possibly give you that information here. There are full-time employees who live on the estate and part-timers who come in from outlying areas."

"I can appreciate that. How many workers all together?"

"In the summer when the foliage grows rapidly and the fruit trees need harvesting ...perhaps ten to fourteen."

Fred returned to his desk as the phone rang. It was an urgent message. "Please forgive me, Miss Chavez, there's been a shooting and murder at one of the local liquor stores. Can we meet when we're not pressed for time, when I'm off duty and you can get away? Maybe we can go over a few details while enjoying some refreshments."

Chavez pursed her lips, tugged at the hem of her dress and stood while Amado reached for his jacket on the back of his chair. She regarded him quizzically and replied, "Detective, I hardly know you, and I'm not sure that what you're suggesting is entirely proper."

"Sorry if I gave you the wrong impression. I was merely thinking we could have a sort of quasi-business affair."

Her large eyes widened. She looked askance. "That word *affair* concerns me."

Amado smiled then laughed. "Give it an innocent interpretation. Can I suggest an after hour's drink at Charlie Chaplin's place? You know, the Montecito Inn?"

"I'm not sure, I..."

"Please find the time, or I'll park myself at the hacienda and start rummaging through..."

She held up her hand, then opened her handbag and gave him her business card. "Call me at this number after seven tomorrow evening."

"Thanks. Look forward to the meeting." Fred hurried to open the office door then watched as she ambled down the hallway. Her snug-fitting dress outlined contours which formed a delectable figure eight. Had she looked back, she would have seen his warm appraising smile.

In the six years he had been on the force, there had been an occasional liaison, but he had never met anyone with whom he might want a relationship. Not until now.

Chapter 4

The droning voices at the bar of the Montecito Hotel were pierced by bursts of laughter and loud talk. Fred and Isabella at a small cocktail table waited for their orders to be taken.

Amado was captivated by Isabella's incredible beauty. Her dark hair framed an oval face of alabaster skin; her haunting topaz blue eyes seemed to dance with excitement. She wore a white blouse with a string of pearls that enhanced her delicate swan-like neck. A white linen skirt seemed molded to her hips and thighs.

He bent his head toward her and said, "Forgive me, if I appear to be staring, but I enjoy just looking at you." He looked around and said, "Trouble is, I can't hear a word you're saying above this damn noise. Would you mind if we left and found a quieter place?"

"Detective, I..."

"Call me Fred. Mind if I call you Isabella?"

"Yes, if you wish."

"What did your señora call you?"

She smiled. "She called me by a number of endearing names: Mi Dulce, Mi Corazon, Mi Querida."

Fred nodded. "I should remember one or two of those names."

"No, no. You cannot call me by any of those names."

"Why?"

"They are much too personal and too intimate."

"I'd like to be personal and intimate—with you."

She put her hand to her mouth to conceal a smile and looked away.

Amado offered his arm as they walked toward the exit, but she did not accept it. He held the door open for her. Outside she breathed a sigh in the clear, quiet evening air. They walked without talking toward his car in the parking area. He held the car door open until she settled in.

"Thank you," she said and smiled.

With that, he felt relief. Clearly, she was not offended by his flirtatious manner or anything he had said. He knew he was capable of turning a woman off by coming on to her in a tactless, insensitive way, saying something he would instantly regret. Too much time had passed since his last date, when he had managed to anger a woman who refused to see him again. Now he was not about to let it happen with this very special creature, one who personified elegance, style, and filled her clothes just right. Even his madre would approve of her.

"Sorry about the tumult back there, I should have known... look, it's early, how about a drink at the Miramar lounge. I know the bartender, Joey, who gives me special treatment."

"Lead the way, kind sir," she said.

The crowd at the Miramar bar was less noisy but intrusive enough to interfere with normal conversation. Amado leaned across the small cocktail table to hear Isabella's soft voice. A candle from the small glass chimney on the table cast a subdued light on her exquisite features. Emboldened by his Martini, Amado reached across the table to touch her hands that held a glass of Cabernet when the table shook.

"Hey, hey, looka here, will ya?" A loud, gruff voice erupted from a craggy-face with a pugilist's nose like a deformed lump of clay thrown onto a pock- marked surface. The head rested on a trunk-thick neck, and a barrel-shaped chest. The intruder leaned into Isabella's face. "Whatcha doin' with this gumshoe, you bee-yoo-ti-ful little lady? Get rid of this slob, and I'll show you a really good time."

Amado looked up at the man. "Well, well, Horse Face Hoskins. When the hell did they let you out?"

"A week ago, on parole, and don't call me Horse Face."

Amado stood, hiked his pants and went nose-to-nose with the ex con. "Listen, Horse Face, if you've got any sense, you'll get the hell out of here. Being in a bar, you've already violated your parole."

Noise in the bar suddenly subsided; the patrons' anticipation of trouble moved them away. Horse Face pushed up the sleeves of his jacket, then threw a wild round-house swing that Amado easily ducked. With the momentum of his swing, the ex con fell forward overturning the glasses on the table. Isabella jumped up and stepped aside, but the red wine had already splotched her white linen skirt.

The bartender and waiter rushed to stop the fracas and lifted Horse Face off the floor. They tried to restrain him, but he managed to lunge free and punch Amado in the face. Momentarily dazed, Amado shook his head. With his left, he blocked another punch Horse Face threw and landed a solid right to the solar plexus that knocked the wind out of the ex con. As Horse Face bent over gasping, Amado caught him with an uppercut and a left-right combination that sent him back against the wall. Barely conscious, he fell forward onto his knees, then face down on the floor. As he hit the floor, a pistol slid out of the inside pocket of his jacket. Amado picked up the 9mm Glock.

"You dumb sonofabitch. You violated all the terms of your parole: carrying a weapon, assaulting an officer and creating one hell of a disturbance." Amado removed the clip from the Glock and stuck the pistol in his own belt.

With the siren sounds of a police car, Amado assured the battered Horse Face that he could expect a long lease on a cell in the Santa Barbara County jail and probably a return to prison.

Isabella, although impressed by Amado's fistic prowess, was furious that her skirt was stained by red wine. Dabbing it with a napkin, she glared at Amado. "This is *so* humiliating. Please take me home—now."

Two uniformed police rushed in with guns drawn, pulled Horse Face onto his feet and handcuffed him. Horse Face was in no condition to resist and had to be supported by the officers as they led him out. Amado briefed the officers and told them he would make his report in the morning.

He led Isabella through the crowd that surrounded them. Outside, she said, "I've got to get out of these clothes."

There was little conversation in Amado's Plymouth coupe as it sped toward Casa Del Caudillo.

As soon as Amado's vehicle approached the eight foot high steel gates of the casa, the headlights revealed a German shepherd leaping at the gates, barking, growling and baring its fangs. Amado remembered the silhouette warning trespassers. He leaned out the window. "Whoa, doggie, we come as friends."

Isabella, recovered from her anger, laughed as she stepped out of the vehicle and walked toward the gates. The dog stopped barking, wagged its tail and whimpered in anticipation of her greeting. Isabella disengaged the alarm system that also opened the ornate steel gates that creaked as they swung slowly inward. The dog stood on its hind legs to lick Isabella's face. She turned her head, pushed the animal aside and scolded it without rancor. "Enough, Lobo. Go back to your doggie house." The dog ignored the command, wagged its tail and walked beside Isabella to the entryway. "Stay!" she commanded; the dog obeyed.

Lights went on in the second-floor servants' quarters. A window opened and a voice called, "Señorita Isabella?"

She stopped and looked up. "Carlos, it's only me." A rapid-fire conversation in Spanish ensued that Fred did not fully understand.

They took several steps into the dark foyer before Isabella

snapped on switches that flooded the spacious living room. Light came from a large black, round metal chandelier holding light bulbs that lit the middle of the room while wall sconces resembling torches provided additional light. The room revealed a curious mélange of southwestern Indian-Mexican décor, contemporary and antique furnishings.

The portrait of Franco and Señora Montenegro fascinated Fred who was drawn to it. Franco's bulging eyes seemed to follow him; Fred returned the stare while walking behind Isabella who slowed her pace. He bumped into her and stopped suddenly, holding onto her arms to steady himself and her. "Sorry about that." Contact with her backside caused an immediate physical response. He released her arms slowly—they were soft, smooth and quite feminine. She turned to look into his eyes but then turned away quickly.

"I'm going to get out of these clothes, then we can have something from the bar."

"What are you serving?"

"Anything you wish."

"Oho, little lady, you let yourself open there. I'll tell you what I wish..."

She cut him off. "Listen, Mr. Detective, I'm talking about drinks, nothing more. If you persist in this silliness, you'll have to leave."

How can I be so damned stupid as to turn her off? Slow down, Fred, you're not talking to some floozie. "My deepest apologies, Isabella. My heart speaks before consulting my brain...what little I have. I have only the highest respect for you, and if you don't mind I'll have a beer."

Fred Amado's eyes feasted on her lovely form as she walked away. He looked around the room; the portrait of the general and the lady again drew his attention, and he studied it closely. *What was their relationship?* He looked to find an artist's signature in the right lower corner. *I'll be damned. This is an actual painting—not a blown up photograph. That's hours of posing ...more than a casual relationship there. How could anyone love that sonofabitch?... he killed over a half million.*

Isabella returned wearing a loose-fitting ecru silk blouse and a black gabardine skirt. When she bent forward to place a silver tray with a frosted glass and a bottle of beer on the cocktail table, her blouse dipped to reveal a cleavage of creamy, delectable skin. She sat, crossed her legs to expose her lower thighs. Amado experienced an extra heartbeat, cleared his throat and took a deep breath.

"You look absolutely smashing. Anytime you want to model a bathing suit, give me a buzz."

She smiled tolerantly but said nothing.

The leather club chair whooshed as he dropped into it. He picked up the bottle of beer and poured it into the frosted glass. "Nice touch, thank you." Isabella nodded, then sipped her Port wine. "Tell me about Señora Montenegro. What was she like? How long did you know her?"

Isabella looked around the room before speaking; her eyes turned to the darkened top of the spiral staircase, then slowly toward the painting. "Strange, I still feel her presence in this room. The señora was a beautiful woman who treated me kindly enough." She stopped to look at her fingers entwined on her lap.

Fred slid forward in his chair. "And?"

"I was seven years old in 1931 when she found me in an orphanage run by nuns just outside Madrid. My parents were killed when they fought in an uprising against wealthy landowners."

Fred interrupted. "The year 1931 was a brief period when the Second Republic took charge after King Alfonso abdicated. The liberals took over then."

Isabella, wide-eyed, stared at Fred. "That's right! How did you know?"

Amado with a complacent smile leaned back in his chair. "I was a history major at Berkeley. Since my forebears, on my father's side were Spanish, I took a special interest in their history... submitted a paper on the Spanish Civil War. Of course, that required research covering the rise of Franco, and it gave me an opportunity to form my own opinions about him."

Isabella sat forward in her chair, filled with wonderment as she listened with renewed interest to Detective Amado. "What was your opinion of Franco?"

"Generally speaking, I'd say he was a two-bit dictator, overly-ambitious, greedy with the soul of a pig. He wasn't too bright but not too stupid, and now he's in charge of a country going nowhere. The government remains repressive. He established military tribunals for Republicans, those against his regime, and sent thousands to their death. Only Catholicism was tolerated and Catalan and Basque languages were forbidden—even Catalan and Basque names for newborns were forbidden. He barred labor unions and created secret police to spy on citizens. You know, of course, that he was the poster boy for Hitler and Mussolini before the start of World War Two. Those bastards supplied planes, tanks, cannons, ammo and the soldiers to fight with his forces.

"At Franco's urging, they bombed Guernica, mass annihilation of men, women, children and farm animals, the first aerial attack of its kind in history. Picasso painted a mural of it that's in the Museum of Modern Art in New York. It's probably the most moving condemnation of war ever created."

Amado went on to flaunt what he knew: "Pablo Neruda wrote a poem about Franco in hell. It translates roughly as the Evil One, neither fire nor hot vinegar in a coven of volcanic witches, so forth and so on, and he goes on to describe some pretty horrific torments the General is suffering in hell."

"Ah, Neruda!" she exclaimed. "I love his poems." Now she was impressed and sensing as much; he was gratified. Perhaps she was thinking that any man could us his fists to pummel someone but wondered how many knew history or could recite poetry. She said, "I'm impressed. You are so well informed. I could listen to you for hours."

"Could we make that pillow talk?"

Isabella's eyebrows tented and she tilted her head. "I don't understand."

"Not important," he said. *Now why in the hell did I say that? Why can't I keep my big mouth shut?* "Tell me about your relationship with the señora. You grew up in her home, right? Did she adopt you?"

"Oh, no."

"Why was that?"

"Her husband, Colonel Armando Hidalgo Montenegro was opposed to me coming into his family, bearing his name or claiming his coat of arms. Family history was important to him. He could not have an orphan of low-caste freedom fighters inherit his family crest or fortune."

"Señora had no children of her own?"

"No. But she gave me all the advantages of a child born into wealth and privilege. I was sent to the finest school for girls in Lausanne, then to a finishing school in London. I learned to act like a lady, you know, serving tea properly, using silverware and dinnerware just so. I trained in horseback riding, dressage, and sports like badminton and tennis. I learned the fundamentals of ballet, ballroom dancing, and spent hours listening to operas and concerts."

"That's quite a cultural background. Do you have a boyfriend who is as refined?"

"I've had"...She paused. "How does all this chitchat about my personal life solve the señora's murder?"

"Background material is important. It goes to establish motive, means and opportunity. Did anyone know the señora as well as you?"

"I don't know." She drew back and pursed her lips. "Wait a minute, does that mean I'm a suspect?"

Amado did not answer. Instead he asked, "Who else knew her well?"

"A number of people: Father Ignacio at the Montecito Catholic Church, some neighbors, her niece and nephew..."

Amado made notations as she spoke.

"You didn't answer my question. Am I a suspect?" Isabella's eyes bore into his.

"We haven't had a chance to interview everyone around here. Bill Connors is calling in the employees one-by-one and questioning them."

"I hope he understands and speaks Spanish well."

"He has an interpreter." Fred leaned back in the soft chair and contemplated Isabella's composure. "I hesitate to change the character of this idyllic moment, but where were *you* when the murder took place? According to the coroner, the shot that killed the señora was fired ten to twelve hours before she was discovered by the maid. That means the murder took place between eight and ten o'clock the night before."

Isabella folded her arms across her chest and raised her chin. "As well as I can recall, I was in my room, two doors from the señora's. There's a linen closet between our rooms."

"And you heard nothing?"

"I can't recall any unusual sounds."

"Nothing like a gun shot? No dog barking?"

Becoming irritated by his persistence, she said, "I might have been in the shower. I heard nothing."

"Usually you would hear the dog barking?"

"He barks when a rabbit, cat or other creature scampers by. Certainly he would carry on if a stranger approached."

Amado made a few more notes, then looked up. "You turned off the alarm system when we came here tonight."

"That was for the front gate. Anyone could scale the walls around this property. We've had attempted break-ins before... kids looking for money, jewelry, small items."

"Even with metal bars on the windows?"

"There are no bars on the workshop or laundry room windows. Those units were built later, and the señora did not bother to install an alarm system for them."

"Are there any rooms I haven't seen?"

"There's the colonel's den. The room has been locked since his death over two years ago. It's opened every month or so for dusting, but otherwise it's..."

"Would you mind showing it to me?"

"I'll get the key from the señora's room." She returned and led him down a hallway to a closed door. As they approached it, she explained, "The colonel, as you'll see, was an avid hunter and fisherman."

Opening the solid door required some force. Having shoved it open, Isabella flipped the light switch and walked over to the casement window, which Amado opened. "That's better...get some of the musty odor out. You can see, it's a typical sportsman's room." She pointed to the mounted animal heads from Africa and India. "This snarling lion makes me shudder every time I... Did I lose you, Fred?"

Amado was studying a display case of small arms recessed in black Styrofoam. "Sorry, this caught my eye. There's a gun missing here."

Isabella walked to his side. "Oh, really? I can't imagine..."

"Who would have access to this room?"

"Besides me and the señora? The cleaning or maintenance crew, I suppose. I never really thought about it."

Amado closed his notebook and placed it in his inner jacket pocket. He looked at his watch. "It's been an interesting evening, but it's close to the witching hour. I apologize again for the fracas at the Miramar and for getting your skirt soiled. I'd like to make it up to you."

"In the grand scheme of things, it matters very little." Isabella stood and smiled. "I can't remember who said that, but it seems appropriate here." She looked at Amado with more respect but also with curiosity.

"Isabella, I'd like to see you again, I have a few more questions."

"As you wish, Mr. Detective. In spite of the little mishap tonight, I enjoyed your company."

Her approval pleased him.

She came forward and held out her hand to shake his. He reached out and drew her to him, then leaned over and kissed her on the lips. She became rigid and tried to push him away. He held her firmly until her resistance ebbed and she succumbed to his embrace; her lips parted slightly and she sighed.

He placed his hand at the back of her head. His heart raced; she felt wonderful in his arms. The soft, smooth skin of her face and arms, her firm bosom against his chest and her perfumed hair were intoxicating. He wondered if she was aware of his tumescence. "I better go, sweet girl, before I insist on staying. Will you walk me to the car and protect me from *The Hound of the Baskervilles?"*

She laughed and turned to lead him out of the house. When the front door opened, the dog waited with a wagging tail. Isabella held Fred's hand as they walked to his car. He held her closely once again and kissed her. His hand moved down towards her derriere as she moved even closer to him. The dog barked.

"Lobo, it's all right. This nice man is not hurting me," she assured the animal. She watched as Amado drove beyond the property, then thought, *this man appears rough around the edges, but he is well-schooled and respectful of me. I feel safe in his presence, and yet, I'm not quite sure what he thinks of me.*

Chapter 6

Absorbed in the afterglow of those last minutes of intimacy with Isabella, Fred realized he was already north on Hollister Avenue, just minutes from his apartment. He hadn't known that kind of sexual arousal since his Marine Corps days at Camp Pendleton when he and his buddies would head south to San Diego on weekends to attend the servicemen's dance. After a couple hours of jiving, they'd try talking their partners into shacking-up in a motel, or if necessary, doing it in a car. If one had enough scratch, the motel was better. A guy could buy a little hooch and enjoy some frenzied fucking with encores lasting all night. Some of those coeds knew more tricks than professional hookers... *But this was altogether different. No one night ram-bam-thank-you-ma'am stuff. No sir. This is one fine gal.*

Trouble is, how can I confide my feelings for this woman to anyone? Jeezus , she's a prime suspect in the murder of the señora. A relationship would violate every damn rule in the book. Could I really be objective? If the chief finds out, he'd yank me off the case, maybe demote me, or worse, have my badge. And I know, he'd be right. What I'm doing makes no sense. It's just plain stupid. C'mon, she's just another broad. Stay clear of her, dummy... yeah, fat chance.

<hr/>

"Think forensics will have anything for us?" Bill Connors asked as he took a brisk step-and-a-half to walk in cadence with Amado.

"We should get a blood-typing from those drops on the señora's vanity bench and a report on fingerprints, if any were found. My guess is that the blood sample will be the señora's own blood, and the fingerprints, if any, will be smudged beyond critical value. That's usually the case."

The forensics laboratory smelling of chemical reagents and formaldehyde made Fred queasy. The odor reminded him of the morgue, and he wanted to spend as little time as possible there. He approached Dr. Johnson who was poring over a microscope. Johnson looked up. "Well, well, if it isn't my good friend, Detective *Romeo,* the undisputed champion lover of the Santa Barbara Sheriff's Department."

"The name's Amado, Doc, but thanks for the compliment. What do you have on the Montenegro case?"

The doctor picked up a test tube from a rack and held it at eye level. "I've got a blood sample from the corpse at the morgue. It matches the blood found on the vanity bench. We do have a number of fingerprints, but quite frankly, I'm not sure how much that helps us."

"Why?" Connors asked.

"For one thing, at least three or four, probably more people, had been traipsing around that room: maid, secretary, and God only knows who else. If we send our samples to the Finger Print Service at the FBI, we probably won't get an answer for weeks. And if there's no match in their files, where are we?"

Amado's eyes shifted to Bill Connors in an I-told-you-so expression.

Dr. Johnson continued, "In addition, there were some indistinct smudge marks on the vanity, suggestive of gloved hands." He looked at both detectives. "If that's of any help." Amado shrugged and shook his head.

Johnson said, "I talked with Dr. Watkins, the pathologist in Ventura. He said there were powder burns in the hair and on the back of the scalp. Gun had to be pretty close to the target. Are you going to talk with him? Might be a good idea." "Yeah, I'll make the call now, thanks."

"This is Detective Amado from the Santa Barbara Sheriff's Department. Dr. Watkins is expecting my call regarding the Montenegro case. That's right, Montenegro from Montecito. The full name is Juanita Castillo Montenegro, M-o-n-t-e-n-e-g-r-o. No, I don't have her birth date—no, I don't have her social security number." He placed his hand over the mouthpiece and looked at Connors. "Can you believe this? How many autopsies on a Montenegro from Montecito could they have? This damned senseless, incompetent bureaucracy drives me nuts."

"Hello, Dr. Watkins...yes, the Montenegro woman. Go ahead, I'm going to repeat the findings and jot them down as you list them... massive cerebral hemorrhage and destruction of brain tissue ... .22 caliber bullet lodged behind and pushed out the left eye."

Amado interrupted. "Anything under her nails? No? No sign of struggle? What's that? Interesting findings not associated with morbidity? Go on, I'm listening. Recent cosmetic surgery... eyelid reduction...dental work, central and lateral incisors capped. Breast augmentation. Moving down... tummy tuck. Pelvis... uterine suspension and surgical narrowing of vaginal passage. A small tattoo partially obscured by the escutcheon above the mons pubis? Hold it Doc. I haven't the damndest notion of what you're saying. Give that to me in simple terms. Go ahead. At the level of the pubic hair is a tattoo with the words *Por Mi Caudillo.* Yeah, nice sentimental touch. The Caudillo would have to get his face down there to see it. Maybe she had that in mind. Anything else? A beauty mark on her cheek was fake? Uh-huh. Why doesn't that surprise me?"

Chapter 7

Bill Connors stood next to Fred Amado in the courtyard of Our Lady of Mount Moriah Parish in Montecito. They watched the mourners entering the century old church with its steeple and solitary bell.

"Fred you're looking glum. Don't you feel a kind of nostalgia being at a church again?" He didn't wait for a response. "Did I ever tell you I was a choir boy at St. Vincent's for four years? When my voice started to crack, I was asked to leave—in a nice way, of course."

Amado listened without expression. "I was a choir boy for eight years. I was asked to leave also, for different reasons."

"Like what?"

"I was a big kid at age thirteen. When my voice started to change, I became an unpredictable tenor or baritone. One day during rehearsal, the choirmaster asked me to remain in the choir loft after the others left. He said my voice was fine, but I needed extra instruction."

"Jeez, I hope you're not going to tell me he..."

Amado nodded. "You guessed it. The sonofabitch waited until we were alone, then kissed me and took my hand and put it under his cassock. I don't know why he thought I'd go along with what the hell he had in mind, but I hauled off and sent the sonofabitch ass-over-teakettle. He fell off the loft into the seats below. Broke his tailbone and wrist." Amado laughed. "I was asked—no I was told—to leave the church."

"Wasn't the priest held responsible?"

"Nah. Everything was hushed up and the sonofabitch was transferred to another church in L.A. If he remained in the community, my father might have whacked off his cock and balls. That would have been the Indian part of him seeking revenge."

"Is that why you're bitter about the church?"

"Actually, I'm not. As a matter of fact, it was my parish priest, Father Dan Kelly, who encouraged me to enter the sheriff's academy after I finished at the university. Teaching positions for history majors were practically nonexistent, and I didn't want to leave Southern California. Father Kelly wrote a convincing recommendation to the sheriff's academy that paid off. We remained friends until his death, and I'll always be grateful for what he did.

"My mother still attends mass. She likes the ceremony, the pageantry, and deep down, I know she'd like to find a nice church-going girl for me. If I ever find a gal I really like, she'll probably be a stripper, guilty of every goddamned sin known to man."

Amado scanned the arriving mourners. "Look over there, a priest is clasping hands with people who obviously don't know him," he said to Connors. Amado approached the smiling, bowing priest. "Hello Father, I'm Detective Fred Amado."

"Father Julio Allende," the priest replied. "Very pleased to meet you."

Amado guessed that the priest would prefer using his own language, so he responded, "*Tengo mucho gusto en conocerle, padre.*" In Santa Barbara, even store clerks were expected to be bilingual. Amado, however, had been raised in an English-speaking household, so the rest of his conversation with Father Allende was in simple, labored Spanish.

"Thank you, my son, for speaking in my tongue." The priest smiled.

"You are not from here?" Amado said.

"No. I am from Madrid. I flew in this morning. I am, excuse me, I meant to say, I *was* a friend of Señora Montenegro.

We were friends for many years In Spain."

"You are here to pay your respects." Amado said. *Of course, he's here to pay his respects, dummy.* "You have a church in Madrid where you officiate?"

"No, no. I have served as an adviser to Presidente Franco since the start of the Civil War in 1936."

"Will you perform the funeral rites for the departed señora?"

"I shall leave here shortly and go to the cemetery to prepare the Rite of Committal." The priest excused himself as he approached another mourner.

Connors stood by waiting for a translation of the conversation. Amado said, "The padre is an old friend of the señora who apparently was well-connected to the big honchos in Spain." Amado scratched the back of his head. "I'm no expert on Spanish dialects, but that priest has the damndest accent I've ever heard."

Watching the mourners pass through the courtyard to enter the church, Connors leaned towards Amado. Out of the side of his mouth, he said, "Did you see the limos in the parking area? More Packards, Lincolns, and Cadillacs than you can count. The señora knew some pretty affluent amigos."

"And amigas," Amado added.

"Yeah, whatever." Connors eyebrows tented. "By the way, what exactly are we looking for here?"

Amado shrugged, looked aside, and dug his hands into his pockets. "I don't know. Anything that even smacks of a clue, anyone who looks suspicious, and don't ask me what the hell that means." He seemed testy and annoyed, not at Connors, but at himself for acting intuitively and probably foolishly. Maybe he wanted to see Isabella again, but he couldn't admit that to anyone, not even to himself. Being at the church defied any rationale, but his gut feeling told him he should be there.

He watched as people left their vehicles to walk toward the recessed arched entry of the church. Three elderly men emerged from a well-maintained pre-war Pierce Arrow sedan. All wore dark suits: two with homburg hats and walking sticks. The third held leather gloves in one hand and sported a monocle. Amado watched them closely.

Meanwhile, Connors watched Amado. "What d'ya think about them, Fred?"

"You mean the Magi? I could smell the mothballs from their suits. They look like rejects from a movie casting studio. From the way they walk and talk, I'd say they're retired military—foreign."

"Foreign?"

"Yeah. If you listened, you would have heard real Spanish, not Mexican paisano Spanish."

"You got all that in just forty-five seconds? That's amazing."

"I'm sure they're friends of the señora or her late husband, Colonel What's-his-name."

After the last mourners arrived, the detectives entered the church and remained in the back. Two ushers closed the thick wooden doors behind them. Of the twenty rows of bench seats on either side of a flat rock aisle, the first two pews were occupied by family members and dignitaries including the three elderly foreign men. The estate workers and their families sat in the last rows. As the services were about to begin, two youngsters yelling their objections to confinement were hustled out by an embarrassed mother.

The mass to be conducted by the popular Monsignor O'Hearn from Los Angeles, was an honor accorded to the departed who had supported the archdiocese generously. The señora's will specified a gift in perpetuity to the church.

A hush blanketed the congregation as the Monsignor, wearing an elegant purple chasuble, strode in, faced the apse, paused and bowed to the life-size image of the Savior on the Cross. He turned to the lectern, took a moment to confront the mourners, looked heavenward, then began the mass for the departed.

Connors whispered to Amado, "Where's the coffin?"

"At the sanctuary in the cemetery. From there she's going

into a mausoleum to be placed next to her husband."

"No kidding? Man, that's living."

Amado looked for Isabella in the first pew. He spotted her wearing the black veiled hat she had worn in his office several days before. Seated next to her, a handsome young man with chiseled features and dark wavy hair leaned toward her and whispered in her ear. Fred wondered: *who in the hell is that?*

Connors watched as Amado fixed his gaze on Isabella and the guy next to her. He poked Amado with his elbow and whispered, "You thinking about that señorita in a romantic way, huh?"

Fred turned quickly and with a scowl said, "No, of course not."

"If you're falling for that little filly, you could be in a heap of trouble. She's a suspect. So far, our only suspect. You could get yourself thrown off the force."

"Goddammit, shut up! You don't know what in the hell you're talking about!"

"Sorry Fred. I just…"

"Forget it. Go out to the parking lot and get the license number on that pre-historic Pierce Arrow, then call it in. I want to know who owns that sled."

An hour of prayers, homilies and tributes ended the doleful mass. Amado, standing in back of the church, waited as the orderly procession of mourners left the pews. When Isabella approached the exit, he stepped in behind her, insinuating himself between her and the handsome young man who had sat next to her. Startled by Fred's presence, she said nothing until they reached the courtyard. She lifted her veil, smiled sadly, then reached out to touch Fred's forearm. He wanted to embrace her but dared not.

"Detective Amado, this is Anthony Garcia, the señora's nephew." Isabella looked around, then caught the attention of an attractive young woman. "And this is Angela Garcia, Anthony's sister. Both of these beautiful young people are students at U.C.L.A. Anthony is a second year pre-law student, Angela is finishing her first year in social studies." Fred shook hands with both and expressed his condolences. He scrutinized the young man whose dark suit was impeccably tailored.

Anthony returned Fred's visual assessment and said, "Are you the officer assigned to find my aunt's killer?"

"Yeah, I'm the detective in charge."

"Detective Amado, I hope you won't be offended by what I'm about to say, but I'm thinking of calling in a private investigator to look into my aunt's murder."

"Do whatever you want. Just be sure whoever you hire doesn't get in my way."

Isabella cleared her throat to interrupt the conversation that was becoming edgy. "Anthony, I think we can discuss this at a later time. Will you and Angela be going to the cemetery? Father Allende is going to conduct the Rite of Committal, and I think the family should be there."

"If you don't mind, Isabella, we'll leave now. We want to avoid the late afternoon traffic back to Westwood. I'm sure Auntie would forgive us. Do you have a ride to and from the cemetery?"

"I'll see that she gets there and back," Amado said. He turned his back to the young man, placed his hand on Isabella's arm and directed her toward the parking area. As they approached the detectives' car, Amado said to Isabella, "Seems like the nephew has his own agenda about investigating the murder."

"He's a bit overzealous and making a show of authority that he really can't afford," she said.

"Explain that to me."

"Anthony and Angela depended upon their aunt's generosity. She paid their tuition and gave them more than adequate allowances for living expenses. Now, of course, that money will not be available."

"Their aunt left nothing in her will for them?"

"Oh, yes, quite a bit."

"I'm confused. Then the nephew will be able to hire a private eye."

"My señora was shrewd. In her will she stated that no money would be provided to her niece and nephew, in the event of her death, unless they had completed their studies at the university. She knew that if they were to inherit money before graduating, they might not continue their studies. Without the means of wasting money, as Anthony had been doing, he is not going to be able to afford a private eye. I hear they're pretty expensive."

"You hear right," Amado replied. "At least twenty dollars an hour plus expenses."

Connors sat behind the wheel of the Ford sedan, his sleeping head rested on his chest. When Amado opened the door, Connors jumped and reached for his piece.

"Take it easy, Bill. Put the cannon away. I'm going to drive Miss Chavez to the cemetery. Did you get the IDs on those license plates?"

"Yeah. Want me to tell you what I found?"

"Hold it for later. Do me a favor, get on the horn and ask for a ride back to the station. While you're waiting for a ride, ask the church secretary for a photocopy of the mourners who signed the attendance book."

"Hey, that's a tall order, Fred..." Connors' voice faded in response to Amado's icy stare. "But, no problem there, no sir. I'll get right on it."

Chapter 8

The white Italian marble of the mausoleum, set on a grassy knoll, reflected the sun's rays against a cloudless azure sky. Designed like a miniature Parthenon, the mausoleum had been created as a showpiece among less obtrusive granite markers that jutted out around the park-like grounds. From here the departed had a view of Santa Barbara's scenic harbor, as well as the gentle sloping expanse of the Montecito Country Club Golf Course. Amado and Isabella sat in the unmarked car near the mausoleum and waited for the arrival of Señora Montenegro's corpse.

"This mausoleum is sort of ostentatious, isn't it?" Fred observed, then looked at Isabella for affirmation. He got none. "I mean this Greek-type monstrosity holds the bones of a guy who was on the wrong side of the angels. He fought for Franco, so how good could he have been?" Fred's voice climbed an octave with the last question. "Now his wife's bones will join his. Can't you just see those two skeletons doing a tango or a Charleston?"

Isabella looked at him but still said nothing.

"Forgive my lousy attempt at humor. I don't know when to keep my trap shut." *Jeezus, who the hell asked for my smart ass comments anyway?*

Both turned to watch the hearse moving slowly up the curved road. It stopped behind Amado's car.

"Father Allende is probably with them," Isabella said.

The uniformed driver and two helpers slid the carved

rosewood coffin with gold-plated ornamentation out of the hearse and onto a four-wheeled carrier. All three lifted the carrier over the curb, then rolled it toward the mausoleum.

The driver, in charge of the detail, reached for a key in his pocket to open the mausoleum door. He was about to insert the key in the lock, when he turned to look at the other men. "Who unlocked the door?" The men shrugged. The driver pushed the heavy door that moved slowly on squeaking hinges. He took a step into the chamber, then backed out. His face turned ashen and contorted. He leaned against the coffin to keep from collapsing.

"What the hell is it?" Amado yelled and ran to the driver's side.

Unable to speak, the driver pointed over his shoulder to the mausoleum. Fred walked to the partially opened door and pushed it completely open. Isabella behind him, peered around his shoulder. A piercing scream from her, startled Fred. She turned and ran out toward the hearse, took several deep gulps of air, then started to cry uncontrollably, gasping and snuffling.

Amado walked further into the mausoleum to see the staring eyes of the bloody, disfigured face of the priest, Father Julio Allende, the man with whom he had spoken just two hours before. He had difficulty comprehending the horror before him. The naked, bloodied and grotesquely battered corpse lying on its back with the head bent backward over the edge of the plinth, revealed a missing nose and a bloody something protruding from the mouth. Amado looked at the groin. He did not want to believe what he was seeing. The priest's penis was severed at the base and stuck in his mouth.

The corpse lay next to the sarcophagus of Colonel Armando Hidalgo Montenegro. It occupied the space reserved for Señora Juanita Castillo Montenegro. A ray of diminished light from a slit-type window at the top of the back wall cast a ghostly glow on the figure.

Amado, careful to avoid the pool of blood that had

collected on the marble floor and avoiding any physical contact with the corpse, studied the deeply traumatized bald head. A depression in the center of the scalp with ropy columns of coagulated blood that had gushed out of it was only a part of the horror he observed. A stilled fountain of blood had issued from the hole in the face where the nose had been hacked off. The confining airless room had already begun to emit the offensive stench of death. A pool of dark blood collected on the marble floor beneath the mutilated head and face. Amado tip-toed around the bloody mess and saw shoe prints beyond the irregular border of pooled blood.

Examining the rest of the corpse, Fred saw further signs of mutilation. An incised cross extended from the neck to the groin and from nipple to nipple.

Deputies arrived and stood guard around the mausoleum. Amado gave a cursory report before returning to the sedan. He felt a twinge of pain when he saw Isabella curled up in the back seat, shivering and crying, her head buried in her hands. Amado removed his jacket and placed it around her shoulders, then gave her a gentle hug. Although he felt an obligation to remain at the crime scene, he wanted to take Isabella back to the estate where she could find relief from the terror of the day.

Chapter 9

Amado and Connors, standing at a discreet distance from the dissecting table, watched as Dr. Watson poised his scalpel above the corpse's skull. "Crushing blow to the skull with a blunt object resulting in a stellate fracture radiating off the central depression. Immediate death. No doubt about it. No one could have survived that trauma. Nose hacked off and the crucifixion-form incisions were done after the head blow. Some crazy act of madness or vengeance, I'd say. How else could one explain the penis jammed into the mouth? I saw it once on Kwajalein. Never thought I'd see it again."

The brain lay sectioned on a metal tray. "Look at this." He called the detectives to view the organ. "The cortex is suffused with hemorrhage."

"What kind of blunt object could have done that?" Amado asked.

"Use your imagination. A baseball bat, a sledge hammer..."

"A bottle?" Connors asked.

"Not likely. The object had to carry real momentum—something on a lever arm," Watkins said.

"Anything else of importance?" Amado asked.

"Just the usual age-related things: atherosclerotic changes in the cardiac vessels, old pulmonary infiltrates..." Watkins voice diminished as he remembered something. He uncovered the groin. "There is something else, a scar above the bloody scrotal sac. I think an implant had been inserted."

"You're losing me, Doc. I don't know what you're saying,"

Amado said.

Watkins held the scrotal sac in one hand and incised the skin to remove the testicles. "This left one is stone hard, quite abnormal. If my memory serves me correctly, the Nazi doctors, a notable example was Joseph Mengele, believed that supermen could be created by manipulating certain organs and giving certain hormonal injections. They experimented with substances, such as testosterone, ovarian extract, pulverized pituitary, thyroid, and adrenal glands. In addition, they tried to improve racial characteristics by selecting and breeding certain body types: blond hair and blue eyes for example.

"One of their methods of improving body structure, defying aging and sharpening mental acuity, they thought, was to implant whole organs from recently deceased bodies."

"Did any of those procedures work?" Amado asked.

"Of course not. The experiments were disgustingly unscientific, inhumane and born out of the minds of delusional, egocentric maniacs who tortured their victims to suffer experiments that no rational person could have conceived."

Amado watched as Dr. Watkins became visibly shaken by his own account of the atrocities. "What does this have to do with the padre's cajones here?" Amado asked.

"Someone implanted testicular tissue or some other substance with the intention of improving the priest's sexual prowess," Watkins said.

"The priest's? You mean the priest was victimized? Another unwilling soul in this madness?"

"Perhaps the priest was conned into thinking the operation would enhance his potency."

"Wait a minute, Doc, you're talking about a priest, a celibate guy, one who took vows..."

The coroner nodded. "Yes, yes, Amado. For a seasoned cop, you're pretty naïve. What a priest professes and what he does may not have much in common. He's a man, just like you, just as horny, and porking women in his flock. Put yourself in his place. Say, you're getting older. Your cock isn't coming to attention like it used to. So someone offers to restore your youthful vigor allowing you to fornicate all night long. Tell me that's an offer Detective Amado could refuse."

"Hold on. It's not about me. Let's get back to the priest."

"All right, try this scenario: the priest presents himself as a lay person with marital problems. He can't get it up and submits to this weird surgery. He'd like erections on demand.

"Here's some relevant background to my thinking. You're a Spanish history buff. You know Franco signed a nonaggression pact with Hitler and Mussolini in the spring of 1936. The Axis wanted Franco to keep the Strait of Gibraltar open—they in turn would supply Franco with bombers, artillery and soldiers. About that time Hitler had given Mengele free rein to carry out experimentation on political prisoners. In his twisted mind, Mengele thought he could change the physiology of a person with some outlandish surgical procedures. Most operations were too unorthodox or horrible to contemplate. It's possible that the priest, this Father Allende, traveled to Germany after he read or heard of Mengele's experiments in human sexuality. The implantation of irradiated monkey testes was promoted as a cure for male sexual inadequacy."

"Were the experiments successful?" Amado asked.

"See for yourself." Watkins held the testicles in his hand. "Whatever was implanted turned into an amorphous, non-functioning mass. This is the result of complete and unadulterated bullshit."

"What other surprises do you have Doc? Were there signs of a struggle? Strange hairs, fabric threads? Anyone else's blood in that slaughter chamber?"

"We isolated some specks of earth at the edges of the scalp wound. The cross-like incisions on the body were done with a sharp blade, if that's any help. Find the bloody instruments that did all this. That'll be a good start. Better yet, find the person or persons who hated this guy enough to kill with a wild, hateful vengeance."

"There's got to be something symbolic about this hack job." Amado said.

"I'm a pathologist, not a psychiatrist. If symbolism is a part of this, I'd say cutting off the penis was a vengeful act for his sexual assault on someone. Cutting off the nose could be interpreted as that which was poked into places where it didn't belong, or maybe one that brown-nosed some despicable character." He pointed to the cross extending from the base of the neck down to the groin and from nipple to nipple. "This could mean someone's contempt for the victim's claim to piety, or the belief that the victim desecrated the meaning of the cross. I'm sure any psychologist could offer more interpretations for this goddamned unholy act."

Chapter 10

Amado sat at his desk, his spring-loaded chair allowing him to lean back and put his feet on the desk top. He supported the back of his head with interlaced fingers. Connors sat opposite him with his legs outstretched.

"I've been thinking, Fred, I bet the murders of the señora and the Spanish priest are related."

"That's a safe bet. What exactly are you thinking?"

"To begin, the señora and priest both knew each other in Spain for years. The priest told us that. Secondly, they were pretty darn friendly with Franco. The priest was Franco's adviser on religious matters, and she was–well, she was his you-know-what."

"Mistress?"

"Yeah, that's it. And since they were Franco's people, they must have had a lot of enemies."

"Bill, you're becoming a regular Sam Spade or a Mike Hammer. Now tell me something I don't know—like who was that Pierce Arrow registered to? The crate those three old farts came out of in the church parking lot."

"That's what I wanted to tell you before. I got that information from the DMV and put it on a slip of paper in my wallet." Connors pulled the paper out and read, "The car is a 1938 custom-bodied four door sedan, manufactured by the Pierce Arrow Motor Car Company, Buffalo, New York. It was shipped to a dealer in Los Angeles and purchased by the I.A.T. Company that year." Connors handed the paper to Amado.

"What the hell is the I.A.T. Company?" Amado asked.

"I had Mabel at communications look it up. I.A.T. stands for Iberia-America Trading Company, established in 1937. It has offices in Madrid, New York, Miami and Los Angeles."

Amado reached for his pocket notebook. "Who's in that company, and what are they trading?"

"Gee Fred, give me break, will ya? I was happy getting that much information."

Amado sighed and looked at the ceiling. "Listen, Billy Boy, what you have here is minimal. It may be the start of something important, but in itself, it is not. The real nuggets in this magilla are the names of the owners and their game. If they're buying and shipping corsets and brassieres, that's one thing, but if they're ..." The phone rang.

"Amado here...uh, yeah, put her on." Amado turned his back to Connors. Connors left the room; Amado spoke softly into the phone. "...yes, I would like to see you again...a nice quiet spot...a glass of wine... my taste runs to beer or hard liquor...no, I never get drunk. Look forward to seeing you." As he was hanging up, Connors returned.

"This meeting with the Undersheriff, Marv Rabino, what's he like?" Connors asked.

"Marv Rabino is one sonofabitch, but he's our sonofabitch. He's all protocol, but he's fair. Thinks like a military man and cusses like one. Chews cigars like candy. He runs the department, including all of Santa Barbara County and the unincorporated areas. In World War II, he served as a fighter pilot and was credited with six kills in the Pacific Theatre. Attained the rank of lieutenant colonel at age thirty-one. He's maintained his military bearing and is well respected. Respected, mind you, but not necessarily loved."

Amado and Connors sat and waited in Rabino's office. Connors asked, "Rabino, is that Spanish or Italian?"

"Spanish, as a matter a fact, it's Sephardic, meaning rabbi.

He says he can trace his ancestry to a Portuguese cartographer, who was on Juan Cabrillo's sailing team off this coast in the mid-16th century. Don't ask him about it unless you've got an hour to spare."

Rabino charged into the room, tossed an abbreviated salute to the men, then slammed two manila folders onto his desk. While standing he tapped the folders and said, "You guys are handling two of the hottest murders in the county—both within one week. We've never had two prominent deaths to investigate concurrently. Ordinarily, we'd have another homicide team take this latest murder, but as you know, those guys are on another case. If you think the job is too big, I'll see that you get help." Rabino waited for Amado to comment.

"For now, I think we can manage," Amado said.

"That's fine." Rabino paused, drew in his breath; his steely blue eyes homed in on Amado's. Speaking deliberately but with a rising voice, he said, "Do you have one goddamned bloody clue in this Montenegro case?" He leaned forward, with his hands in his back pockets. "How would you like to sit at this desk and listen to reporters and nudniks all day, asking if any progress has been made in these murders?" He did not wait for a response. "Complaints are coming in from neighbors scared shitless about their safety. And I offer them some goddamned vapid excuse like, 'we're working on it.' Hell, I don't know diddly about what we're working on."

He put a cigar in the corner of his mouth and clamped down on it. "Amado," he pointed his forefinger at him, "can you tell me what the hell you have on this case? Let me warn you. If you tell me nothing, I'm putting you on a walking beat in Old Town Goleta." Rabino leaned back in his chair, folded his arms across his chest and said, "All right, now, enlighten me."

Fred Amado had listened to Rabino's melodramatic haranguing too many times to cower at his threats. He respected the man, even liked him, but he could not solve all homicides with a snap of the fingers, and he knew that Rabino knew it, too.

This was a game they played, especially in the presence of a third party—in this case, the novice detective, Bill Connors. "You have all the information we have," Amado said. "We're in the process of questioning and re-questioning all the help. One of them is going..."

Rabino cut him off. "I want the principal players brought to this office." Tapping the desk with his knuckles, then looking through pages in a manila folder, he said, "Let's bring in Isabella Chavez, the secretary." He turned the page and continued, "Maria Guerrero, the maid, Carlos Estevan, the caretaker, and John G., the chauffeur. Does anyone know what the G stands for? No? Okay, let's get started."

"Will you want to ask them questions about the visiting priest's murder?" Connors asked.

"Hell yes. Why wouldn't I? We'll interview them separately, of course. Round up these people." He looked at the calendar on his desk. "Bring in the first one, the secretary, on Monday. You have two days to line up your dominoes. Any questions? No? Okay, get to it." Rabino dismissed the detectives—then as they were leaving, he called out, "Fred, I'd like a word with you—alone." Connors walked on as Amado returned to the office and closed the door behind him.

Rabino, slightly shorter than Amado, faced him closely. "Fred, all that talk about pulling you off and giving you a foot beat is bullshit. You know that."

"Yeah, yeah. You want to impress the new kid. I've already told him you're a bastard."

"Thanks. How's he doing? Is he helpful?"

"He's okay. About as helpful as I was when I started."

"That bad, huh? Only kidding. What are your thoughts regarding the señora's death? And now this wild hack-job on the padre?"

"There's got to be one or more crazies floating around that hacienda with a need to kill...probably revenge murders with a big time payback."

Rabino started to chew on his cigar. "You've excluded the

possibility of outsiders?"

"No, but I think that's less likely. The place is forti-
fied, surrounded by a high wall, an alarm system and a
watch-dog."

"Fred, I know you're giving this your best shot, but I need
more action. Dan Black is catching hell from Sacramento, and
when that happens, Dan leans on me. Do you want a twenty-
four hour surveillance on the estate? Maybe a tail on one of
the employees?"

Amado shook his head, reached for the doorknob, then
turned to face Rabino. "Marv, I'll do whatever you suggest.
Right now, I don't know what else to do except ask more questions and become a bigger pain in the ass to some of the help."

"That's it—become a bigger pain in the ass, if that's
possible, but get some answers."

Chapter 11

"Head south," Amado said to Connors. "Let's go to the Montenegro place again. We've got to ask that chauffeur more questions. He was the last one to see that Father Allende before he got chopped up."

"You mean the last one besides the actual killer," Connors said.

"What makes you so damn sure that the chauffeur isn't the killer?"

"I dunno, but it's like you always say, 'What's the motive?' I don't know whether the chauffeur had the opportunity or the means. Geez, when I think about that priest's chopped off nose and that whacked off dick stuck in his mouth—that's wild man, really wild. When you saw that and the crucifix cut on his body, did you want to puke? I think I'd have tossed my cookies, cripes!"

Amado lit a cigarette, opened his window and blew out the smoke. He stared through the windshield and became contemplative. "After my gig in the Pacific, nothing hassles me. But I'll tell you, some of our boys treated the Japs the same way. When a guy gets a terrible mad on, like when one of your buddies standing beside you, gets his legs or his head blown off, you go crazy and want to kill and torture—well, you get the picture."

"I thought you were a pilot, Fred, like Rabino—away from ground fighting."

"Yeah, until I was shot down." Amado made no further

attempt to talk about his war experiences, as the mansion loomed in front of them.

John Gruenwald was bent over the front right fender applying touch-up paint when he looked up to see Amado and Connors standing behind him. He stood up, wiped the brush on a rag, smiled and extended his hand. "Just doing a little touch-up on this old chariot. I'm sorry Miss Chavez is not here. Can I help?"

"We'd like to ask a few more questions about the day you drove the priest to the cemetery," Amado said.

"Certainly. Would you like to come into my apartment for a cup of coffee or soft drink?"

"No, why don't we sit in this old crate and get out of the sun," Amado said.

The chauffeur opened the rear door for the detectives, then opened his door, sat behind the steering wheel and turned in his seat to face the detectives.

Detective Connors gaped at the spacious passenger compartments and ran his fingers along the velvety seats. "Hey, this is all right, fresh rose buds in vases on each side and a robe on a bar." He picked up the passenger phone. "I'll be damned, a telephone to the driver and a fold-away liquor bar. This is better than a Pullman car." He wrinkled his nose and sniffed. "What's that smell, Lysol?"

The chauffeur quickly opened both front doors. "I didn't realize the odor of the cleaning fluid would last this long."

Amado reached down to feel the carpeting. "This is still damp. I hope you weren't trying to get rid of blood stains or..."

Gruenwald interrupted. "No, no. Lobo our dog was sick, and I had to take him to the vet. He got dog shit on the floor. I had a devil of a time cleaning up."

Amado opened the door next to him. "You drove the priest to the cemetery, right? Did he stay at the chapel?"

"No. He insisted that I take him directly to the

mausoleum."

"Did he say why?" Amado asked.

"No, and I didn't press him. He looked as though he wanted—how do you say—solitude?"

"So you left him there—alone?"

"Yes. I knew the hearse would be bringing Señora Montenegro's body there soon. The chapel in the cemetery is only five minutes away."

"Did you see anyone else around the mausoleum?" Amado asked.

Gruenwald shook his head. "I can't remember...oh, yes. There were grave diggers close by, but I didn't pay any attention to them."

"They were using shovels, pick-axes, things like that?"

"I don't know, I suppose," Gruenwald said.

"How long is the ride from the church to the cemetery?" Amado asked.

"Maybe fifteen minutes or so."

"When you were questioned before, you said you were gone for about one hour. What took so long?" Amado asked.

The chauffeur paused momentarily, then said, "I stopped at a gas station and then at a food store."

Amado and Connors left Gruenwald and walked to their vehicle. "What d'ya think, Fred? Does the guy sound kosher?"

"About as kosher as Patty Murphy's pig."

Chapter 12

The Santa Barbara Biltmore, one of Isabella's favorite places for brunch and a glass or two of Chenin Blanc, served as a meeting place for her and Amado. Initially, he was reluctant to meet in this up-scale restaurant but consented after Isabella insisted. He agreed to sit with her, but said he wanted only a beer.

She protested. "Fred, I refuse to eat alone. Order a sandwich or salad—order something. I don't want you watching me while I eat. Don't shake your head, and don't worry about the bill. I have an open account here."

"You make me feel like a kept man."

"Don't flatter yourself. Your importance to me falls somewhere between Carlos, our foreman, and Lobo, the dog." She stifled a giggle then reached across the table to tap Amado's hand. "I'm only teasing. Actually, I think I'm growing quite fond of you."

"Glad to know I'm not last on your list."

A tuna salad sandwich cut in four sections accompanied by fries was brought to the table. Isabella requested an empty plate, then placed two sections of the sandwich with all the fries on it and slid it over to Amado.

Looking at the plate then at Isabella, Amado said, "I don't think you understand. I said I didn't want to eat."

"I do understand, but you're a big man, and you need food."

"You sound like my mother, but for some reason, I don't resent you."

"Good. Now, ask me whatever you wish." Isabella dabbed the corners of her mouth with a napkin and smiled.

"The question I've got to ask again is, did you kill Señora Montenegro? Don't laugh, I'm serious."

Isabella closed her eyes, shook her head, and assuming an air of forbearance, said, "Fred stop trying to act like a big, bad policeman. No, my dear, I did not kill my beloved señora. Now eat your sandwich and fries."

"I need your help. Someone or some ones in that mansion wanted the señora and the priest dead. Do you know of anyone..."

"Fred, we've gone over all this before. I simply do not know."

"Murder is usually the result of money or love problems. I'm making the assumption that the problem here is money."

She paused, placed her sandwich on the plate and gave Amado her complete attention. "More money than love," she said.

"Okay, what're you thinking?"

"The señora had a good mind for business. On the estate there are several acres of orange and lemon groves. The crops are harvested and purchased by a citrus exchange twice a year."

"Are you saying that brings in enough revenue to cover the upkeep on the estate?" Amado did not wait for an answer. "From what I know about small groves, I'd say it doesn't."

"You're quite knowledgeable, Fred. I'd say you're probably right, but remember, the señora and her husband had considerable wealth before they came to this country. Now, don't ask me where their wealth came from while they lived in Spain."

"You don't know? Or you don't care to tell me."

Isabella did not comment. She caught the waiter's attention and requested coffee.

"What exactly were your responsibilities in that organization?"

"I had many. I was the señora's confidante. I handled all incoming and outgoing correspondence, made bank deposits and withdrawals, made appointments at the beauty salon, scheduled massages and chiropractic treatments and helped select her wardrobe." She smiled, tilted her head and spoke joyfully. "We spent hours, like school girls, giggling over the men who wanted to date her—such delightful moments." She became wistful, placed her chin on the back of her hands and gazed out the window.

"The men you referred to, those dating or trying to date the señora, who are they?"

The question snapped Isabella's reverie. "Oh, yes, the men. There's Attorney Cornelius Spingarn, we called him 'Corny', a wealthy widower who tried a number of times to invite the señora to dinner at his hillside mansion. He handled legal matters for the Montenegros and was quick to become overly-solicitous after the colonel died two years ago. But he was physically unattractive and too old for her. Truth is, she was repulsed by him. He became outraged when she told him that she did not care to date him."

"Do you think this Spingarn character could have killed the señora?"

Isabella shook her head. "The man is too old, too arthritic, and besides, how would he be able to...unless he hired someone."

"Always a possibility. We'll be sure to call on him. Did the Montenegros have other active business dealings? We've examined their bank accounts and found that although they had adequate funds, they did not appear to be multi-millionaires. We wondered how they invested the monies they brought from Europe. Of course, they could have stashed hard cash or bullion in a vault somewhere. Did they have investments here?"

"I can only tell you what I know and what I've been told. After the Spanish Civil War, they came to the United States and settled in Santa Barbara. They bought up ocean front properties and a warehouse in Goleta near the railroad station—paid cash. Not all the properties were attractive. In fact, to my mind, none of them were. Some were nothing more than run-down shacks, including two houses of prostitution, a tattoo parlor, and a motorcycle repair garage. Some of the former owners stayed on as tenants."

"Sounds like the colonel aspired to be a slumlord with a penchant for inelegant properties." Fred lit a cigarette and leaned back in his chair. "What about the señora? Anything in her past or business activities that could explain..."

"She took charge of collecting rents, and demanded payments on time. I know she angered some delinquent renters. She went so far as to evict a few. I thought that on more than one occasion, one of those unsavory characters might do her harm."

"Seems to me the playing field is getting larger." Amado continued probing, and Isabella didn't seem to be concealing anything as she recollected her years in the señora's service. The focus shifted from the señora to Isabella herself. She shared some of her tastes with him, offering tantalizing glimpses of what mattered to her. Again she told him how she loved Neruda and went on to sight a few lines from his *Cancion Desesperada,* his song of despair.

Isabella looked at her watch. "Do you realize we've been dining for almost two hours?" She folded her napkin and signaled the waiter to bring the bill. After signing it, she pushed back in her chair. Amado walked behind her to assist in bringing her chair back. She stood, turned and looked over her shoulder to thank him. "Fred, you're so chivalrous, so gallant, and I love you for it."

He resisted an overwhelming impulse to lean forward and kiss her on the neck, but too many eyes were watching, and he wanted no public notice of him being intimate with her.

"Can I drive you back to the estate?" he asked.

"No, thank you. The chauffeur is waiting out in front."

"Why don't you send him home? I have a few more questions to ask and being alone with you in the car will be..."

Isabella interrupted. "Are you sure that's the only reason you want to drive me home?" Before Amado could answer, she said, "Flatter me. Tell me it's not. Besides, we won't have much time in the car. We're just twelve minutes from the estate." Isabella left and returned to the lounge where Amado waited for her. She said, "John has driven the limo back to the estate. Now we can have a few more moments together."

"I'll cherish every moment we're alone."

Lobo barked, and wagged his tail excitedly as soon as Isabella got out of Amado's car. The dog walked between her and Amado and made slight contact with her side to indicate possessiveness.

One door of the four-car garage was open with the front half of the Hispano Suissa facing forward. The chauffeur leaned into the engine compartment, a set of tools rested on a cloth covering the running board. Amado approached him. "Having trouble with the old chariot?"

The chauffeur in a jump suit stood up. "Yes, the timing chain needs adjustment. That happens in these old cars."

"You're wearing gloves. I can't ever remember seeing a mechanic wearing gloves."

"The señorita doesn't like seeing black grease under my fingernails."

Amado picked up a rag with red stain. The chauffeur grabbed the rag, balled it up, jammed it into his pocket and said, "That's my blood on the rag, I cut myself on the fan."

Isabella was at the front door of the estate when Amado came up behind her. "Do you mind if I step inside with you?" he asked. "I'd like to look at the murder scene again."

"Only if you promise to behave."

"I'll make no such promise."

With Fred close behind her, Isabella walked into the entryway, then into the living room. She glanced around, then froze and put her hands to her mouth to muffle a scream.

"What the hell's wrong?" Amado asked.

Isabella, unable to speak, pointed to the large painting of Franco and the señora.

Amado stared, his brow wrinkled. "What kind of shit is this?" He walked slowly toward the painting. Isabella followed closely, her hands covered her mouth, her eyes wide with fright and bewilderment.

Bright red, roughly spattered swastikas almost obliterated the faces of Franco and the señora. Only Franco's right eye had been spared; it seemed to follow Amado as he moved before it. A glob of red paint covered Franco's right hand and drops of paint fell from it like trickling blood. Several drops had fallen on the picture frame and pooled on the floor. Amado, careful to avoid stepping on the paint, held his outstretched arm behind him to warn Isabella not to step in it. He sniffed the paint. "It's fresh, been there just a short while."

Isabella, trembling, said, "It wasn't there this morning. Who could have done this?" She recoiled from the painting. "Oh, Fred, this is so frightening. It's so evil." She clung to Amado who embraced her and held her head against his chest.

"Go ahead and cry, baby. It's okay." He stroked the back of her head.

She grew pale as she looked into his eyes. "Fred, don't leave me now, I need your strength." Her eyes rolled up and she collapsed in his arms. He carried her to a nearby sofa. Kneeling at her side, he reached for a pillow to place beneath her head. He felt her pulse. It was steady and strong. He pushed a few strands of hair from her eyes, then kissed the back of her cold hands and watched her expression closely. Her eyelids fluttered, then opened. Confused, she tried to focus on Amado's face, then she looked around. "What happened?" Amado explained and reassured her.

A weak smile transformed her worried look. "Thank you, Fred." She clasped his hands. "You're sweet and gentle. I've put you through a lot of trouble."

"Where is all the help in this damned place? A person could be dying and no one would know it. How do I get someone here to look after you?"

Isabella sat up with Fred's help and picked up a phone

on the end table. She dialed a single number and waited. "Maria...yes... the living room." Maria Guerrero hurried into the room, stammered expletives in English and Spanish and took immediate charge.

"Okay, doll, you rest," Amado said. "I'm going to look around this museum to see if there's any other damage. Don't let anyone get near that painting. This is a crime scene with vandalism of valuable property."

"Fred, wait! I'm frightened. I don't know whether I can stay here alone." She searched his eyes beseeching him to stay. "I'll have Maria prepare the guest room and..."

Fred's brow wrinkled as he pondered one *helluva* dilemma. While it was not unusual for someone to be given protection, it always involved having a deputy parked outside, not sleeping in an adjacent bedroom. He knew the rules, but Isabella's fear and vulnerability moved him to accept the risk of being caught breaking them. She needed to be protected, that's all there was to it. He looked at the vandalized painting again and dug his hands into his pockets. Seeing Isabella's imploring eyes, he said, "Where's the guest room?"

"Next to mine."

Chapter 13

Amado remained silent, then turned his back to Isabella and rubbed his temple firmly. When he faced her again, she searched his eyes beseeching him to stay.

"Why not have Maria sleep in the guest room?"

"Fred, Maria doesn't have a gun."

Fred's brow wrinkled. "I suppose I could lie down in the next room and listen for any sounds that..."

"Yes, yes! Oh, please do. I would be so grateful." Isabella's pleas came in torrents. "I could even give you a pair of the colonel's silk pajamas."

"Not a chance. I'll remove my shoes, nothing else."

Isabella hurried up the stairs to the bedrooms. Fred followed.

"There's a connecting door between the bedrooms that can be locked from either side. Should I lock my side?" Isabella asked with an almost childlike innocence that belied her sophistication.

"No, don't lock it. If I hear a sound from your room, I'll want to charge in. Lock the door to the hallway."

Isabella, on tiptoes, held the back of Amado's neck and kissed him lightly on the lips. "I can't thank you enough."

Looking around the guest room, Amado thought it more than adequate with an adjoining washroom and shower and certainly better than his own stark quarters. He removed his shoes, placed his jacket on a hanger in the closet, loosened his tie and unbuttoned his collar. The shoulder holster with his Colt .45 jabbed his side. He had never worn it while lying down. He removed the holster and gun and placed them on the nightstand beside him. Suddenly he felt uncomfortably warm and removed his shirt.

After opening the window, he stuck his head out to look in both directions, then above to follow the roof lines. The moonlight provided visibility for about a hundred yards in either direction. He sat on the edge of the bed and picked up the gun to check the barrel, then put it back on the nightstand and shut the nightlight. He lay back on the bed, his fingers interlaced behind his head. He brought his left wrist forward to look at the luminescent hands on his wristwatch: 10:45. Usually he was asleep at that time, but knowing that Isabella occupied the bed in the next room, caused a kind of restlessness. Then the thought of an intruder lurking about, brought him to a sitting position. He swung his legs over the side of the bed and switched on the nightstand lamp.

His hearing, keenly attuned to any sound, kept him alert. The absence of light under the connecting door indicated that Isabella had turned off her lamp and was probably asleep. He wondered if she thought of him, as he did of her. He had never known anyone like her. She was damn near perfect in every way—her movements, her manner of speaking, even the way she flirted, classy and subtle-like and now her almost childlike dependence upon him made her irresistible.

She reminded him of Linda Darnell as she appeared in *Forever Amber*. *Yeah, that's who she looks like, but Isabella is even prettier.* He placed his head back on the pillow, his eyes closed, and finally the world seemed to be shutting down.

A faint, distant click invaded Amado's unconsciousness. He turned his head but kept his eyes closed, until a squeak brought him to full alertness. He bolted upright, slid off the bed, and reached for his gun. As his eyes adjusted to the darkness, he moved toward the door. Then he was startled to see that the connecting door was open. His heart pounded. His eyes searched the blackness. He jerked as something touched his arm, he recoiled and raised his weapon.

"Hey! Who the hell's there?" he demanded.

"Sh-sh. It's all right, Fred. It's only me." Isabella's voice came in a whisper.

"Jeezus, girl, I could have blown your head off. What's the matter? Are you all right? I'll turn on the light."

"No, no. Please don't. I'm wearing a sheer nightie. I couldn't sleep." She found his arm and held it firmly. "Fred, I need your reassurance. I'm worried, I'm terribly frightened. I hope you understand."

"Yeah, I understand, kitten." His voice turned soft and compassionate. "Sit down. Let's talk. I'll bring the other chair over."

Isabella seated across from him, reached out and held his hand. "Fred, I'm terrified. This place gives me the creeps, like there's an evil presence here. I want to run away and leave all this behind. Is that unreasonable? I hate everything about this place. Just a short time ago, it was such a wonderful home, now it's like a slaughterhouse."

"Whoa, baby, whoa. I understand your fears, and I sympathize, but this pile of bricks isn't responsible for what goes on around here. Some damned screwball, some demented crazy is seeking revenge. We'll find out who he is. It might take a while, but we'll get him. Until then, nothing bad is going to happen to you. I give you my word."

"Oh, Fred, I'm so grateful for your strength and understanding. I feel much safer just being near you." She placed her arms around his neck and kissed him lightly on the lips. The delicate fragrance of her hair, the feel of her supple body and soft skin covered only by a silky garment filled him with mounting desire. He brought her into his embrace with a force that took her breath away. His lips covered her mouth, and she devoured his thrusting tongue.

She hungered for his animal-like reaction to her own pent-up yearnings, and she thrust her pelvis against his tumescence. "I love you so," she murmured. Her hand brushed lightly the hair on his chest then slipped below to unbuckle his belt. Quickly, he stepped out of his trousers and shorts, then lifted her nightie over her head. The light of the moon had shown the perfect form of her breasts and the hardening nipples that tilted upward. He bent forward and suckled them as she closed her eyes, bent backward and sighed. She reached down and gently stroked his rigid shaft and cupped his scrotum. She pleasured him exquisitely for several moments before kissing him again on the mouth.

Then, leaning back against his arm, she let him lift her. He set her down softly on the bed, bent over and whispered, "I've got a condom in my wallet, should I get it?"

"No, no. I want to feel all of you."

They lay in each other's arms until the excitement of those magical moments of intimacy were again fulfilled.

As the early morning sun bathed the room, Isabella clutched her nightie and tiptoed toward her bedroom. Awake, Amado regarded her backside, marveling at her perfect gluteal symmetry, the narrowness of her waist and the tantalizing, graciously curving sides of her full breasts.

She was everything he had ever hoped for and more…a lover, a companion, a partner forever. But then cold, bitter reality intruded, a sobering awareness that this moment in paradise was fleeting, and it could cost him dearly. By compromising an investigation he had crossed the line and become a rogue cop who would pay a huge price whenever his offense was discovered. For the moment, still savoring the heavenly intimacy, he was almost able to shut out reality, almost able to convince himself that discovery could be avoided.

He showered and shaved with a guest kit he found in the medicine cabinet and started to hum into the mirror, *Some Enchanted Evening*. Isabella, fresh and happy, walked into the bathroom. She smiled broadly and embraced him from behind. "Thank you for a magnificent evening. I loved being in your arms and making love to you. Do you know, I think I lost count after three." She giggled.

Amado took her in his arms and studied her eyes, then brushed her face gently with the back of his hand. "Your cheeks are rosy."

"Thanks to the stubble on your face." She took a step back, tilted her head and put a forefinger to her chin. "I'm going to outfit you in a custom-tailored suit, Italian shoes, a silk shirt, a cravat..."

"Hold on, kitten. We're a long way from domestic dominance here."

"Are you frightened by my possessiveness? You were the one who had complete control over me last night, and I loved every moment of it." She placed her arms around his neck. "I wouldn't mind making permanent arrangements for that."

Amado nodded. "First, you'll have to learn how to make a few Mexican dishes. Second, you'll have to pass muster with my mother."

Isabella put her finger to his lips. "She'll like me, I promise. As for food—we'll live on love."

Chapter 13

"Bring the Chavez woman in," Rabino said to his deputy. Amado and Connors sat against the back wall of Rabino's office. Isabella, elegant in a trim black suit, stepped into the room, looked about and smiled when she saw Amado. He responded with a curt nod but didn't smile, fearful that Rabino might be suspicious if he detected any sign of warmth between them. She stopped smiling and turned her attention to Rabino, who asked her to be seated. Her back was all that Amado and Connors could see of her.

In a solicitous tone, Rabino said, "Miss Chavez, thank you for coming in. Please understand, we're not charging you with anything, but you are a person of interest. We're dealing with two murders, and we're desperate for clues. Assuming that you're innocent of any involvement in these terrible crimes, you have nothing to worry about. As investigators we are compelled to ask questions as we see fit. No one is exempt. If this causes you distress, I apologize, but it can't be helped." He leaned forward on his desk. "As you know, for the past ten days we've been trying to uncover evidence in the murder of Mrs. Montenegro." He paused as she nodded. "The trouble is, we're stymied. We don't have much to go on, and to make matters worse, we have a second murder, the visiting priest, and again, we're without clues. Oh, don't get me wrong, we'll find the guilty party or parties, all right, but we could use help." He flipped through the pages in the manila folder on his desk.

"In reviewing some statements you made to Sergeant Amado, I'm having difficulty understanding why there were no witnesses. No one saw or heard anything unusual." Rabino's brow wrinkled, and he paused, waiting for a response.

Isabella started to say something, then stopped.

Rabino continued, "If an outsider approached the estate, a guard dog would have barked, isn't that right?" She nodded. "The dog has a loud bark—loud enough to rouse most people on the estate, maybe even the neighbors. Of course, your closest neighbors are a quarter mile away, so it's possible they wouldn't have heard. But, if the dog did bark, and nobody on the estate heard him, that would be unusual, wouldn't it?"

"I suppose so."

"You told Sergeant Amado that you would not have heard the dog if you were showering. Right?" Isabella nodded and Rabino continued, "Does the dog bark at any of the permanent staff?"

"I—I'm not sure."

"I see. Would the dog bark at the seasonal workers?"

"Yes, if they came to the main gate, but they're instructed to go to the workers' entrance. That's fenced off and far removed from where the dog would be guarding. "

"Do the field workers have access to the main house?"

"Not ordinarily. The workers who live on the estate sleep in a separate building. Only the señora and her personal staff live in the main house, and those outside doors are locked during the evenings."

"Who are the personal staff members?"

"Maria Guerrero, the maid, Alicia Montez the cook, John Gruenwald, the chauffeur and I."

Rabino flipped a page. "Sergeant Amado reported a firearm missing from a display case in the colonel's den. Would you know anything about that?"

"No, and I mentioned that to Fred—I mean Sergeant Amado."

Rabino looked at Amado, then at her. "I see." He paused.

"A request made to the Bureau of Firearms in Sacramento, revealed the registration of a .22 caliber Smith and Wesson pistol to a Colonel Armando Hidalgo Montenegro, dated September 14, 1948. There's a good possibility that might have been the gun used to kill Señora Montenegro."

Isabella said nothing.

"Miss Chavez, in a review of Señora Montenegro's will, a copy of which I have here, an article of interest is the distribution of property. As you know, your share of the inheritance is considerable. You inherit the main house and all associated properties. I'm not an attorney, so I don't know what that entails. The point I want to make is that you're coming into a great deal of wealth."

Isabella straightened in her chair. "The implication is that I would have a strong motive for murdering Señora Montenegro?"

Rabino shrugged. "You must admit that..."

"Stop!" Isabella stood. "How dare you! I did not come here to be accused of murdering someone I loved dearly. You have no right to suggest such a monstrous thing." She took a deep breath and exhaled. "As of this minute, if you or anyone else in your department wants to speak to me, it will be through my attorney."

"Miss Chavez, please understand, this is a case of murder, no other crime is as serious. Now we're faced with two murders, and we're desperate for clues. If you're innocent, I will apologize for any inconvenience I've caused you. Until then, we are compelled to ask questions as we see fit. No one is exempt from our investigation."

Isabella turned and cast a baleful glance at Amado, then walked briskly out of the office and slammed the door behind her.

Rabino stuck a cigar butt in his mouth then patted his shirt pockets for a match. The room soon took on the stench from his cigar and Amado opened a window.

"Marv, if you wanted us to leave too, you could have asked us. You didn't have to stink us out."

Rabino ignored the comment. He pointed his cigar at Connors. "I want you to examine Miss Uppity's bank account. Find out what kind of deposits and withdrawals she's made recently. Is she paying off any gambling debts or big ticket jewelry items? Did she buy a fancy car or put a down payment on a home? You know, things like that." He turned toward Amado and studied him for a moment. "What's eating you, Fred? Why the hell are you looking at me like that?"

"Christ, Marv, Chavez isn't a credible suspect—at least, not to me."

"Really? Maybe you have a proprietary interest there."

"What the hell does that mean?"

With a pugnacious sneer, Rabino said, "If I thought for one minute you were cavorting with our only viable suspect, I'd order you to turn in your badge. Expect no quarter, no appeal, no nothing. Is that understood?"

Amado gave no immediate response, then asked, "Are you going to question the foreman now?"

Rabino looked at the list on his desk and signaled his deputy. "Bring in Carlos Sanchez."

Sanchez, a dark, mustachioed man, held a soiled broad-brim straw hat against his chest and approached Rabino's desk apprehensively.

"Do you understand English?" Rabino asked.

"Si', señor, un poco."

"Fred, talk to this guy, will ya? My Spanish ain't great. Ask him if he heard a gunshot on the night the señora was murdered, and if he thinks any of the workers would have a reason for killing her... whether he or any of them own guns. Tell him if he's lying or covering up for someone, he'll go to jail forever. Don't ask him if he's a U.S. citizen. We have enough problems as is."

<hr />

Amado ran his finger along the directory. "Cornelius A. Spingarn, Attorney at Law, room 212. Let's take the stairs,

Billy Boy, stretch our legs."

"Is he expecting us, Fred?"

"Hell no. I never want these guys to prepare lying answers."

Amado spoke softly to Connors. "This waiting room has all the charm of an undertaker's parlor: worn-out leather chairs, overgrown fern plants, and two-year-old *Saturday Evening Posts*."

The frosted glass window slid open and a matronly secretary made a cursory appraisal of the detectives. "Can I help you gentlemen?"

"We'd like to talk with Mr. Spingarn," Amado said.

"If you don't have an appointment that would be quite impossible."

Amado flashed his badge and pulled enough of his jacket aside to reveal his holstered piece. He leaned forward. "Just a few moments of his time would be appreciated."

"I—I think we might be able to squeeze you in. Just a moment, please."

⊷⊷❈━━━❈⊷⊷

Spingarn, a wizened, bald septuagenarian, stared through thick eyeglasses that enlarged the size of his eyes and gave him a surprised look. His prune-like face was liberally sprinkled with liver spots and warts. His head and neck barely cleared the top of an oversized desk. A forced smile revealed bright, even teeth, obviously alien in origin. "Gentleman, what can I do for you? If it's the Annual Police and Fireman's Ball..."

Amado remembered what Isabella had told him about how the señora regarded Spingarn as physically unattractive and was repulsed by him. He could hardly fault her taste.

"Counselor, we've come to ask about your relationship with the late Mrs. Montenegro. "

"Montenegro?" His sustained smile disappeared. "I don't know what you mean. I had no relationship with Mrs. Montenegro."

"But you did do legal work for the Montenegros."

"Yes, and I'm under no obligation to disclose to you or anyone else what I did for them. Ours was a client-attorney relationship that will remain inviolable."

"As you wish. What you may not be aware of, counselor, is that you will be called upon to explain your adversarial relationship with Mrs. Montenegro."

"I still don't know what you're talking about."

"We have a witness who will testify that you became abusive when you learned that Mrs. Montenegro refused to socialize with you."

"Poppycock! I would deny any allegation of that sort."

"You were the attorney of record when certain property dealings were consummated by Colonel Montenegro."

"Goddamn nonsense—all of this. I had no part in any of those shenanigans."

"What shenanigans would that be, counselor?"

"Don't try to get clever with me. You're not going to inveigle me into saying anything more."

"Counselor, you might be a maven when it comes to matters of the law, but let me tell you that the prosecutor won't spare you if he believes you have information that could help solve two murders."

"Don't you lecture me about legal procedures, Mis-ter Detective." Spingarn labored as he emerged from his chair to reach for a cane. He moved toward Amado and Connors and craned his neck to look up at them. "I may be half your height because of this damned spondylitis, but I've got twice your brains."

Amado looked down at the aged attorney bent with a severe flexion deformity at his waist and asked him outright, "Counselor, did you have anything to do with Mrs. Montenegro's death?"

Spingarn swung his cane at the detective. "You ignora-muses. Get the hell out of here, now."

"Your records can be subpoenaed with a court order,"

Amado said as he dodged the sweep of the cane.

"You don't know what you're talking about. Now, get the hell out of my office—go on, git!"

Outside, Amado shared what he suspected with Connors. "I'll bet that old sidewinder is concealing information on the Montenegros that could bust this case wide open," Amado said as he opened the door to the sedan. Getting in, he repeated, "Yeah, wide open."

"Think we can get a judge to issue an order to examine his records?"

"That could be difficult. Maybe impossible." Amado paused and stared through the windshield as he started the engine. "On the other hand, that wily old bastard has managed to aggravate at least two judges who wouldn't mind rubbing his warty nose in a pile of shit."

"How do you know that, Fred?"

"It's a small community. Gossip runs rampant, especially when a snake like Spingarn slithers around."

"Do you think one of our legal experts could initiate an action for those records? Maybe one of those two judges would issue the order," Connors said.

"Almost too much to hope for, Billy Boy. We might have to be a bit more inventive."

Chapter 14

With a phone against his ear, Amado sat back in his chair; his legs stretched and crossed at the ankles rested atop his desk. "Isabella, be reasonable, I've called again and again in the last three days. If you hang up on me, I'm coming over with a search warrant—dammit, don't hang up!" Amado slammed the phone down, bolted out of his chair and headed to the parking lot.

He wove along the serpentine turns of Alameda Padre Serra Drive until he reached the driveway to Casa del Caudillo. At the iron gate, he sounded his horn, leaned out the window and yelled, "Open up! *Abre la puerta!*" Lobo came charging and barked at the horn blast. Carlos, the foreman, hurried to the gate with a flurry of apologies in Spanish.

Isabella, in the grand room, aware of Amado's arrival, stood with her back to the entryway, her arms folded across her chest. Amado approached slowly and tapped her shoulder. She shrugged his hand away. "I come with a peace offering." She stiffened but turned around, then tilted her head and with a show of reluctant acquiescence, said, "Yes?" He handed her a bouquet of red roses.

She had difficulty maintaining her scowl. With pursed lips she looked at the flowers and said, "*Picalo,* you rascal." His pleading expression did not escape her. To Amado's relief, she spoke calmly and without rancor. "You're naughty and you deserve to be punished." She tilted her head and said, "I really shouldn't be talking to you. A fine friend you turned out to be—permitting that awful Sheriff Rabino to accuse me of murder."

"Hold on, Duchess, he didn't accuse you of murder. He merely intimated that you might have motive, opportunity and..."

She interrupted. "What kind of a friend permits talk like that—from anyone?"

"That's the whole point, don't you see? We're not supposed to be *friends*, especially close friends. We shouldn't even be talking like this now. If Rabino knew that we were..." He stopped and took a step back as Maria approached.

Isabella handed the roses to her to place in a vase. She looked at the bouquet again when Maria left. "The roses are beautiful, thank you. I must confess I enjoyed being with you the other night, and I was grateful for your love and understanding, but I'm disappointed and unhappy about the sheriff's and your attitude towards me."

"It's not attitude. It's our job. If you and I are seen socializing, I could lose my job. It's just that simple."

"Then why are you here?"

"Because I'm nuts about you, and can't stand being away for long. Is that so hard to understand?"

"I think it's my body you want."

"I'd never deny it. I simply adore you."

They both laughed and the icy wall that existed between them minutes before had melted completely. Amado pulled her toward him with a force that surprised her. Her immediate impulse was to push him away; but suddenly she put her arms around him. She hungered for his kisses and the strength of his body. Their moment of enchantment ended when Maria cleared her throat at the far end of the room. She apologized for the intrusion and asked Isabella questions about dinner.

Isabella responded, then asked Amado, "Would you have dinner with me here tonight? Just the two of us. Maria will make one of her wonderful Mexican dishes."

"You don't have to ask me twice." Amado looked at his watch. "It's 4:45. I should go home, shower and change...get rid of some of my man stink."

"Fred, you have such a refined way of expressing yourself." Isabella made a show of sniffing his jacket, then holding her nose. "You do smell as though you've put in a hard day. Let me make a suggestion: how about showering here? You can cover yourself afterward with talcum powder. You'll smell like a newborn baby, and I love newborn babies."

"Will you scrub my back?"

"Go, before I change my mind and ask you to leave."

Fred put his clothes and pistol on the guest bed and stepped into the shower stall with its border of colorful Mexican tiles. He luxuriated in the steaming water and fragrant suds while humming *Bali Hai* from *South Pacific*. The soapy suds covered his head and cascaded down his face, neck and chest.

Suddenly he stopped humming and scrubbing. "What the hell's going on here? Who's there?"

"Guess who."

Amado felt a familiar soft body press against his back. Two arms reached around his chest then slid downward over his abdomen to his inner thighs and started a gentle massaging motion.

"Oh, baby, this is one shower I'm not leaving." He turned to face a nude beauty with a mischievous smile. He moved to allow the water to splash on her as she turned her face upward toward the showerhead while he stood behind her.

"Will you wash my back?" She handed him a soapy washcloth.

"With pleasure, baby." He leaned forward and kissed her neck, then brought his soapy hands around to caress her breasts.

"I said, wash my *back*." She giggled; he murmured, "Your breasts are marvelous." Leaning back against him, she replied,

"I love your hands." Their erotic passions mounted after a short period of mutual exploration. Isabella leaned against the shower stall and wrapped one leg around Amado drawing him inside her. She gasped as he penetrated her, bit his neck and clung tightly murmuring something unintelligible. With a shudder she came, then went limp and slumped in his arms; he raised her chin and kissed her gently on the lips.

With the shower still spraying, he ran his hand over her body to remove soapy residue. She remained quiet in the sensuous afterglow when Amado embraced her again. They gazed into each other's eyes with the total understanding and wonder of discovery only new lovers possess.

Isabella reached for her towel hanging over the shower door and left. She called out, "Dinner in thirty minutes, love."

The shower splashed Amado's face when he heard Lobo's bark. He listened while the dog's distant but distinct bark could be heard again... and again...and again.

He toweled himself, then sprinkled talc over his body. He approached the bed to discover that his underclothes had been replaced by neatly folded silk boxer shorts and an undershirt. *Dammit! No one has a right to invade my personal…wait a minute, calm down stupid, you've just had the most wonderful intimacy with the girl of your dreams and you're complaining because your Fruit of the Looms have been replaced? Stop being such a jerk.*

Chapter 15

A table in the alcove had been arranged with a damask cloth, two tapered candlesticks and long-stem wine goblets. The room was suffused with the aroma of sautéed onions, garlic, basil, cumin and other Mexican herbs. Isabella asked Fred to pour the wine.

Amado held the bottle and read the label. "1940 Sangre de Cristo, Madrid. This stuff has to be rare. When were the grapes harvested? The country was at war until 1939."

"Enjoy it. That comes from the last case the colonel shipped from Spain just before he died."

Amado watched with anticipation as an entrée of baked shrimp on a bed of rice was brought to the table.

"Ah, camarones con arroz."

María smiled. "Sí."

The dish was his first true homemade Mexican meal in months. He thought it was tastier than his mother's, but after all, she was born an Anglo—a WASP who had learned what few cooking skills she had from her Latina mother-in-law, too many years ago. Even Maria's flan was creamier and tastier.

The overhead light had been dimmed allowing the candlelight to cast soft shadows on Isabella's face, making her skin appear more lustrous, almost glowing. They made small talk filled with laughter and innuendo. She used the tip of her napkin to dab the corners of her mouth, and that little gesture was so lady-like, Amado thought. It too, set her apart from the others he had known.

Isabella stood, picked up her plate and dinnerware when Maria appeared, as if on cue, insisting that Isabella retire to the grand room with her guest.

In the grand room, Amado sniffed the faint, lingering odor of turpentine used to clean the red paint off the floor below the vandalized picture of General Franco and the señora. The picture had been removed leaving a pale rectangle image on the wall.

Lounging on a settee, with Isabella at his side, Amado looked about the grand room and studied it as though seeing it for the first time. "Beautiful furnishings," he said, "done with eclectic taste but done well."

Isabella reached out to hold his hand. "Don't tell me you're an expert on interior decorating, too. What do you know about such things?"

"More than you might imagine. I can probably name the period and style of most of these pieces and give you an approximate figure of their worth."

"Fred, how in-the-world would you know?"

"My father dealt in high-end antiques, including period furniture and accessories. They also took paintings on consignment. Some of the art work was world-class stuff that could have been in museums."

"You said, 'they'. Who were you referring to?"

"My father and his partner had a large store on State and Camarillo in downtown Santa Barbara. Dad's partner was Ben Goldberg. They combined the initials of their last names and came up with *A & G Fine Furniture and Furnishings*. They catered to the elite, I mean big bucks clientele in the Santa Barbara and Montecito areas. I worked in the store and in the warehouse during holidays and between semesters, until the business went belly-up in 1932. After Dad died, Mr. Goldberg remained in the business but at another location. I learned to identify and appreciate good art and furniture."

Amazed to hear this, Isabella became more curious and a bit dubious. "Let me test your expertise."

"Go ahead."

"Can you identify the dining room table and chairs?"

"And if I give you the correct answer, what reward will I get?"

"I think you've already had it," she answered, with a knowing smile.

Amado walked into the dining alcove with Isabella behind him. He pulled one chair away from the table and regarded it critically. "It has a typical Sheraton shield pattern." He turned it over, examined the underside, running his finger over the wood joints and supports. "It's authentic, all right... approximately 150 years old... museum quality." He bent over the table top and examined the pattern of the grain. "Beautifully matched walnut." On his hands and knees, he scrutinized the underside. "Yeah, this is a real find." He straightened up. "I'd estimate the value at around ten to twenty K at auction."

"Really? I am impressed."

"The señora and colonel were antique collectors?" Amado asked.

"I suppose so, although I can't recall seeing any of these pieces when we lived in Madrid, but furniture and antiques meant little to me then."

Chapter 16

In the undersheriff's crowded office, Rabino looked at Connors. "What did you find out about that Chavez dame's bank account? Any irregularities?"

"She's been depositing $500 a month at the Bank of America for at least two years. Her monthly expenses run about $200 to $400. Checks were made out to: I. Magnin, Saks Fifth Avenue, and The Fashion Shop. No really big-ticket items."

Rabino nodded, then pointed his cigar at Amado. "What do you have on that attendance list from the memorial church services? Any names of interest?"

"None made the F.B.I. 'Most Wanted' list, if that's what you're thinking," Amado said.

"Any local parolees? Any *asesinos*? No? Jeezus, give me something I can use, guys." He sighed. "If the Montenegro murder was not an affair of the heart, and I'm not saying it wasn't, then it had to do with money matters, right?" Amado remembered saying that to Isabella. "What business, besides the nickel-and-dime citrus grove, was the señora into?" Rabino glared at both detectives.

"She had real property and collected rents. Close to $1,000 a month." Amado said.

"That's not enough to sustain the estate and their lifestyle." Rabino tapped the desk repeatedly with his forefinger. "Guys, the numbers don't add up. What's in that Goleta warehouse? Spanish doubloons?"

Amado shrugged.

"I want to know what's in that warehouse. If that Chavez dame says she doesn't have a key or she refuses to open it, tell her we'll get a search warrant."

"On what pretext?" Amado asked.

"If you can't think of one, get the fire marshal to tell her the city can't take any chances on having combustible material in there. Besides, the fire chief has to be sure there are adequate fire extinguishers mounted and loaded...conforming to city code, of course."

"Is there a city code?" Connors asked.

"As of this minute there is—even if there ain't."

———

"Do you know anything about the warehouse or what's inside?" Amado asked Isabella as they rode in his Plymouth north on Highway 101 toward Goleta.

"I've never been inside. In fact, it never occurred to me to ask anything about it. The colonel and the señora seldom referred to it in my presence." Isabella's voice trailed off, her brow wrinkled. "Come to think of it, I do recall hearing snatches of conversation between them and Carlos the foreman about shipments coming in from time to time. I never thought about it until this moment. I thought they were talking about shipments of fertilizer or bricks, things like that." She turned to look at him. "What do you think we'll find in the warehouse?"

"Haven't the foggiest."

"Then why are we going there?"

"Rabino has this queer notion that we'll discover some illicit cache. This could be a wild goose chase, but frankly, I'm curious to know what's inside. Mysterious things appeal to me. For instance—you. You're an enigma like the smile on the Mona Lisa. I can't figure you out completely, but I sure enjoy the challenge."

"There may be a compliment in there, but I'm not sure. Getting back to the real world, are you any closer to knowing who killed the señora and the priest? It's been over two weeks, and there haven't been any arrests. Are there any suspects?" She glanced at him sideways. "I mean, besides me?" She moved closer to him; her thigh touched his. He placed his right hand on her left thigh and stroked it gently. "Please keep your mind on the road, Mr. Detective."

"Yes, ma'am." He turned his head for an instant to look at her. "Tell me, are your nights less troubled? Are you sleeping okay, or are you just as frightened as ever?"

"I'd live elsewhere if I could, but I have too much to attend to. I have obligations to the staff..."

Amado interrupted. "Will there be enough cash flow to maintain that white elephant? When the bills come due at the end of the month, you're going to have to write paychecks for the help and for utilities: electricity, water, gas..."

"Please, don't remind me."

"Some time ago, you said the señora's niece and nephew..."

"Angela and Anthony, the students at UCLA?"

"Yeah. As I recall, you said there was quite a bit left for them in the señora's will. If you've inherited the casa and the surrounding property, what's left for them?"

"I asked Lawyer Spingarn about other heirs. He said the only other people entitled to any of the spoils would be the niece and nephew, and he assured me there was enough for them."

"That old geezer used the term 'spoils'?"

"Yes, I thought that was rather crude and unprofessional."

Chapter 17

In a field adjacent to the Southern Pacific Railroad Station in Goleta, a low end outlying community known mainly for its lemon groves and the poverty of its mostly Latino inhabitants who picked the fruit, was the warehouse they sought. It was a squat rectangular cinderblock building surrounded by wild oats, scrub oak, and brush thick enough to constitute a fire hazard. A dirt road led to a double-door bolted entrance wide enough to admit a truck. Next to the entrance was a regular-size door secured by a large padlock. Dust piled up in the lower corners of the door, and cobwebs triangulated the upper corners.

Isabella removed a ring of keys from her purse and tried several of them to open the lock, without success.

Amado growing impatient, asked for the keys. "The lock is a Schlage, so there should be a matching key." He found it, opened the squeaky door, pulling and stretching the cobwebs that ruptured. He brushed them aside, then stepped into the darkness and groped along the wall for a light switch.

Isabella, close behind, wrinkled her nose in the stale, musty air. Two banks of fluorescent ceiling lights running the length of the warehouse blinked like strobes, then remained on to reveal the two-hundred foot long interior. A narrow central aisle twisted between tall, irregularly-shaped objects covered by movers' blankets. Despite the absence of windows and open wall spaces, light dust had accumulated on the folds of the dark green and brown blankets. Isabella reached for a handkerchief to cover her nose and mouth.

Amado walked several feet along the aisle. Reaching down to lift the lower edge of one of the blankets, he revealed a display case with intricate floral marquetry and hand-carved claw feet. He raised the blanket higher to study the bombé shape of the case and the delicate brass handles on the glass doors. He whistled, then said, "This thing belongs in a castle or mansion...it's magnificent...costly and old."

"How costly? How old?" Isabella asked.

"Probably a couple hundred thou...eighteenth century... wizardry in woodwork."

"Do you think this entire warehouse is full of things like that?"

Amado pulled another blanket aside and froze. He remained immobilized by what he saw. Stacked against the wall and extending toward the aisle were paintings framed in baroque and rococo gilt. One painting of a mother caressing a child in almost luminescent oils like pastels beckoned him.

He examined the painting more closely, then backed off. Rubbing his chin, he murmured, "Jeez, I know this painting."

"You know this painting?"

"That's a Mary Cassatt. Beautiful, isn't it? It's from my father's place."

"Your father's place? What's it doing here?"

"I sure don't know, but I'll bet there is someone who could tell me." Amado picked up the painting and studied the backside for a date.

Isabella expected to hear a name. "Who can tell you?" she asked.

"Ben Goldberg, my father's old partner. I haven't talked with him in several years...hope he's around. There's a phone in the office in front of this barn. I'll get Mr. Goldberg's phone number and talk with him. C' mon, you can listen in on the conversation."

"Mrs. Goldberg? How are you? This is Fred Amado. Do you remember me? I'm Romero Amado's son...how is Ben?" Amado looked at Isabella and crossed his fingers... "Ben is well...good...but he's gone...to Europe on a buying trip. Are you expecting him home soon?... three weeks. Can I ask a favor? When you talk with him would you ask him to call me at this number during evening hours." Amado started reciting his numbers but stopped. "You don't talk with him by phone because the reception is so bad and so costly?...yes, l understand. I would like to talk with him when he returns. Please have him call." He hung up and turned to Isabella. "There won't be any quick answers there."

They walked back into the warehouse and Amado picked up the Cassatt painting again. "I love this painting. Yeah, don't look so surprised, an ex-marine, sentimental about a picture of a mother and kid... it always pulled me in." He spoke slowly. "I really should have had a kid or two of my own, by now." He held the paintings at arm's length and said, "Look how the artist used colors to form a delicate life-like transparent quality to the skin, and notice the folds and filigree in the clothing...it's all so real, it makes you want to touch it."

"Fred, you're what I always suspected, a softy under that cloak of machismo. I think that's wonderful. Maybe that's why I love you. Now tell me, why is that painting here?"

Amado shrugged. "It was left in my father's place on consignment in 1934 as I recall; it had a price tag of 500 bucks. Probably worth ten times that now." He pulled the painting gently forward to find behind it a Camille Pissarro, a self-portrait. Behind that, a Monet painting of flowers in a remarkable array of vivid colors in the artist's garden at Giverny.

Amado awed, shook his head in disbelief, wondering *were they authentic or copies? Who brought them here? How many are stashed in this warehouse?*

Isabella, noticing Amado's sudden quietude, asked if he felt all right.

"Huh? Yeah, I'm all right. It's just that all this is kind of overwhelming. This stuff should be stored in an ambiance controlled for temperature and humidity— with an armed guard in attendance. "

"Where did these paintings come from?" she asked again. "And why are they here?"

Amado ran his hand through his hair and shook his head. "I get the impression that the Montenegros left this vale of tears without confiding all their secrets to you." Before she could respond, he asked, "Are you sure you knew nothing about all this?"

Isabella glared at him. With hands on hips she said, "Amado, you're insufferable. After all this time, and all we've been through, how could you be so cynical, so distrusting as to ask me that? Just when I thought you might understand my loss, my grieving, you ask a dumb question like that." Her voice escalated. "Why do I even bother associating with you?"

He dug his hands into his pockets. "Because I'm dumb; you take pity on me, and besides, I love you."

She evaded his embrace and walked toward the door. "Take me home."

"Look, Sweetheart, you gotta forgive me. I can't help asking stupid, dumb-ass questions. Remember, I'm a cop. These things just pop out of my mouth."

She stomped off.

He lifted another cover. A man-size steel safe set on a concrete block with gold lettering on the door, read, "Diebold Safe Co. Made Especially For ..." Amado dropped the cover and spoke to Isabella who had turned to look at him and was waiting impatiently. "Have you got the combination to this beast? He asked."

"No, and I don't care to know what's inside, either. Take me home now."

Chapter 18

Rabino's cigar smoke filled his office during a briefing with the two homicide detectives. "Get someone from the S.B. Art Museum or the university to authenticate those paintings and someone who knows about that fancy furniture. From your description, Amado, those gems are worth more than Daddy Warbucks can afford. How do we know they weren't stolen?"

"Have any claims been made against them?" Connors asked.

Rabino glared at him. "If any claims had been made, do you think for a minute they'd still be here?"

"No, sir." Connors lowered his head. A moment of painful silence followed.

"That's all right, kid. It's not you. It's me. I'm acting like a jerk. I keep getting calls from Sacramento that are driving me crazy. The state's attorney keeps threatening to send down his boy scouts. I don't want his prissy darlings prancing around here telling us what yokels we are and how brilliant they are." Rabino blew out a cloud of smoke that obscured his face. "Is there a chance that all that stuff belonged to the Montenegros, and they shipped it here from their home in Spain?" Rabino asked Amado.

"I doubt it. There's just too much of it. I'm guessing that someone or some ones gathered this stuff from a number of places and deposited it there for safekeeping or for sale at a future date. Now that the Montenegros are gone, we might never know."

Rabino clenched the cigar in the corner of his mouth.

"There could be instructions or an agreement with someone and we're not privy to that—just yet."

"The will has been read. There are no hidden secrets there," Amado said. "But as you mentioned, there could have been an oral agreement with someone to avoid probate. I'm no attorney, and I know zip about wills and trusts, but I'm willing to bet that dried up old fart, Spingarn, knows enough to blow the lid off this case. Maybe he's waiting for the dust to settle before making his move."

Rabino waved his hand in front of him. "That's all speculation. Anyway, we can't do anything about that."

"If we can get into his files…" Amado started to say.

Rabino cut him off. "There's no legitimate way of doing that, so forget it." Rabino sent out another cloud of smoke, as if to punctuate his remark.

Both detectives sat in the unmarked black Ford sedan. Amado looked at his watch, then glanced at the light in the third-floor office across the street. "5:30. Time for that old bastard to go home." Amado picked up binoculars from the seat. "The secretary just walked in; she's talking to him… holding his jacket. Why that old sonofabitch just pinched her ass. She's turning around, saying something like she's mad. He's talking fast. Now she's smiling."

Connors said, "He's bent like a goddammed pretzel. Think his pecker is straight?"

Amado disregarded the question. "This goes to show the bastard's character. Officer of the court, upholder of civil and constitutional laws. Hah, wouldn't trust him with the silverware…old fool." He continued to stare at the window and pursed his lips. "We've got to get a look at his files on the Montenegros."

"Think we can break in without tripping an alarm or something?"

"I didn't see any wires on the door or windows."

"Maybe we can go in as service workers."

"I thought about that," Amado said. "You mean like window washers or telephone repair men? Know anything about telephones?"

"Heck, no."

"Maybe we'll pick a lock or two after hours."

"Fred, that's awful chancy. There could be armed guards and a security system. I just don't know. I'd be awfully wary."

"Look, Billy Boy, we need to take some chances, even if we get shot at. But there's no gunplay here, just old-fashioned second-story rubber-necking. It's not like stealing a million bucks. All we want is a look at some papers. We don't even have to take them out of the files."

"Somehow, it just doesn't seem right. If we get caught that'll be the end. Rabino will slam the door in our faces."

Amado watched the lights go out in Spingarn's office, then looked at Connors. "You're probably right. I don't have to involve you in this caper."

"Now wait, Fred, I didn't say I wouldn't go along. It's just that I don't think…"

"Forget it, Billy Boy. Maybe it is a dumb idea. We'll play it safe and keep clear of that old sonofabitch." *The kid doesn't need to know what I have in mind.*

Chapter 19

"Look, baby, I don't know how to apologize except to say I'm sorry and get down on my knees to beg forgiveness. I'll bring you a dozen roses, a box of chocolates, even a diamond ring... that's right...no, not a five-carat diamond, but one that'll set me back a few months' salary. You're laughing. Does that mean I can come over? Good. Why don't you tell Maria to take the night off? Tell her to take in a movie at the neighborhood cinema... I promise to behave. We can talk and hold hands. Just talking to you on the phone like this gets me excited. Be there in thirty minutes."

Isabella, framed in the doorway, held Lobo's leash and pushed the button to open the gate allowing Amado's car to enter the grounds. Amado held a box of chocolates and attempted to embrace Isabella when Lobo came between them; his bushy tale struck Amado's legs repeatedly. Isabella pulled on the leash. "Stop, Lobo, sit! Now stay." The dog sat next to Amado and looked at him with an expression suggesting a broad grin. His tail swept the ground.

"I believe he likes you," she said.

"I could have guessed that. Dogs and old ladies are fond of me." He looked over Isabella's shoulders. "By the way, where is Maria?"

"She was happy to have the evening off as you suggested, so if you wish to steal a kiss, you need not worry about being interrupted."

"Stealing a kiss isn't all I had in mind."

Isabella led Amado through the grand room toward the settee where she sat with her legs curled under her. She patted the pillow next to her for Amado.

"You may be interested to know that I'm having a monthly visitor now, so our intimacies will be limited to hand-holding and kissing. Truth is, I'm grateful for the appearance of the red devil since we had unprotected intercourse. Now, if that displeases you, you can leave, but your candy stays."

"I'm not leaving. I'm going to enjoy that candy, too." Amado sat next to her and placed his arm around her shoulders, then leaned over to kiss her lips.

The door chimes sounded.

Isabella hurried to the door. She held a brief conversation with someone, then closed the door and returned to the settee. "That was John, the chauffeur. He wanted to know if I would need his services tonight. He's taking Maria to the cinema. They've been quite solicitous since the señora was..."

"Murdered?"

"I have difficulty saying that. It still sends shivers up my spine."

"Are John and Maria dating?" Amado asked.

"I hope so." Isabella laughed. "They're married."

Amado looked puzzled. "I don't understand. From that roster of employees' names you gave me, there were no two names suggesting a mister and Mrs. relationship."

"Fred, you continue to amaze me with your ability to recall. You're right. Maria Guerrero has been with the Montenegros since they arrived here. I don't know why she doesn't use her married name. John joined the staff in Madrid at the end of the Spanish Civil War in 1939. He and Maria have been married at least ten or more years."

"What is John's surname?"

"It's Gruenwald, actually, Johannes Gruenwald."

"That's not a Spanish moniker. Come to think of it, he doesn't talk like a Spaniard—more like a kraut."

"I vaguely remember the señora saying he was an

engineer. She was pleased to have someone who could keep her precious, cantankerous old limousine in working order."

"What was her special attachment to that old crate?"

"She enjoyed the spectacle, the notoriety, the instant recognition it gave her. People would stare and point to it knowing the famous Señora Montenegro was riding in her chariot while her proud chauffeur sat tall and elegant."

"Sounds like she was pretty much self-absorbed."

"Perhaps, but she was generous and provided me with a wonderful education. I loved her dearly, although many times I resented being sent away to this academy or that finishing school. When she came to visit me, I didn't want her to leave, I was so proud to introduce her to my friends. I would cry bitterly when she left. As beautiful and as generous as she was to me, she was disliked by some. I believe that was the reason she sent me away to the English countryside and to Lausanne, Switzerland."

"Explain that to me."

"The Spanish Republicans threatened members of señora's party, the Nationalists. I know the señora received hate letters. She feared that I would be kidnapped or harmed. That's why she sent me out of the country. The terrible irony of all that is that my biological parents were loyal Republicans who were killed by Franco's forces. The entire matter is insane and much too painful to talk about." She looked into Amado's eyes and hoped he understood. "Now you know why I need someone who is strong and protective."

"Like me."

She poked his arm. "You'll do until someone with some polish and sophistication comes along...and that might happen at any time."

"Thanks." Amado got off the settee. "How about an after-dinner drink?"

"Fine. I can show you something that you might be interested in."

"If it's you in the buff, I'll be right over."

"No, silly. Come here." With Amado standing next to her, Isabella reached under the bar countertop and pressed a button. She smiled awaiting Amado's response as the glass-faced wall began to turn slowly revealing another wall with shelves stocked with a variety of liquors, most of them costly and some with rare labels.

"Well, I'll be damned." Amado shook his head. "What the hell was the reason for this?"

"Usually you're the one to explain this sort of thing to me. As I understand it, this building was remodeled in the early 1920s just after Prohibition was enacted. The owners of the mansion wanted to conceal their display of alcoholic beverages, so they had this hideaway contraption built. Isn't it neat?"

"That was the stupid Volstead act," Amado said.

"There are a number of wonderful and scary secrets about this old building that I still know nothing about. Señora told me there is a wine cellar somewhere down below, although I haven't seen it." Isabella looked around before she said in a whisper, "I was also told there was a burial vault down there too."

"Terrific. Now, if you don't mind, I'll have that drink."

Isabella poured Courvoisier into two snifters, then handed Amado one. They clinked glasses.

"This is real class. I could get used to this kind of lifestyle."

"You have to earn it, my love"

"Really? The way the señora did by cozying up to a sonofabitch who murdered a half million? No thank you. One can make a lot of enemies that way. Among those enemies, at least one could be mad enough to want you dead."

Isabella's brow wrinkled—she seemed pained, then bewildered. "You think those murders were acts of vengeance?"

"You bet! Whoever committed those murders must have been seething with hatred. No one hates that way unless he or she has been terribly wronged and is determined to get even. It looks like revenge to me. Besides wanting to find the sonofabitch who did it, I have what Rabino would call a vested interest."

"Meaning?"

"Your protection, baby. I'm claiming you as my own."

Isabella hugged Amado tightly, covering his face with kisses, then she backed off. "Why would anyone want to kill *me*?"

"I'm not sure anyone does, unless there's something you haven't told me about your past."

"You know everything there is to know about me."

"Maybe not. I can't believe you haven't been involved with a man before. You're beautiful, talented, warm and loving—everything a guy could possibly want. So what don't I know about you?"

"You're not entitled to know any more about my personal life, until I know about yours. You've been of marriageable age for fifteen or twenty years. You'll never convince me that some little tootsie didn't show you her wonderful wares and promise to be a dutiful wife."

"Touché . However, no one has thrilled me as you have."

Amado took a nougat from the box of chocolates he brought and popped it into his mouth. He walked to the door holding Isabella's hand. "As soon as this case is solved I'm putting in my bid for your hand, for keeps."

He opened the door and turned back to kiss Isabella.

A shot rang out!

Amado fell.

Isabella screamed.

Chapter 20

Three deputy cars with flashing lights surrounded the entrance while estate workers clad in night clothes gathered around the entrance to watch the turmoil. Rabino approached Isabella who was hovering over the pale Amado lying on the sofa holding a towel over his right arm.

Rabino approached. "You all right, ma'am? Don't worry about Amado. The ambulance will be here soon."

Obviously shaken and anxious, she looked up at him. "Are you sure he'll be all right?"

"You have my word," Rabino said. "Now, I'd appreciate having you call everyone on the estate to come out here."

Isabella looked at her watch. "It's almost midnight, are you sure this can't wait until morning?"

"No, ma'am. This is a grave offense against a sheriff's deputy. Someone on these premises did this. Would you step outside and see if every worker is here and if anyone is missing?"

"Maria and her husband, John the chauffeur, are not here."

"Where are they?"

"The Arlington Theatre. They have the night off."

Rabino made a notation in his notebook and looked at Isabella. "Please tell the workers we're taking them by bus to our crime lab. They are not to leave here, and they are not to wash their hands."

While Isabella gave the message to the staff of twelve, Rabino whispered to Connors, "Take charge of the group. See that everyone boards the bus and gets back on it. I'm going with Amado in the ambulance."

The ambulance careened around the dark foothill curves of Montecito on its way to Cottage Hospital in Santa Barbara. Amado remained calm, lying in the semi-recumbent position with a pressure dressing on his right arm.

Rabino sat next to him and shook his head. "What the hell were you doing at the estate at this hour?" He looked at his watch. "It's 11:45. Don't tell me you were chasing down more clues."

"Actually, I was," Amado said.

"Yeah, and I'm the good fairy."

Amado smiled weakly. "I always knew there was something sweet about you. "

"Cut the crap. Tell me again, what happened and don't leave out any detail."

"I was in the doorway saying goodnight to Isabella—I mean Miss Chavez —I heard a shot and felt a burning pain in my arm. Then it bled. That's all."

"That's all?"

"Well, not exactly. I purposely hit the ground and Isabella started screaming. I pulled her down to protect her, waited a minute, then hustled her back into the house. Then I called you guys."

Rabino shook his head again. "In all the years I've been in the department, I've never seen the likes of you. You just gravitate toward trouble. You see a gorgeous mug, a hefty pair of knockers, a firm ass, and ka-boom— you're taking orders from your stand-up cock. When are you going to grow up?"

Rabino and Dr. Hanson stood next to Amado's bed in recovery when Amado's eyelids began to flicker as he was coming out of the anesthetic. He squinted trying to focus on those around him.

Dr. Hanson felt his pulse, then put the stethoscope to

his chest. He leaned toward Amado's ear. "Fred, you're out of surgery and you did well. Your arm is going to be fine. Look over here. You've got a visitor." Amado turned his head, blinked, then he closed his eyes again.

The doctor said to Rabino, "The wound was relatively superficial: no bone involvement; the nerve tissue and large vessels are intact." Dr. Hanson went on to explain, "We had to clean the path of the bullet, teased out fabric fibers, did a lot of irrigation and inserted a drain. Several days of antibiotics and a tetanus booster should be all he'll require beside a couple of aspirin for discomfort. I'll see him in two days to remove the drain. We'll give him a sling, and he can leave here in about an hour."

"Can I talk to him now, Doc?" Rabino asked.

"Sure, you might get some goofy answers, but go ahead. No harm trying." The doctor made notes in the chart and left the room.

Rabino bent over and shouted into Amado's ear, "Hey, Fred, can you hear me?"

Startled, Amado jumped. "Christ! Stop yelling. I can hear you, and I can smell your cigar stink, too."

"Listen, this is a helluva way to get a few days off." Rabino's voice had a sobering effect on Amado who attempted to sit up. He winced when he moved his arm. Looking at Rabino, he asked for help.

Rabino dragged the visitor's chair and placed it near the head of the bed, then looked around. He spoke softly. "Amado, you and I have got to talk. Right now I'll do the talking and you'll listen. In case you haven't figured this out, you're in deep shit. I don't know what you think you're doing playing footsies with this *puta* suspect..."

Amado's eyes narrowed. "Wait a goddamned minute, Rabino, she's no puta."

"Uh—huh, protecting your little friend, that's what I thought." Rabino sat back in the chair, a smug condescending expression crossed his face. "You couldn't keep your pecker in your pants long enough to maintain objectivity. Okay, you fucked her, and now you've fucked yourself, but good. You violated basic rules of a deputy's code. What in the hell were you thinking? I'll tell you—you weren't thinking."

Amado looked away and made no comment.

Rabino stood, ran his hand through his hair. "Shit," he mumbled. "There's no goddamn defense for what you did. It was just plain stupid. If Internal Affairs gets hold of this..."

"Marv, I'm not in any mood to argue. I'll turn in my badge and..."

"Shut up, you damn fool! I don't want your fucking badge. I need to figure a way of keeping you out of trouble and protecting my own ass. Who else knows about your affair?"

"I guess the help at the estate— Maria, and I suppose her husband, the chauffeur."

"Does Connors know?"

"I never told him, but he might suspect."

"He shouldn't be a problem," Rabino said. "As for you, you're going to take sick leave and get the hell out of town. You'd better not see that dame again until these murders are solved. Do you understand? If you tell anyone about this conversation, I'll deny everything. Don't set foot near headquarters or talk to anyone on the force until I tell you to. After you make your last visit to the doc, call and let me know where you'll be vacationing."

At the door, Rabino turned and said, "The nurse looking after you here has a nice ass and big tits. She might offer you something to take your mind off that..."

Amado cut him off. "Hey, what about the sonofabitch who shot at me? You doing anything about that?"

"Way ahead of you, Amado. All the help are getting their hands checked for gun powder and getting fingerprinted. Got two rookies beating the bushes, looking for shells, shoe tracks or whatever. I don't know how much they'll find in the darkness. We'll give the area a thorough going over during the day. Come to think of it, wasn't there supposed to be a watchdog?"

Chapter 21

"Isabella, baby, I've just come from Doc Hansen's." Amado balanced the phone between his shoulder and his ear while placing underwear and socks in the suitcase on his bed. "Yeah, the drain is out. Sutures come out in a week to ten days. Any doc can do it... you think you can do it? Well, that's what we need to talk about... Rabino's given me fair warning about losing my job if word gets out that we've been—you know—seeing each other. Better tell Maria and her husband not to say anything to the other workers about us. Baby, I don't want you to know where I'm going. Knowing you as I do, there's a better than even chance that you'll be out to see me as soon as I settle in."

"What you can do is cooperate with the sheriff and ask questions around the estate; find out who owns a .22 caliber gun. By the way, why didn't Lobo bark?... The dog's been at the vet hospital for distemper? That's really conveniently coincidental."

"...Of course, I'm driving alone. My right arm is fine. I can shift gears, and I can bring a fork or spoon to my mouth. If you were here, I'd show you how well I can use my right arm, and there's nothing wrong with my kisser either. I could kiss you until you'd beg to come up for air. I might weaken to the point where I tell you where I'm hiding, but you've got to swear not to tell anyone. On second thought, I'm not going to tell you. I'll suffer through a few wet dreams rather than have you come down here... love you too, baby."

Chapter 22

Professor Chadwick Grobstein of the university's fine arts department motioned for Rabino to sit on the other side of his desk. In a high-pitched voice, he said, "Please don't light that cigar. I abhor the stench of cigar smoke, and I'm highly allergic to it. It makes me cough and my eyes tear. Smoking is so unhealthy. I really don't know why anybody would do it." Obviously vexed, he pursed his lips and crossed his arms over his chest.

"Yeah, well, this is one of my lesser vices, Doc. Sorry, I didn't mean to upset you. What can you tell me about the paintings in that Goleta warehouse?"

The professor referred to a tablet on his desk and with his forefinger pointed to the names of the paintings. "I saw these four paintings which covered the Impressionist Period—the late 1800s to the early 1900s. I can tell you without fear of contradiction that those oil paintings are original."

"No kidding?"

"An examination of the pigments revealed them to be of that period, and the canvas fibers are like those used at that time. Each painting is a fine example of a recognizable painter of the time. Their value to western culture and to the world of fine art is inestimable.

"I also found something exceedingly interesting. Those treasures were not purchased by any American collector or any American museum."

"Wait, Doc, I'm not sure I understand. How did they

get here?"

"I meant to say the paintings were not commissioned by any American individual or American museum. They were acquired originally by private Europeans, mostly from dealers in Paris."

"You're losing me, Doc. Like I asked—how did they get here?" Before the professor could explain, Rabino went on. "Someone here had to buy them. Since they're in a storage barn belonging to the Montenegro estate, wouldn't they belong to the Montenegros?"

"I've traced the provenance of just four of those paintings. I know there are many more. What troubles me is that the Montenegro name does not appear in any owner's register of significant works. In the art world, the owners of masterpieces are usually well-known to one another."

"Interesting. What value would you place on those paintings?"

The professor rubbed his chin and shook his head. "I can't predict what the frenzied bidding at an auction would bring. My answer would be a mere guess, but simply stated, they're worth millions."

"How in the hell did those paintings wind up here?"

Chapter 23

With his left hand, Amado carried his suitcase across the expansive lawn of the mansion designed in harmony with Mexican-American motifs. He placed his suitcase down at the wide carved wooden door and rang the chimes.

An elderly man with a belt line dipping far below an ample paunch stood in the doorway with outstretched arms. "Fernando! Welcome, my dear boy, to Castillo Del Fuego. Let me look at you. You are more handsome with a few gray hairs and a face with the character of a seasoned caballero."

Amado gave him an abrazo. "Uncle Juan Carlos, cut the flattery. I'm happy to see you, too, and grateful to take advantage of your hospitality for a week or ten days..."

"No, no, Fernando," the older man protested. "Stay as long as you wish. I am leaving. I shall be visiting my friends in Jalisco for a month. I am happy to have you occupying this old castle while I'm away. Choose any of the five bedrooms as you wish. You will not be disturbed, except for the gardener who comes twice a week, the pool man who comes once a week and the maid who comes three times a week to clean and cook."

Amado followed his uncle into the large living room furnished in old southwestern décor, complete with serapes draped over leather club chairs and sofas darkened by the patina of aging. Amado had fond memories of this room going back to when it was newly furnished twenty-five years ago. Little had changed.

The larger-than-life studio portrait of the stunning movie

star, Dolores Del Fuego, still hung above the mantel on which a single memorial candle flickered. A spotlight in the ceiling illumined on her coquettish smile and her sensuous dark eyes. A lacy mantilla on her head and shoulders draped carefully, revealed enough cleavage to stir a response in Amado. She was well endowed, truly a *chichona.*

"Ah, my son, you remember your aunt. She was the love of my life... *mi corazon,* until that fatal accident seventeen years ago."

Amado looked askance. "She was my aunt? You two were married?"

"Well, yes and no. The studio didn't want her fans to know she was married, so we lived as husband and wife without a license...may Jesus, Mary and Joseph forgive me."

Amado followed his uncle, who avoided stepping on a large white bearskin lying in the center of the room. Noting how his uncle was careful not to step on the rug, Amado did likewise, prompting his uncle to voice his appreciation. "Thank you, Fernando, for not violating the sanctity of this magical rug."

"You had magical moments on this bearskin—you and Dolores Del Fuego?"

The older man sighed and closed his eyes. "Many times— mystical, rapturous, glorious, tender, heavenly moments like two young wild cats sniffing, pawing, licking, exploring one another until we burst with complete and utter consummation."

"Uncle, that's raw emotion—pure poetry." Amado clasped his uncle's shoulders then studied the bearskin for a moment. "Now I have a profound appreciation and reverence for this." He bent down and brushed the fur lightly. "Should the opportunity arise for me to use the bearskin in a similar manner, would you object?"

The uncle roared with laughter and placed his arms around Amado's shoulders. "Son, there is an old Latino saying, 'He who would make love on the hide of a bear will remain potent for all the days of his life.'"

"Thanks—words to live by. Now, if only I can find a she-cat who thinks like me..."

Chapter 24

Amado's room on the upper floor overlooked the pool with its sparkling water made bluer by the aqua tiles. He imagined Esther Williams emerging from the pool side, clinging to the polished chrome ladder and smiling her wonderful smile, then pulling off her swim cap and shaking her hair. She was a great swimmer, not a bad actress; he wondered how she might be in the sack. He chided himself for allowing such stupid daydreaming to interfere with his attempt at analysis of the murders and the recent gunshot intended for him or Isabella.

On a legal pad he listed events in sequence and boxed in the names of the victims. Someone with an intense hatred of Señora Montenegro killed her, that was obvious, maybe someone she knew and trusted. That hatred lasted even beyond the señora's death since her portrait with Franco had been defaced. Then there was the death of that visiting priest from Madrid whose mutilated body was found in the mausoleum. What were the common points? He drew arrows from one box to the other. Both victims were members of Franco's Nationalist party. What about the art treasures in the warehouse, and what does that wretched little attorney know about the Montenegros and their estate? Why the hell is he so secretive? As soon as I can, I'm going to break into his files.

He placed his pen on the pad and studied the boxes as well as his doodling, then shook his head. Nothing seemed to gel; no answers emerged.

Staring out the window, he beheld the San Jacinto Mountains that formed a backdrop to the landscape, and the tall palms swaying gently around the estate were like majestic sentinels. And yet, in this picture-perfect setting as in a movie, Amado felt a gnawing in his belly when he thought about the two murders and the attempt of a third, possibly his. Most troubling of all was the suspicion that Isabella was somehow involved. He tried to dismiss it, tried to maintain a shield of innocence he had built around her. But he couldn't deny the fact that his judgment was not to be trusted where she was concerned. He adored her, wanted only to be with her. She was so beautiful, so smart and worldly-wise—hell, maybe she was out of his class, and yet he seemed to satisfy her as a lover. Maybe she was too good or too clever for him, and yet she made love to him as though she were sincere. She professed her love...

His conflicting reflections were disturbed by the door chimes. Consuela, the maid, engaged someone in conversation at the door for several minutes before Amado heard the door close. Perhaps some delivery man left a package or an itinerant had been turned away.

Amado sat at a desk with his back to the door. The warmth of the desert sun had caused drowsiness, and his sleepy head fell onto his chest. Two hands covered his eyes. He jerked backward, grasped the wrists and pulled the arms forward causing a body to slam against the back of his chair.

"Whoa, mister! I come in peace." Isabella laughed and complained in the same breath. "Is that how you treat a lady?"

Amado stood up, whirled around, dumb founded. He grabbed and embraced Isabella, kissing her face and mouth repeatedly. He stopped suddenly, then pushed her away. "You dumb little bunny, I could have killed you. How did you find me?" He pulled her toward him again and held the back of her head against his chest. "Answer me? How did you find me?"

She mumbled, "You're smothering me. I can't talk."

He released her and feasted his eyes on her face, her bosom and her legs. "Did you know I'd been thinking about you day and night?"

"Then you're really happy to see me?"

"Happy to see you? I could eat you up."

"I may give you that opportunity." She smiled and held his face with both hands, mesmerizing him with her eyes. He clasped her hips and drew her to him. She became aware of his male response. "I'm pleased that your friend is so happy to have me near, also."

"He's ecstatic."

"What about the maid downstairs?"

"She won't disturb us." Amado, still embracing Isabella, turned and kicked the door shut.

Isabella started to unbutton his shirt. He pulled her blouse out of her skirt, then over her head. She unbuckled his belt and unzipped his fly. Amado quickly stepped out of his trousers while Isabella loosened her skirt that fell to the floor. She stood in a lacy bra and sheer matching panties that revealed a dark, triangular escutcheon covering her vaginal area.

Amado reached around to undo her bra, but she quickly unfastened the hooks herself and slid the shoulder straps off allowing the bra to fall. Putting her arms around his neck, she moved her pelvis in a kind of circular motion over his protuberance. He stepped out of his jockey shorts. She reached down and stroked his engorged member. Having brought him to maximal readiness, she led him to the bed. She lay down, and he surveyed her magnificent soft curves, the fullness of her breasts with their pert nipples and the slight hollow of her abdomen. He knelt over her. She moaned with ecstatic pleasure as he began to suckle her breasts. "I dreamed of this moment," she sighed and ran her hands through his hair. She gasped as he penetrated. Their rhythmic copulation increased until he stopped suddenly and withdrew.

"Darling, what's wrong?" she asked.

"I want this to last longer," he said.

"Please don't stop. Let it happen. We have the whole night for encores."

They lay on their sides like nested spoons, her back against his front. He cupped her breasts and nuzzled her neck. In two hours of petting and experimenting they had enjoyed repeated arousal and exotic episodes of bliss, until they lay exhausted.

"I could lie like this forever," she said. "I feel so safe and secure in your arms."

"Good. Should we make this arrangement permanent?"

"Darling, as soon as the estate is settled..."

"Uh-huh. Reneging already," Amado said.

"No-no. Only one thing makes me hesitate."

"What's that?"

"It's your job." She turned on her side, leaned on her elbow and looked into Amado's eyes. "I would worry every day about your safety, your life."

"Okay. Here we are—we're not married. Are you worried about me now?"

"Yes, of course, but suppose we were to have children. I would want them to have a father who comes home to dinner and spends time with them, and..."

He interrupted. "Most cops' wives don't live in constant fear of their husbands being killed."

"Well, I would. I've suffered too much tragedy and personal loss. I want my love to be near me forever. Do you understand? Forever."

Chapter 25

Even as Amado was enjoying a blissful leave in Palm Springs, Rabino was carrying on with the investigation Amado had begun and having little joy in it. Trying to pursue leads in connection with the art cache Amado had discovered, he returned to Professor Grobstein's office and sought more help.

"With all due respect Professor Grobstein, and I'm not doubting your analyses that prove these paintings are real and worth a bundle—my question is: who do they belong to?"

Grobstein was clearly ready to dismiss the whole matter. Secure in his academic womb, he could care less about crime solving in the real world.

"If provenance cannot be established, then the U.S. Justice Department should be notified." Grobstein's lack of knowledge about returning stolen art to its rightful ownership, was a matter of least concern to him. "Look here, sheriff, my consultation fee covers verifying the authenticity of these paintings, that's all. The history of their ownership is an entirely different matter, one that I cannot be concerned about. Maybe the old maxim: possession is nine-tenths of the law should apply here. If no one else claims ownership of a painting, then that painting should belong to the one who has it in his or her possession. To me, that's a simple solution." Grobstein's tone indicated a cavalier and dismissive attitude.

Rabino stood and shook his head as he prepared to leave the professor's office. "You're not that naïve, professor, and

I'm not that gullible. If a famous painting is stolen from a private collection or from a museum, that painting remains stolen property, no matter who has it."

"Yes, yes, of course," the professor said. "Now if you will excuse me, I have a seminar to lead."

Chapter 26

Isabella and Amado remained in bed. He ran his hand gently through her hair and kissed her forehead. She grabbed the afghan on the bed to cover her nude body and got up to use the washroom. When she returned she had managed to drape the afghan into something looking like a sarong.

"Why the sudden modesty, baby?" Amado had no inhibitions about his own nudity. He climbed out of bed, stretched, yawned, then scratched his behind. Isabella looked away. Amado headed for the shower stall. "Want to share the shower with me, love?"

"We've played that song before," she said.

A pretty Girl Is Like a Melody. He sang the tune, embraced her and tried to coax her into the shower stall.

"If you don't mind, I'll shower alone," she said. "I'm not up to any more gymnastics. I've got to put certain body parts at rest."

"The maid left early this morning. We've been left to our own devices for breakfast, or I can take you to *The Pantry* if you wish. The food is good enough, and we won't have to clean up afterwards."

"Darling, how about allowing me to test my domestic skills. I think I'm capable of preparing bacon and eggs, waffles, or pancakes..."

"Pancakes sound good." Amado sat in the den and read the morning newspaper while Isabella rattled pots and pans, opened and closed the refrigerator and slammed kitchen cabinet doors. Forty-five minutes later, she called out in a plaintive voice, "Fred, do you want your pancakes sunny side up or scrambled?"

He walked over and stood behind her as she moved about, harried and frustrated. In a patient voice, he said, "Sweetheart, how about toast and coffee? I'll make the coffee." He turned to conceal a smile. "Your domestic skills hardly reflect your expertise in the love-making department."

"You're not angry?"

"Being with you, baby, is all I want."

Seated side-by-side on a love seat in the living room, Amado put his arm around Isabella. "Now, you little vixen, tell me how you knew I was holed up here."

"Promise you won't be angry?"

"I promise."

"Sheriff Rabino told Detective Connors where you were, and told him not to say a word to anyone. Connors told his girlfriend, Lupe Rodriguez—in the strictest confidence, of course. She told Maria, my maid, since they attend the same church, and Maria told me." Isabella smiled broadly. "It was the most exciting news I could have hoped for. I kissed Maria, then packed my overnight bag and voila! Besides, I love driving my Cadillac on the highway with the top down, the radio blasting and my hair blowing in the wind. Best of all, I was going to see you, and the thought of being in your arms and making love to you is more wonderful than anything in all the world."

Amado held her face in his hands, and leaned over to kiss her lips.

"Fred, I must confess, I've never felt this way about anyone. I not only love you, but I trust you to protect me. I'll concede that I will worry about your safety if you continue as a homicide detective—so much so, that I will insist that you quit the force. Oh, don't worry about making a living wage. There's plenty of money. I've inherited enough to support us quite comfortably. You could be the major domo looking after the estate, guiding our children...I guess what I'm trying to say, and I see no reason to wait any longer—will you marry me?"

Before he could answer, she went on, "We could find a justice of the peace here, then plan a big wedding in Montecito later. I'd really like that." She looked into Amado's eyes. "Wouldn't you?"

"If we married now, you wouldn't have to worry about me quitting the force."

"What do you mean, darling?"

"Rabino would toss my butt into a trash bin. A married man can't testify against his wife."

Isabella gasped and put the back of her hand to her mouth. "Fred, you still harbor thoughts..."

"It's not what *I* believe, sweetheart, it's what *they* believe."

He hesitated a moment, choosing his words carefully. "I believe you had nothing to do with those murders, and I'm terribly afraid that you might be in danger from whomever it was who committed them."

Reassured, she kissed him and said, "I know you'll protect me. I trust you with my life."

Chapter 27

Amado's arm healed quickly. He was able to discard the sling and rotate the shoulder to keep the joint from achy stiffness.

"Do you still have pain, darling?" Isabella asked.

"Very little, and none when I'm making love to you." Amado stroked Isabella's neck lightly then ran his finger down over her bosom. "I love your body."

She brushed his hand aside. "Your arm seems sufficiently healed to me. When are you driving back to Santa Barbara?"

"Rabino said he'd let me know when to return. Besides, I'm entitled to sick leave, and the thought of sharing a bed with you—well, I might never go back."

"Sorry to disappoint you, darling, I'm leaving in two days. I know I've a pile of paper work on my desk..."

Amado put his finger to her lips. "Don't spoil this idyllic moment with that intrusive crap. Think wonderful thoughts, like magnificent fucking in the pool on a balmy evening..."

Isabella frowned and shook her head. "Fred, really! Must you be so vulgar? You're like a horny teenager with an insatiable sexual appetite."

"I'm in total agreement, but that's part of my charm." He lit a cigarette and took a long drag. "Okay, I'll get serious. There's a lot I still don't know about you. Tell me about your life from the time you were a youngster to your life with the Montenegros. What do you remember as a kid?"

"My childhood? I will never, ever forget it."

"What about your home and your parents?"

"Our home was charming, a sunlit cottage on the outskirts of Madrid. My mother would bring flowers in from our garden; we had music—both my parents played the guitar, and we sang. They were young, beautiful expressive people. I was an only child, and they lavished their love on me. The three of us did so many fun things together." Isabella smiled wistfully.

"What did your parents do?"

"Mother was an instructor in cultural studies at the University of Madrid. I had a nanny who looked after me since my parents were gone most mornings and afternoons, sometimes even in the evenings."

"You had no relatives to look in on you?" Amado asked.

"My father's family was in the Ukraine. He came to Spain in the early thirties as a young Communist to organize the youth against the growing Falangisti movement, that is the Fascists."

"But your name...Chavez?"

"That was my mother's maiden name. My father's name was too long and too foreign sounding. My maternal grand-parents lived in Toledo, much too far for babysitting and my mother's only sister lived in Guadalajara—long distances from us."

"Tell me about your father."

"He was an officer in the defense forces of Madrid during the Civil War." Isabella cleared her throat, then paused before continuing, "One day, over a thousand soldiers in Franco's army were rounded up and murdered by my father's army, the Republicans, outside Madrid in a place called Paracuellos." She hastened to add, "But my father was not a part of that massacre, and when he learned of it, he was terribly distressed. There was a fierce outcry by the families of the victims who demanded revenge."

Isabella broke down and wept uncontrollably, her shoulders heaving; she looked away and dabbed her eyes and nose with a handkerchief. "Sorry," she said. "This is all too painful to recall. My parents were ardent liberals, idealists.

They made no attempt to conceal their hatred of Franco and his fascist Nationalist army."

"After much more bloodshed, Franco's armies conquered Madrid. A door-to-door search for Republican holdouts was made. We were celebrating my tenth birthday when our front door was smashed in by enemy soldiers. I stood off to the side and saw my dear parents gunned down by a thousand bullets. The noise was deafening. I can still hear the frightful sounds of those guns. My parents fell against each other, then collapsed on the floor... blood spattered everywhere. It was more horrible than I can describe." She cried and held her head in her hands..

Amado held her closely.

Between sobs and snuffling, she said, "As long as I live, I'll never forget that. I threw myself on their bodies. I refused to believe they were gone forever...taken from me...never to talk or sing or hold and caress me. I wanted to die with them. I lay on their bloodied bodies and screamed hysterically until one of the soldiers picked me up and carried me away. I kicked and beat him with my fists, even though he tried to calm me.

"That evening of horror has never left me. Even now, I have nightmares that awaken me in a screaming, sweating fright. I can still see my sweet mother's eyes that remained open in death as though she saw me and wanted to tell me something."

Isabella's tearful eyes looked into Amado's. "Fred, I've never told anyone about those horrible moments. I could never talk about it before." She remained silent for a moment. "I'm sorry I had to share my pain with you. Now you know more about me than I intended."

Amado nodded and embraced her. "What happened after that?"

"I was taken to an orphanage run by nuns."

"Your relatives couldn't take you in?"

"We learned some weeks later that my mother's parents were killed in an aerial bombing like the one at Guernica where every living soul, including the children and farm animals were destroyed. My aunt and uncle were never heard from after the fierce fighting in their home town."

Chapter 28

"What about your life in the orphanage?" Amado asked.

"The nuns were very kind, even motherly, but I was determined not to become a part of their world. I wanted to be left alone. I would curl up on my cot in that cold, barren room and cry almost constantly."

"How long were you at the orphanage?"

"A couple of months. About two weeks after I arrived, the orphanage was put on alert. That meant important people were coming to visit and possibly select orphans for adoption."

"Were you hoping to be adopted?"

"I can't remember how I felt, except that I remained terribly resentful and hated those who robbed me of my loving..." Isabella began choking and paused to clear her throat, then looked away for a moment. "Like the other girls in my section, I stood in line wearing the dreary, ill-fitting black and white uniform of the orphanage. I watched an entourage of military officers and wives inspect us as though we were pet animals waiting to be adopted. I wanted the ordeal to end, so I could go back to my own world of isolation and misery.

"One couple stopped in front of me, and this attractive woman dressed exquisitely, smiled and attempted to chat with me. I was determined to be rude because her husband wore the uniform of Franco's army, and I showed my feelings. I wouldn't even speak to her.

"After the inspection, the mother superior called for me. I

feared she would reprimand me for being insolent to the señora and her husband. I made up my mind, I would never consent to being adopted. I decided I'd remain in the orphanage, as much as I detested it, rather than go with *those* murderers.

"Contrary to what I expected, the mother superior was patient and sympathetic. She said, 'Isabella, you are a pretty and intelligent child, and I respect your wishes, but the opportunity to live with people of wealth and influence is rare and might not occur again. Señora Montenegro spoke to me. She understands your resentment, but she assured me that she would welcome you with open arms and do her best to create a good life for you, if you were to change your mind. You would be the cherished daughter she had hoped to have. She has not had children of her own.'

"I remained adamant. I shook my head and told her that under no condition would I consent to..."

Amado interrupted. "What changed your mind?"

"I requested a work assignment in the flower beds and in the greenhouse next to the main building. I hoped working among the lovely roses, dahlias, azaleas and other blooms, would relieve some of my sadness. My duties consisted of gathering young roses and rose buds and bringing them into the greenhouse where varieties were selected and prepared for the market place. I worked long hours, often alone, after the others left the flower fields.

"A brutish, demented oaf, hired by the nuns, carried heavy boulders and sacks of fertilizer. He would leer at me and became uncomfortably close on more than one occasion. I avoided him as best I could. One day as the sun was setting, I was alone in the greenhouse sorting out rosebuds, cutting stems and gathering them in bouquets when this creature came toward me. I watched him out of the corner of my eye. My heart pounded so hard I thought I would die right there. He kept coming toward me with a crazy look. He unbuttoned his pants, then lunged at me.

"With his dirty salivating mouth, he kissed me. His

breath was horrible. He pushed me against the table, lifted my skirt and jerked my panties down. I screamed as loud as I could and kicked him. Nothing stopped him and no one heard me. I reached behind me and grabbed the scissors from the table and swung it wildly at his face. The point pierced his eye.

"He bellowed like a wounded animal and held his eye with one hand. With his other hand, he ripped off my blouse. I wiggled out of his grasp and ran to the main building screaming hysterically. Two nuns hustled me to safety. They barred the door and phoned the police. I can still remember shaking uncontrollably.

The following day, the mother superior talked with me. She praised me for my bravery, apologized for the frightful experience and assured me that the monster would never harm anyone again. He was imprisoned for the criminally insane. She looked at me a long while, then asked, "Isabella, wouldn't you be happier living with the señora and Colonel Montenegro?"

"No!" I answered like the stubborn creature that I was. In her wisdom, the sister said, "Would you like to spend the rest of your life like the hard-working nuns here? They are married to our Lord Jesus and perform duties in His blessed name. The frivolities of the laic world are forbidden here. Although we do have choir music, we sing hymns of praise and rejoice in the name of the Lord. As you know, our clothes are quite simple and our food is plain but wholesome.

"In short, we have pledged our lives and souls to the glory of the Lord God and His only son Jesus Christ. We eschew all worldly and temporal rewards. Some say our lives are humdrum, but that is not true. We aid the poor, the infirm, and the elderly. Our work is fulfilling, and the good Lord willing, we will be rewarded in the glorious hereafter."

I looked around the sister's office: the stark bare, brown walls interrupted only by a cross on which a bearded, skeletal Jesus hung with His crown of thorns, His eyes turned beseechingly upward, and a cloth draped across His loins.

What a sharp contrast this was to the joy of lively colors, tiles and pictures that decorated the walls of the home I knew. I remembered the gentle sweet songs my parents played on their guitars and even the bawdy ones my father sang with his comrades. They drank wine and laughed and stomped loudly when they danced with castanets clicking and guitars strumming loud chords. It was all so magical and wonderful.

I knew the austere life of the nunnery was not for me. Perhaps the mother superior was right after all in trying to convince me to seek a different lifestyle.

She leaned across her desk and said, "Isabella, should I call the señora to tell her you have consented to live with her? Child, if you are unhappy living with her after a month, you will be welcomed back."

"Obviously, you chose to stay with the Montenegros," Amado said.

"When I saw the señora, she embraced me so tightly, I was practically smothered. We spent days trying to find clothes for me in the Madrid stores, but couldn't find any that pleased her. She was much more concerned about my clothing than I was. She called her friend, General Franco, and believe it or not, he arranged to have his six-passenger De Haviland fly us to Paris for a shopping spree."

"You remember those details well, even the name of the plane."

"Señora Montenegro told me it was a gift to Franco from the English Prime Minister, Mr. Chamberlain. The British and French really wanted Franco to win, so they gave him extravagant gifts.

"The clerks at the Bon Marché in Paris fawned over the señora and me, and she bought me more clothes than I could possibly wear for the next two years."

Chapter 29

All the stress and frustration of overseeing investigations wore heavily on the sheriff. But Rabino had the support of a loving wife who maintained a home to which he could retreat and find temporary relief from the pressures of serving and protecting the public.

Rabino's home took on the welcoming warmth of the Friday evening Sabbath with the fragrances of freshly-baked challah, chicken soup and beef brisket. The dining room table was decorated with Rachel Rabino's Belgian linen, fine silverware, and English china reserved for the once-a-week dinner. A pair of polished brass candlesticks that had been in the Rabino family for over a century awaited Rachel's lighting after she put on her prayer shawl.

The family sat and watched as the Sabbath Queen, Mama Rachel, in silent prayer, asked for God's blessings—not for herself, but for her family and thanked Him for the bounty they were about to enjoy. She made an addendum plea for her husband's safety, stealing a glance at his holstered gun lying on the server behind him.

Marvin Rabino sat at the opposite end of the table with his twin seventeen-year-old daughters, biblically-named, Ruth and Miriam, to his left and his fifteen-year-old son, Monte to his right. Monte was named for a deceased grandfather, Montefiore Perez.

The sweet Carmel wine over which a blessing was made by Rabino loosened tongues sufficiently so that conversation flowed more freely and became increasingly loud. While Mama served the roasted brisket, the twins collected the empty chopped liver and chicken-soup plates.

"All right, what news is there from my beautiful daughters? Tell me, what lotharios am I going to pitch out on their heads this week?"

Miriam started but hesitated, then began again. "Daddy, a boy asked me to go to his senior prom." She looked at her father for approval.

Rabino held his knife and fork upright. "So? Tell me about him. What's his name, and is he worthy of my daughter's attention? Where did you meet him and what does he do?"

"Daddy, he's a senior at our high school. His name is Peter Periera; he's co-captain of our football team, and he's quite handsome." The words tumbled out. "He's a business major, and he's going to Santa Barbara City College in the fall."

Rabino nodded slowly and looked at Ruth. "And what news does my other princess have to tell me?"

"I was asked to the prom, too, by a neat guy. His name is Larry Beneveniste."

"And what about this Don Juan with the Sephardic name?"

"I met him during services at the synagogue a month ago. He was there with his parents. He's been accepted to M.I.T., and he's brilliant." Ruth, like her sister, could hardly explain herself rapidly enough.

Rabino looked at his wife across the table. "Rachel, do you have questions for our daughters and their current beaux?"

"Who's going to chaperone the girls on their dates?" She asked.

In unison, the girls turned toward her and said, "Oh, Mother!"

Rabino added, "Keep reminding your boyfriends that your father keeps a loaded pistol with him, and he won't hesitate to use it if…"

Obviously appalled, both girls looked at him and said in unison, "Oh, Daddy!"

Rabino looked at his son. "All right, Monte, what startling news do you have? Any clandestine rendezvous?"

"Nope, but if any girl refuses a date with me, I'll tell her my dad carries a gun."

Rabino smiled, nodded and continued eating, then stopped to look at the girls. "What were those family names? Periera and Beneveniste?" The girls nodded.

Rabino excused himself to make a phone call in the den.

"Hello, Amado? Listen, do the names Periera and Beneveniste ring any bells? Don't say 'no' so damned fast. Remember the names of those visitors at the señora's burial services at the church... yeah, yeah, that's it... members of the I.A.T.... Iberia America Trading. Let's look into that... maybe a glimmer of connection. By the way, hope you got to fire off your cannon a few times... you can reload here... but not with the Chavez dame."

Chapter 30

"Boy, am I ever glad you're back," Connors said as Amado sat in the passenger seat and lit a cigarette. "Things were getting kinda dull around here. There's always some excitement when you're around. What's on the docket?" Amado reached into his jacket pocket for a notebook and flipped some pages. "Rabino thinks we ought to pay a visit to the Perieras up on the Mesa. He wants to know if Periera has a connection to the paintings and the antique furniture in that Goleta warehouse."

"Think he had anything to do with the murders?"

"I don't know, but if we don't keep pushing, turning over every rock, we won't have anything. The fact that we have no damn good leads to two big-ticket murders speaks to piss-poor detective work. Dammit, we ought to be doing better than that."

Connors glanced at Amado. "What exactly is the thinking here? Maybe Periera and his partners had something to do with those paintings and fancy furniture in the warehouse?"

"Maybe. Rabino thinks we ought to check him out, that's all. Remember, Periera is a name that appeared on the guest list at the señora's church memorial service. Rabino says the name is Sephardic."

Connors gave him a questioning look.

"Sephardic, meaning a Portuguese or Spanish Hebrew name. Maybe he's a member of a cabal..."

Connors interrupted and pointed upward. "Hold it, Fred.

Look up there. This is the address. I'll park on the street. Better than taking the car up that narrow incline. Why do people want to live on top of a hill, anyway?"

"The view of the coastline and the valley is terrific." On the ridge top above them were mansions with sweeping views of the harbor and the mountains to the east and west across the channel to Santa Cruz Island. "Besides," Amado added, "there's prestige in location... big bucks to construct also." Half-way up the inclined driveway, Amado pushed the lid of his fedora up and wiped his brow.

Connors said, "Whew, I'm winded. We should have taken the car up."

Amado looked through a large window next to the entryway, then pushed the doorbell. The door opened and a maid glanced wide-eyed at Amado's badge, then asked him what he wanted.

"Who's there, Amalia?" A voice called out from another part of the house. A clickety-clack of heels striking the tile floor preceded the appearance of an attractive, smartly-dressed woman in her forties. She looked at the men and said, "Yes? Can I help you gentlemen?"

Amado removed his hat and introduced himself and Connors. "Is Mr. Periera in? We'd like to ask him a few questions."

"You could have saved yourself a trip by phoning him at his office in Ventura. What is this about?"

Amado hesitated with the maid present, and Mrs. Periera sensed that. She dismissed the maid and invited the detectives to follow her. She walked into a large living room, bright with sunlight streaming through ceiling-to-floor windows. "I was preparing to go out, but I can spare a few minutes." She smiled. "It's not often that two handsome detectives come calling."

Amado looked around, made a mental note of the luxurious furnishings. He ran his hand along an intricately carved breakfront. Mrs. Periera noticed his apparent interest. "Do you appreciate old furniture, detective?"

He nodded. "This is an early nineteenth-century Austrian piece... well preserved, nice detailing."

"You're kind. I think it's atrocious, but my husband received it as a gift from his uncle, and we're stuck with it."

"Is Mr. Periera in the antique furniture business?"

"My husband? Heavens no! He's an attorney. It's his uncle who's in the import and export business. He has offices and a warehouse in L.A."

Amado chatted with Mrs. Periera for several minutes, about the magnificent view. Then said, "We won't keep you any longer. Not everyone is as cooperative or pleased to see us detectives. Would you have Mr. Periera's uncle's address and phone number?"

She hurried to another room, then returned with a business card. "I think you fellas do a great job— besides, I know your boss, Sheriff Rabino." She laughed. "This really is a small community. My son is asking one of his daughters to the prom."

Connors put the car in gear and pulled away. "Boy, oh boy, that's a lot of coincidences, Fred."

"How so?"

"Periera's kid and Rabino's daughter are dating and the Periera kid's great uncle is in the import business. Some pieces of the puzzle might be falling into place."

"The Jewish community here is small and tight," Amado said. "They all seem to know one another. Before the war there was some nasty anti-Semitism here, the KKK tried to get started but the Jews and Catholic Latinos succeeded in running them off. After the Holocaust, public sentiment wouldn't tolerate any overt racial hatred."

"I know what you're saying. Kick one and the whole tribe comes down on you. Those people are like that, but I think they care mostly about themselves, Jews, I mean. They're pushy bastards."

Amado turned toward Connors, his steely gaze made the novice detective do a double-take. "Did I say something wrong?"

"Yeah, wrong and stupid. I'll let you in on something you didn't know. I wouldn't have mentioned this, but this is as good a time as any. Just after you came aboard, I was pissed off. I told Rabino I didn't want him assigning you as my partner, you were too green, and from what I could see, not too bright."

"Gee, thanks, old buddy," Connors said.

Amado continued, "Rabino sat me down and drove home a few points. 'Listen,' he said, 'the kid has got to start somewhere, and you're the one who can teach him.' Then he went on to say that he had a good feeling about you and would put his badge on the line if you fucked up. Not too many guys are willing to make that commitment, especially for a green butt recruit."

"Gee, Fred, I meant no disrespect when I said that, and I have nothing personal against Marv Rabino. I don't think..."

"That's right." Amado interrupted. "You don't think. Listen, Mr. Pale Face Anglo: this community was settled and inhabited primarily by Latinos and Indians and then secondarily by outsiders. The so-called white man came on the scene later. In case you've forgotten, those early settlers migrated up from old Mexico. My father's people were among them. You make any more stupid remarks about peoples' origins, races or religions, and you'll find yourself holding the shitty end of the stick."

Connors said nothing, but now he had a hang-dog expression.

Amado slumped in his seat, crossed his arms and became reflective. "Marv Rabino and I go back a long way. Our families were in the area for generations. He and I joined the Air Force together. After the war, we both qualified for the undersheriff's position, but I lost out. Know why?"

"Sure don't, Fred. Why?"

"Booze and dames—that's why. I was a big shot with a

badge and a gun and thought I was untouchable. Complaints came in against me. I thought my so-called vices never interfered with my job, but too many straight arrows in the department resented me...didn't like my free-wheeling life style. Guys I thought were my buddies turned their backs on me. The disciplinary board wanted my ass, no doubt about it. I was ready to pack my bags and leave. Trouble was, I had nowhere to go."

"What happened?"

"One guy thought my ass was worth salvaging. He busted his balls for me and pleaded my case privately before every member of the board. No one asked him to, certainly not me. I thought I was beyond redemption. This guy saved my worthless ass. You know who I mean? Yeah, that's right—Marv Rabino. We still have differences, and there are times when I feel like slugging him. But I'll always be grateful to him, and no one can say anything bad about him, his family or his people—not to me, not ever. Do you understand that?"

"Yeah, I do, Fred, and I'm damned sorry for the stupid things I said."

Chapter 31

7:30 p.m. The professional building offices were dark. Traffic downtown slowed to a trickle, not unusual for Santa Barbara at that hour. Homicides, although relatively infrequent, took on special importance to Amado. He felt justified at the prospect of breaking and entering into old Spingarn's office. He needed to plow through his files to discover any shady connection with the Montenegros. Such information could give clues to the murders. He'd bet his Smith and Wesson on it.

⋆⟵⟶⋆

Amado's 1948 coupe, mud-spattered and with fender dings, appeared unobtrusive along the curb, opposite the Santa Barbara Professional Building. A dim light in the lobby suggested the presence of the evening cleaning crew or security.

He sat in the car surveying the building for activity, then slumped down in his seat when a couple walking by gave the car a cursory glance. Amado removed a container of talcum from the glove compartment and sprinkled his hands, then slipped them into rubber gloves. He reached for a briefcase on the seat, and took a flashlight out of it. Looking up and down the street, and seeing no one, he opened the car door, stepped out and closed it quietly. Taking long strides in his sneakers, he crossed the street quickly. A tall juniper, one of two bordering the entry, provided further camouflage for his black jacket and trousers. His face was partially obscured by his turned-up collar and navy stocking cap pulled down over his ears.

He hiked his left shoulder and rotated it slightly forward to feel the holstered gun—an unconscious movement made countless times during the day. Now he did it with awareness. This unauthorized caper, this crazy derring-do that his spirit longed for, was essentially a rebellious act against every restrictive protocol that smothered his fighting spirit. Unless he risked this break-in, he reasoned, these murders might never get solved. The required stealth and proximity of danger excited him in a way he remembered from his Marine Corps days...hand-to-hand combat...jujitsu...

Moving sideways toward the entrance, he tried opening the door, not really expecting it to open, but when it did, he stepped hurriedly into the lobby and hugged the wall. Turning a darkened corner, he stopped to listen for any sounds, then opened the door to the stairwell next to the elevator. He cursed the squeaking hinges. When the door closed, he was immersed in total darkness causing momentary disorientation. He reached for his flashlight to get his bearings and began ascending stairs slowly. At the second-floor level, he stopped to listen to the muffled sounds of a vacuum cleaner. He hoped the cleaning crew had finished work on the third floor where Spingarn's office was located.

The third floor remained dark and quiet with only the distant humming of the vacuum cleaner and indistinct voices from the cleaning crew below. Amado remembered that Spingarn's office was to the right of the stairway. Shielding the beam from his flashlight, he located the office door and turned the knob—it was locked. He placed the flashlight on the floor and opened the briefcase to remove a ring of keys. He reached for a master key and told himself to remain calm. The use of this key required patience and finesse. Amado felt his body heat rising. An interminable minute-and-a half later the door opened.

Hurrying through the waiting room, he entered the business office with its file cabinets, and directed the light beam onto the letters in front of the cabinet drawers. Pulling the handle of the drawer with the initials L-M., he found that it too was locked. *Dammit!* The recessed lock near the top of the cabinet required a small key. He reached for the key ring in the briefcase, then stopped to listen again for any noises. One voice had become louder and more distinct. No stopping now. He had to find the Montenegro file. The first small key from the ring of keys did not work; he tried a second key, then a third. None worked.

From the briefcase, he pulled out a thin screwdriver to force into the key slot, then thought of trying one more key. Bingo! It slid in. The lock turned. The L-M drawer slid forward with an easy pull. The flashlight on the tabs above the folders revealed the names: Mason, Mettler, Michaelson—ah! Montenegro. He reached for the thick folder when he felt something pushing against the back of his head.

"Stop right there, or I'll blow your fuckin' head off!"

Amado cursed. He didn't see this coming, but he wasn't going to let it all end here. He released the folder into the cabinet drawer, then brought his hands to his sides. Whoever it was, stepped back and switched on the light.

"Put your hands up! Now turn around."

The voice sounded like that of an older guy, breathless, wheezy, maybe a chronic boozer who had just labored up a flight of stairs. "I said, turn around," the voice demanded.

Amado planted his feet firmly and did nothing more.

"You deaf? I said turn around, you sonofabitch."

"Fuck you, buster," Amado said in a low, steady voice.

The man grabbed Amado's shoulder to force him to turn around.

In a lightning move, Amado turned and caught the man's wrist, pushing it sideways. With his other hand, he twisted the gun out of his hand. Then he tripped the watchman with a foot sweep and set him on his backside. Crashing to the floor, spread eagle, the watchman's eyes were wide with fear and confusion. His gun had skittered across the floor. Amado bent forward, picked up the gun and tucked it in his belt. His conjecture of the watchman couldn't have been more accurate: a pot-bellied, fiftyish man lying terrified, shaking; his pants darkening at the crotch with urine.

"Sorry to inconvenience you, buster." Amado held his own gun on the watchman. "What's your name?"

"J-Joe. Please don't shoot me. I got kids—grandkids."

"Tell you what I'm gonna do, Joe. I'm going to walk out of here, and no one is going to know how you fucked up, providing you keep your mouth shut. If you call the cops, I'll drop a note to management and tell them how badly you fucked up. Now, do we have a deal?"

The watchman answered quickly, "Yeah, yeah, sure."

As Amado helped the portly man stand, the wail of a siren could be heard in the distance. Amado grabbed the watchman by the lapels. "Did you call the cops before you came in here?"

The watchman didn't answer immediately, then said, "No, no, I swear."

Amado knew he was lying. Never taking his eyes or gun off the guard, he pulled up a folder from the file cabinet, stuck it in his briefcase and ran out. He had to use the rear exit since the cops would be coming through the front. The exit sign warned: *To be used in emergency only.* He opened the door and stepped out onto the fire escape landing, three levels above the dark alley. Two police cars pulled up to the front entryway. Getting down to the street level by elevator or stairs was not an option.

Suddenly the third floor was flooded with light. Four police with guns drawn began a search of every office. The guard, huffing and wheezing, tried to keep up. He directed two of the police to the rear exit door.

They opened the door and charged onto the fire escape landing. No one was above or below, and no one was in the alley.

In a far corner of the roof of an adjoining building, Amado sat huddled, his collar turned up and his stocking cap pulled down; his briefcase at his side. After twenty minutes, the noise of the search ended and the third floor lights went out. With a flick of his flashlight he looked at his watch: 8:52. Crouching, he moved toward the front of the roof and looked down to see the last patrol car pull away. *Good. I'm freezing my ass up here. I'll give them ten more minutes, enough time for them to circle the block and return to the crime scene. I know the drill.*

Chapter 32

Like a true athlete, he raced down the fire escape, then released his arms and dropped six feet to the dark alley. After glancing in both directions, he ran to the car, tossed the briefcase on the passenger side and whipped off his stocking cap. After inserting the key into the ignition and starting the engine, he reached for a cigarette and took a long drag. A loud rapping on the driver's window startled him. *What the hell!* He squinted through the dirty window to see the beaked hat of a steely-eyed officer motioning him to roll down the window.

"What's the trouble officer?" Amado didn't recognize the young face confronting him.

"Your left tail light isn't working."

Amado exhaled but tried to conceal his relief. "Sorry, I'll see that it's repaired in the morning." He was about to shift into first gear when the officer beamed his flashlight on the passenger seat revealing the briefcase, stocking hat and the powdery residue between Amado's fingers resting on the steering wheel. He took his hands off the wheel and placed them at his sides.

"What are you doing here at this hour?"

"I was planning to rob a bank." Amado smiled with false bravado. "Just kidding. Actually, I came from the YMCA... worked out... did some weight lifting." He looked at his fingers. "I guess I didn't get all the powder off my hands."

The officer nodded, then looked at his watch. "The 'Y' closed an hour ago."

"You're right. Truth is, after my workout, I met a friend. We talked for awhile before she had to leave…well, you understand."

"Uh-huh. Your driver's license, please."

Amado reached for the wallet in his back pocket, then placed his sergeant's badge on it.

The officer directed the light beam onto Amado's face. "Sergeant Amado? Gee, I'm sorry, sir. I had no idea…"

"Not your fault. I held off purposely to observe your approach. I like your style. You're a credit to the department. Put your name and badge number on a slip of paper. I'll want to tell your chief about you."

"Thank you, sir, I'd appreciate that." The officer gave an abbreviated two-finger salute and stepped back. "Have a good evening, sir."

Amado returned the salute, put the car in gear and hurried off.

After entering his apartment, Amado placed the briefcase on the kitchen table and pulled up a chair anticipating the discovery of valuable information. He flipped the briefcase cover and pulled out the folder. He glanced at the first page and blanched. His brow furrowed, his shoulders sagged. *Oh, shit! How could I have been so stupid? Goddamn it!* He looked at the name again. *This is Michaelson –not Montenegro. How could I have picked up the wrong goddamn file?* He pounded his forehead with his fist, then picked up the file and threw it across the room.

He dropped onto the sofa, folded his arms across his chest and sighed. *I placed my career on the line for that damn thing and got it wrong.* He walked toward the cabinet above the refrigerator where he kept hard liquor and reached for the Jack Daniels.

The phone rang; he looked at his watch: 10:32. *Maybe they got my ID and they're coming to pick me up. Hell no, they wouldn't be calling to tell me that.* Snatching the phone off its cradle, he snarled, "Amado here."

When he heard the voice, his angst disappeared, and he

smiled as though he had just won a year's supply of Budweiser. The melodious voice of Isabella was more wonderful than anything he could have imagined.

"Fred, darling, I hope I'm not disturbing you at this late hour. I just read an article in the art section of the Santa Barbara News Press by a Professor Lundstrom from Sweden. I got so excited, I had to share it with you. He says that the art world has been deprived of thousands of art treasures that were stolen and many destroyed by the Nazis. They looted homes of Jewish patrons of art as well as museums in occupied countries."

"Look, baby, I'm overjoyed to hear your voice, but the professor's news is a little stale. Tell me something I don't know."

Isabella read on, "Members of several prominent German Jewish families who had migrated to the United States, England and Canada are demanding a return of their art from the German government or appropriate compensation."

"Good luck to them," Amado said laconically.

Isabella continued, "Claims have been made for the return of paintings by such famous artists as: Toulouse-Lautrec, Picasso, Matisse, Léger and many others."

"Okay, baby doll, I thank you for that information. Now tell me how much you love me."

"Not until you hear me out. Listen, the Nazis declared many paintings to be the work of degenerates who did not paint in good German tradition."

"Well, la-di-da. What else did the barbarians say, or is that all?"

"No, that's not all. Many of the paintings were sold under duress by their Jewish owners for much less than their real worth. The owners were anxious to escape and sold their art to get money to leave Germany hurriedly. Those people were forced to sell to unscrupulous dealers." Isabella paused expecting Amado to comment. "Are you listening, Fred?"

"Yeah, yeah. You got me thinking, baby." *Those dealers probably contacted well-heeled Fascists and offered them the art. The Montenegros may have been among them.*

Chapter 32

Connors glanced around. "This drive to L. A. is a real pain in the ass...never saw so much damn slow traffic. The address we're looking for is near Olvera Street. I'm gonna get some good Mexican tacos, maybe chili rellenos. I love that stuff. Trouble is, it makes me fart so bad."

Amado turned slowly to look at him. "We've got a long ride back. I'd suggest you eat something else—and avoid the refried beans."

The factory, a red-brick, two-story, pre-World War One building in need of tuckpointing, stood as an oddity in an area of light-colored, stucco-faced commercial establishments of more recent origin. A brass plate bolted to the right of the entrance read: I.A.T. Co. Est. 1935. Before pressing the doorbell, Amado read the printed message on the door: *By appointment only.* He looked at Connors. "Maybe this'll turn out to be an exclusive men's club."

Connors smiled. "That'd be okay by me."

A woman's voice called out from a black box above the entrance. "Can I help you?"

"This is Sergeant Amado from the Santa Barbara sheriff's office. I'd like to talk with Mr. Periera."

After thirty seconds of silence, Amado became impatient and rapped at the door. "Open up, please."

"Just a moment, I'm trying to locate Mr. Periera."

Amado pulled Connors back from the door and whispered, "I'm going around the back to see if anyone is getting into a car. You go inside the building when the door opens."

In a parking area behind the building, a polished black 1938 Pierce Arrow formal sedan was backing out of a parking space. Amado ran toward the driver's side, held up his badge and commanded the driver to stop. When the uniformed driver did not stop, Amado struck the window with his fist and shouted, "You're pushing your luck, buddy boy. I could have your ass hauled in for attempting bodily harm to an officer and resisting a command to stop."

The chauffeur rolled down the window, apologized and said that the sun had obstructed his vision.

"Save the excuses," Amado said.

A voice from the back of the vehicle called out, "What's going on? Why are we being detained?"

Amado stuck his head in the driver's compartment and looked at the elderly man seated in the back. "Mr. Periera?"

"Yes, what is it? Who are you?"

"I'm Detective Amado, from the Santa Barbara sheriff's department. I'd like to ask you a few questions."

"Why didn't you make an appointment? I'm a very busy man with a full schedule. I don't have time to..."

Amado cut him off. "This involves the murders of two people. One you knew, sir, Señora Montenegro—the other was a Spanish priest."

The older man's voice took on a conciliatory tone. "Yes, of course, forgive my abrupt manner." He leaned forward and tapped the chauffeur on the shoulder. "Wilson, go to the warehouse and tell Sibyl to call my business associates and tell them I'll be late." He looked at his watch, then at Amado. "Will thirty minutes be sufficient?"

"Can't say for sure, but we'll aim for that." Amado looked at the chauffeur who was leaving. "Would you ask Detective Connors to come here?"

Periera signaled Amado to join him inside the limousine.

Connors arrived minutes later and introduced himself. When he and Amado were inside the limo, they pulled down the jump seats facing Periera.

Periera leaned forward in his seat. "Detective, how did you know that I knew Señora Montenegro?"

"You and two other men riding in this vehicle, which is quite noticeable by itself, attended her memorial service in Montecito." Amado pulled out his notebook, moistened his forefinger at his lip and flipped several pages. "According to the guest register, you arrived with a Mr. Perez and a Mr. Beneveniste."

Periera nodded. "My partners."

"Mr.Periera, how did you know Señora Montenegro?" Amado asked.

"We had mutual business interests."

"And what would that have been?"

Periera hesitated. "I don't mind cooperating with the law, but that question invades privacy privilege, and I'm uncomfortable revealing that information."

"Just because you feel uncomfortable, doesn't excuse you from telling us. Let me put this in proper perspective, sir. Two murders have been committed, you know one of the murder victims. You are obliged to give us any information that might help us in our investigation." Periera glared at Amado and started to respond but stopped and turned away.

Unwilling to be dismissed, Amado persisted. "All right, let me ask you this: what can you tell us about the art treasures in the Goleta warehouse?"

Periera turned to face Amado, then shook his head. "I don't know what you're talking about."

"Sir, do you deal in old furniture...valuable old furniture?"

"One might say that." He leaned forward and placed his gloved hand on a walking stick.

"Do you deal in art treasures—costly paintings?"

"Detective, I refuse to answer any more questions, and furthermore, I resent any implication that I engaged in some kind of illegal activity. Besides, what does all this have to do with those murders?"

"That's what we're trying to determine, sir. I'd appreciate having you answer my questions. If you don't answer them here, you'll answer them in court. If you give us false answers, you'll be guilty of lying and obstructing justice."

"Don't threaten me and stop assuming the role of prosecuting attorney. If you persist, I'll charge you with harassment, and you'll be served by my lawyer."

"Maybe we'd have better luck with your lawyer. What's his name?"

"Why should I tell you?"

Amado stared at him. "Why won't you tell me?"

Periera snorted a "Humph," and wouldn't answer. Clearly, the conversation was not going to be productive.

Connors, eager to break the hostile stalemate, said, "Mr. Periera, I just spent a few minutes in your warehouse, and I was really impressed. Boy, you've got an awful lot of stuff in there. Do you buy those things here or overseas?"

Periera, regarded Connors thoughtfully and almost smiled. Unlike Amado, the young detective was not being intrusive or threatening. He was genuinely impressed by what he had seen and was simply expressing appreciation. "Young man, I'm not disposed to discuss business operations with outsiders, but your obvious interest deserves an answer. Briefly stated, yes, I do go overseas to select my furnishings from European dealers."

"How long have you been doing that, sir?" Connors asked.

"Since 1934." He looked out the side window. "Now, if you'll excuse me, I see that my chauffeur is returning, and I have a business engagement. Should you have further questions, make an appointment to see me." From his wallet he removed two business cards and gave one to each detective.

"Thank you for your time, Mr. Periera," Amado said. "I'm sure we'll meet again."

Chapter 33

"What were your impressions of that old geezer, Fred?" Connors, driving, slipped into traffic going south. "Do you think he knows more than he's letting on?"

"You damn well know he does. He's as innocent as a whore in a cathouse. Did you see the expression on his face when I asked him about the Goleta warehouse? We just have to figure out what if anything, that has to do with the murders."

Connors nodded. "Fred, I kinda figure you have a special, well, sort of a close friendship with Isabella Chavez. I don't mean to pry or anything like that, but do you suppose she would know something about the business dealings between old man Periera and the Montenegros? I mean, wouldn't it be hard for her *not* to know something about what went on between them?"

"She said she knew nothing about the Goleta warehouse before we went there two weeks ago. Why should I doubt her?"

"No reason, it's just that...with all those high-powered treasures and Periera doing business with the Montenegros..."

"She probably didn't even know Peiriera and his partners."

Connors gave him a quick glance. "Then why did she kiss him at Señora Montenegro's memorial service?"

Amado's brow furrowed. "So what? That doesn't mean anything. She probably kissed a lot of mourners she didn't know. Just a way of thanking them for being there."

"Sure, Fred, sure. There's something else I was thinking about: Pereira's old Pierce Arrow..."

"What about it?"

"Well, isn't it kind of funny that the Montenegros had an old bus, too? What's it called?"

"You mean the Hispano Suissa?"

"Yeah, that's it. Why do you suppose that is, Fred? Man, you never get to see ancient sleds like that, unless you go to an old car meet. Takes a lot of moola to restore and maintain those old crates. 'Course, I guess that's no problem for Periera or the Montenegros. Maybe the Montenegros had one because the Hispano was made in Spain..."

"It was made in France, but that's not important. However, you raise an interesting point—Periera and Colonel Montenegro liked old cars. They had that in common... maybe they liked a few other things as well."

<hr />

Amado's coupe approached the gate at the Montenegro estate. He sat in the car and looked to either side then upward toward the roof line and the second-floor windows with their small balconies where a gunman could be lurking. That gunshot wound to his right arm had sensitized him to the possibility of a nut case drawing a bead on him again. He saw nothing suspicious and the estate grounds were cemetery quiet. After two short horn blasts, Lobo came tearing out of nowhere barking and baring his fangs as the gate opened slowly.

"It's okay, Lobo. It's only me." As soon as the dog heard Amado's voice, he stopped barking, wagged his tail and made little yipping sounds of anticipation. Amado pulled a dog biscuit out of his pocket and gave it to the dog who chomped it hurriedly, then with imploring eyes watched until Amado fed him another. Walking at Amado's side, Lobo looked up at him for yet another treat.

Isabella stood at the entrance smiling, approving of the little domestic drama. Amado approached the dark-haired beauty whose eyes shown as he neared. He lifted Isabella as though she were weightless and whirled her around.

She laughed, then protested feebly when he squeezed her derriere, and she pushed his hand aside.

"Why must you be so physical?" she said.

"Just how I express affection."

"Try being gentle, more caring."

"But, I am, I am."

"Are you going to hold me in the air like this, the whole evening?"

"Uh—uh. I'm going to get you in a better position for what I have in mind."

"Okay, Tarzan, put me down, and let's talk like two adults. I want to know what progress you've made in the past week."

Amado told her of his failed attempt at stealing the Montenegro file from Spingarn's office and the visit with Periera.

"Why don't you concentrate on someone around here? Don't you believe someone working here murdered the señora? Is that so difficult to understand?"

"We've questioned every employee, taken fingerprints and so far, we've come up with zip, zero, nada. We don't even have a motive yet, but I think we might be getting close."

Isabella looked at her hands, then passed her thumbs over her fingertips. "Fred, I don't remember having my fingerprints taken."

Amado shrugged, raised his brow but said nothing.

Isabella persisted. "Why weren't they taken?"

"I don't know...an oversight, I suppose."

"I don't believe that. For all the suspicion the sheriff had about my guilt in the señora's murder..."

"All right." Amado, annoyed at her insistence, said, "Damn it, I didn't want your prints taken."

"But why?"

He hesitated. "I didn't want your prints showing up anywhere near the scene of the murder."

Isabella's brow wrinkled. "I don't understand."

"You want me to draw pictures? I didn't want to give anyone more ammunition to suspect you. I have more than a casual interest in your future—and mine."

"Fred, you're sweet, but I don't mind having my fingerprints taken."

He cut her off. "I know what I'm doing, baby."

"If you're trying to protect me to get at my money, you could be terribly disappointed."

"What I want from you, baby, is what you give me between the bed sheets." Seeing her look of disapproval, he added quickly, "Only kidding."

"You have such an elegant way of expressing yourself."

"It's one of my more charming attributes."

"All right, Prince Charming, what really brings you here? Don't tell me you came merely to see me. Even when we're making love, you usually spoil the evening by asking questions. Sometimes I feel that I'm just being used …"

"Shush." Amado put his forefinger to Isabella's lips. "Don't ruin these precious moments with such mundane thoughts."

"Well, it's true. Now, tell me what you really want."

"Besides you? I want to take another look at the colonel's den. Something about that musty room piques my interest."

<hr />

She led him back to the colonel's den, which appeared unchanged since their first visit. It was still as musty and unfriendly with the wall-mounted heads of a snarling lion, tiger and leopard creating the same visceral reaction from Isabella when the lights went on. She looked away to avoid them.

"Glad those cats are stuffed," Amado said. He walked toward a rhino head and studied it momentarily. "His horn is dusty. How often does the cleaning crew come in?"

"Every two weeks or so. They should have used a feather duster on those poor defenseless beasts," she remarked.

"Poor defenseless beasts?" Amado asked. "You don't approve of hunting big game?"

"Certainly not. Not big or small unless it is necessary for food. What gives one the right to kill a creature for mere sport? That is so barbaric. Fortunately, most cultures have strong prohibitions about killing men."

"Yeah, which they can put aside for any cause or excuse whatever—patriotism, ideology, ethnic hatred. Eleven million in our civilized twentieth century alone have been slaughtered in spite of any civilized prohibitions. And how do you feel about an individual act of revenge or vengeance when you have no lawful recourse?" Amado asked.

"*Vengeance is mine, saith the Lord*", Isabella replied.

"Can't argue scripture. Glad to know you're incapable of killing."

"I could make an exception in your case," she said, laughing.

Chapter 34

Amado studied the colonel's desk and picked up a gold-plated pen and pencil set on an onyx base. He read a scrolled dedication: *To my dear friend, Colonel Montenegro with warmest regards, General Hermann W. Göring.* "Now, there were two bastards of the same stripe."

"What was Göring's role in the Spanish Civil War?" Isabella asked.

"He was head of the German air force, the Luftwaffe, and conducted practice bombing in the Basque country with Blitzkrieg techniques that were later used in WWII. To them it was just target practice. Another example of how they used Spain as a training ground for the invasion of Poland. Innocent men, women, children, farm animals...hell, they were all expendable."

Amado walked to the gun collection in the oak cabinet. The indentation in the black Styrofoam where a .22 caliber pistol was missing again caught his attention. "If the only people who come into this room are the cleaning crew..." He spoke softly as though to an imaginary third person while he rubbed his chin.

"You interrogated those elderly maids, Fred. You told me that accusing them of any crime would take a *blank* stretch of a fertile imagination. I remember your statement because I scolded you for using the *blank* word."

"Yeah, yeah, you're right." He turned to study the floor-to-ceiling book shelves and noted the set of leather-bound books of Shakespeare's plays on the top shelf along with volumes of the Encyclopedia Britannica. At eye level the shelf held books showing wear on the spines. With his forefinger he pointed to a book on Hegel's Philosophy next to a collection of works by Nietzsche. He ran his finger along the other books and stopped at the *Philosophy of Schopenhauer.*

"Are you acquainted with those works?" She asked.

"These old birds formed a chapter or two in my Philosophy 101 class at Berkeley. From the wear on the book covers, I'd say the colonel had an interest in the concept of man's superiority. Nietzsche, for instance, wrote about the Ubermensch, superman. He also rejected Christianity..."

Isabella interrupted. "Fred, that wasn't the colonel's thinking at all. He was a devout Catholic. He would have joined the Crusades if he could have."

"Well, someone was interested enough to study these miserable bastards." He reached for a well-used book. "Here, for example is the epitome of evil demagoguery, unmitigated anti-intellectualism, *Mein Kampf,* written by the sorriest excuse for a human being ever spawned, Adolph Hitler, the antithesis of everything or anything remotely good about mankind." He riffled the pages, then shoved the book back into place.

At a distance of about five feet, Amado studied the craftsmanship of the book shelves and noted the exquisite matching pattern of the walnut grain. Something caught his eye, some tiny irregularity, a loss of luster in the finish along a vertical support.

"What are you staring at, Fred?"

He did not respond but walked toward the shelves, studied them closely and ran his hand lightly over the marred finish of the wood. He applied pressure and the muffled, high-pitched whirring of an electric motor sounded. The entire wall of book shelves pivoted outward exposing a dark opening in the wall. Isabella gasped and ran to Amado clutching him tightly.

"I'll be damned." Amado approached the opening, a foreboding maw of darkness that carried the stink of sewer gas and the smell of damp earth. Isabella, hung onto him, wrinkled her nose and pulled back.

A light switch, almost concealed by a plate with the same wood finish, was affixed to the right side. "Let's hope this turns on a light," Amado said. He pushed the lever up; the hollow clicking sound produced no light. He flipped the lever up and down several times. "Damn! I'll go to the car and get my flashlight. You wait here."

Isabella hurried to walk beside him. "Oh, no. You're not going to leave me here alone."

On the cement pad where Amado had parked his car, Isabella inhaled deeply. "This air is wonderful after that awful smell from down below." She shivered in the cold evening air and crossed her arms across her chest. "I'm frightened, Fred. Where do you think that passage leads to?"

"I don't know. Maybe Dante's Inferno, but we'll find out. What I find hard to believe is that after all the years you lived here; you never knew that concealed opening existed?"

"Fred, that room was the colonel's private sanctuary. It was always locked, and I had strict orders never to enter it."

Isabella pulled on Amado's shirt sleeve as he took a flashlight out of the glove compartment. "Fred, would it be too much to ask of you to leave your gun in the car?" Her eyes implored him.

"You really are afraid of a gun, aren't you?" He patted his shoulder holster. "Sorry, baby, this little *shmiesser* goes everywhere I go...on duty or off. It's mandated by the department. What frightens you about my gun?"

"Suppose you shoot some innocent person?"

"Suppose someone shoots at us or threatens to? It's already happened. Remember?"

"You're right. It's just that I know everyone here and..."

"You've got to trust my judgment. I know how to respond to an emergency, it's what I've been trained to do." Amado closed the car door quietly, locked it, and again made a quick survey of the grounds and the main house. He took Isabella's hand and both walked toward the entrance. Instinctively, he kept his head down to make a smaller target for any sharpshooter.

For Isabella, the house, no longer provided a safe haven, in fact, she had not regarded it as safe since the señora's murder one month earlier. The discovery of the secret passage in the colonel's den was just one more frightening development.

Amado approached the door to the den and turned the knob. He peered over his shoulder at Isabella and whispered, "Might be better if you stayed out here."

"Forget it. I'm not staying here alone. I'll be right behind you."

Amado opened the door slowly. He stopped. The room was not as they had left it. The moveable book shelves were back in place. He pulled out his gun, held it ready and walked warily into the room. He looked under the desk, behind the leather recliner and sofa...no sign of intrusion. Isabella held onto his shirt.

At the bookcase, he applied pressure to the vertical wood strip. Again the whirring sound of a motor preceded the opening movement of the book shelves. Amado directed the flashlight beam into the dark opening and discovered about ten wooden stairs with hand rails that led down to a short platform. The stairs continued downward at a right angle from there.

Amado whispered, "I'm keeping both hands on my gun. You take the flashlight, walk behind me and a little to my right, so I can see my way down."

"Fred, I'm frightened. Shouldn't we have more police here?"

"Do me a favor, stay here. I'll go down myself."

"Oh, no you won't. I'm not staying up here alone."

Amado, holding his pistol with both hands, took three steps down while Isabella held the flashlight. Her curiosity caused her to deflect the light beam to either side of the staircase. She whispered, "There's a lot of stuff stored down here... old furniture, paintings..."

Amado cut her off. "Keep the light on the stairs, so I can see where I'm going."

"Sorry. It's just that all this stuff looks so fascinating..." She bumped into Amado just beyond the landing and dropped the flashlight. It thumped as it struck several stairs then rolled off the side to the floor with a lens-shattering crash. "Oh no!" Then she murmured, "I'm so sorry."

The shaft of light from the den above disappeared with the sound of the whirring motor as the bookshelves moved back into place. "What the hell goes on here? Why did those damn shelves move?" Amado asked.

Immersed in total darkness they remained absolutely still. They heard only the sounds of their breathing. Isabella experienced a wave of panic, then nausea; she held onto Amado more tightly and began to whimper.

"Sh-sh. It's all right, baby." He placed one arm around her waist. "We'll stay here until our eyes adjust to the darkness... only six to eight steps before we reach bottom."

An outline of the stairs gradually appeared allowing them to descend to a cement floor. Again, they stood still; the fetid odor of sewer gas became more pungent; then they heard the faint sound of a different humming. Amado took Isabella's hand and walked slowly toward the sound. In the distance, a sliver of light penetrated the darkness and the sound grew louder.

Isabella's hand became clammy in Amado's firm grip. Slowly, they continued toward the source of light and sound. Amado released her hand to hold his pistol with both hands. He crouched as they advanced toward a partly-open door to a room from where the light and sound issued.

Amado pulled the door open several inches and held the gun ready. The room was a workshop with lathes, band saws and assorted tools hanging in order of size on the wall. Metal shavings lay on the floor.

Bent over a lathe, Gruenwald, the chauffeur, wearing a shop apron and an oily baseball cap, held a file on a rotating metal part. When the moving door disturbed his peripheral vision, he turned around abruptly. "You gave me a scare." He turned off the lathe, glared at Amado, but gazed softly at Isabella. "What are you both doing here?"

Replacing his gun in its holster, Amado said, "I've got some questions for you." He looked at his watch. "10:10. Why are you here at this hour?" Before Gruenwald could explain, Amado pointed upward. "And what about that concealed opening in the colonel's den? Was it you who closed that damn opening in the wall—twice tonight?"

Gruenwald removed a metal part from the lathe and placed it on the work bench. Moving methodically, he didn't bother to answer Amado as he wiped his hands on a mechanic's red rag. Then he said to Isabella, "You must forgive the appearance of the workshop. Usually things are more orderly, but I rushed to complete this job." He turned to pick up the steel part from the work bench to display it. "This is a starter motor-mount to replace the original one that cracked from fatigue." He shook his head sadly. "Can't buy these old parts anymore. I do what I can to keep that old vehicle running. I want the engine to work properly because I enjoy driving Miss Chavez around town. She looks so regal in it, and it befits her station." He paused and smiled at Isabella.

Amado, annoyed and impatient, said, "Okay, that accounts for you being here and the noise. What about those magical bookshelves up there, and why is there a stink around here?"

"We could use larger sewage pipes. That was a project the señora was going to take care of before her...departure."

"Murder, you mean." Amado said.

Gruenwald nodded.

"Now, what about that secret passage from the den to this place?" Amado asked.

"Mr. Detective, that question would have to be asked of the colonel, and, of course, he is no longer..."

"All right, all right. Who the hell closed that magician's

now-you-see-it-now-you-don't opening in the den?"

Gruenwald smiled. "That is the result of a timing device that allows eight minutes of open time—more than enough time to go up and down the stairs. The colonel wanted to be sure that the opening in the wall would not remain open by someone's carelessness."

Amado asked, "Who else knows about this secret passage?"

Before Gruenwald could answer, Isabella said, "Please show us the quickest way to the outdoors...not that convoluted passage to the main building. I know that route, and I want to avoid it. I'm not feeling well. Oh, yes, there's a flashlight on the floor somewhere. Look for it in the morning and return it to me."

The chauffeur opened a work bench drawer and handed Amado a flashlight, then moved close to whisper in his ear, "Remind me to tell you why the moving wall was really installed, but be sure the señorita is not with you."

Chapter 35

With a cigar stub lodged in the corner of his mouth, Rabino, growled at the seated Bill Connors. "What the hell did you guys say to Moses Periera that made him sic his gonif lawyers on our department? And what were you doing in L.A., anyway? You had no authority to go there. You guys were way the hell out of your bailiwick." Rabino put the cigar with its soggy misshapen end on an ashtray, then pounded his mid-section and reached for two Tums in his desk drawer. Making a sour face after belching, he continued, "What did you two geniuses discover that you couldn't find out by making a phone call?"

Connors detailed his report of their meeting with Periera and his impressions of the East Los Angeles warehouse.

"So, what did you conclude from all of that?" Before Connors could explain, Rabino said, "Do you think that stuff in the Goleta warehouse came from Periera?"

Connors shrugged. "Periera denies any knowledge of the Goleta warehouse."

"Sure. That's why he's having his shysters demand that we stop asking questions." Rabino put the cigar back in his mouth and chomped down on it. "Too bad about Periera, that old sonofabitch. He doesn't know what real harassment is. By the way, when you see Amado, tell him he can expect a good ass-chewing."

Chapter 36

Amado, lying next to Isabella, supported her head in the crook of his arm as she lay on her side facing him. In the exhilarating and delightfully exhausting moments after sex, she gazed at his handsome profile, reached over and absently played with the hairs on his chest. "Fred, I love you so much. I hope you love me as much as I love you."

He smiled without opening his eyes. "More, baby... but..."

She bolted upright. "But what?"

"Nothing, it's just that sometimes I think you're holding back...not telling me some dark secrets about the Montenegros." He was still wondering what Gruenwald wanted to tell him in the workshop. Amado sat up leaning against the headboard and reached for a cigarette on the nightstand. "The señora's relationship with her husband had to be goddamned strange. She was Franco's mistress, everyone knew that. Her husband had to be one dumb cuckold." He paused a moment. "On the other hand, maybe he wasn't so dumb. Was it possible that he encouraged her affair with Franco?"

Isabella hesitated before saying, "Perhaps."

"Perhaps? What does that mean?"

She rolled toward the edge of the bed, sat up and reached for her underclothes on the bedside chair. "The colonel and señora lived almost separate lives. The day I was taken from the orphanage, I knew the señora loved me, but he remained distant and uncaring. I don't recall a time when those two acted like loving married people—certainly not like my own wonderful parents. I've often thought that the señora needed me to listen to her. The colonel must have been afraid of Franco."

"Either that," Amado said, "or Franco made it worth his while to be his pimp. If he had any pride, he might have murdered her, but he didn't. So who did? And why? The señora gave someone a reason to murder her. She must have been goddamned guilty of something." Amado moved out of bed and reached for his Jockey shorts and undershirt. "Did they argue much?"

"Oh yes, at times there was absolute bedlam. The señora had a fiery temper. She would shout bloody curses and throw things at him. Funny, now that I think about it, he never responded in kind."

"Why was that?"

"I think he wanted to avoid confrontation. As you're suggesting, he reacted passively or even approved of the señora's relationship with Franco."

Amado stubbed out his cigarette in the ash tray. "Either the guy was limp as a noodle or guilty as hell about something, or the señora could have been holding it over his head. But none of that answers questions about *her* murder...unless she was guilty of some heinous crime...hell, she had to be. We talked about this before, but I'm not sure the question was answered to my satisfaction. How did the estate support itself? Don't tell me the citrus harvest was sufficient to maintain the salaries of the workers and the upkeep of this place."

Isabella slipped into a silk robe, then straightened the bedding. "Fred, believe me, there was much I didn't know. I never asked questions about finances or estate expenses. Because I feel close to you, I can tell you that I have complete control of the estate's business transactions now. There are over a half-million dollars in the Bank of America account. I don't know how long that will sustain the estate. Fortunately, I've had advice from the accountant and attorney Spingarn."

"How well do you know Periera, the man I interviewed

at his warehouse in L.A.? Connors suggested you must have known him well, since you kissed him at Señora Montenegro's memorial service."

Isabella smiled. "Of course, I kissed him. Mr. Periera is an old family friend. He was always kind to me. He brought me things like candy, books and dolls."

"What was the purpose of his visits?"

"Business, I suppose. He always carried a briefcase. After a few minutes with the three of us, he, the colonel and señora went to the library. I, of course, was sent away. I would hear arguing—mostly between the señora and Mr. Periera."

"And you didn't know what they were talking about?"

"No, and I never asked. I avoided involvement in matters I knew nothing about. I was always saddened when I heard their angry talk. I would escape to a safe place, like a corner in my room to read my books. Sometimes, I would saddle up Daisy, my beautiful sorrel pony, and ride the trail around the estate. Daisy gave me wonderful relief from the nastiness of those arguments. I loved Mr. Periera, but I dreaded those meetings he had with the señora and the colonel."

Amado listened and nodded to prompt more of her recollection. "Do you think Periera's anger with the señora resulted in his murdering her?"

Isabella gasped. "Oh, Fred, what a terrible thought. Mr. Periera was too kind, too thoughtful..."

"That wasn't my impression of him during our meeting in L.A. He acted like a mean old bastard. Were there any other visitors who caused shouting matches?"

Shaking her head, Isabella said, "Not that I recall." Taking Amado's hand, she asked, "Before you go home, would you like a nightcap in the bar downstairs?"

"You don't have to ask me twice."

⟵◦❧ ✿ ❧◦⟶

Seated at the cocktail table with their drinks, Amado gazed with unconcealed insatiable yearning at Isabella.

Aware of his staring, she said, "A penny for your thoughts."

"You're a remarkably beautiful woman. I could spend a lifetime admiring you, actually lusting after you."

"Is that a proposal?"

"Yeah, for the twenty-fifth time, I think. As soon as we nail down these two murders, I'm giving you my name."

"Really? I like my name just as it is, thank you." She laughed softly and reached out for his hand. "But I like *your* name even more. I must confess, I've written *Mrs. Isabella Amado* a hundred or more times. I like the fact that Amado means *beloved*. Do you think that really describes you?"

"Not a chance, but my mother probably had high hopes for me. Speaking of mothers, tell me about the señora who acted as your mother for the past fifteen or more years. What was she really like? We know about her fascination with Franco. She was in bondage to the guy and let it show."

"What do you mean?"

"She had a tattoo right above her vagina."

"Are you serious? What are you talking about?"

"I'm only telling you what the coroner said. Just above the hair line on her crotch, she had a tattooed message: *Por El Caudillo*. That's the kind of broad, sorry, I mean woman, she was. No gal with a nickel's worth of refinement would have done that or paraded around with Franco, that tubby fat-ass pop-in-jay. On a morality scale, she couldn't even register a blip."

Isabella closed her eyes and shook her head, obviously unwilling to hear any more unsavory details. In defense of the woman who had mothered her, she said, "She gave me a lot of love and affection."

"That gives her some redemptive points, I suppose. Did that pussy have many tomcats sniffing around her?"

"Fred, when you use that kind of language, it's so—well, so degrading. I just don't appreciate it."

"Just so we understand each other, baby doll, I have no respect for the likes of Franco or his bimbo. In my book they're the dregs of humanity. But make no mistake about my intentions. I'm going to get her killer and the priest's. That's my job. Makes no difference to me if the victim is the lowest form of life, I gotta find his or her killer. That's what I get paid to do."

"Bravo! How eloquent and reassuring. I'll be able to sleep better tonight knowing that the bravest detective in the Santa Barbara Sheriff's Department is on the job—protecting me."

"You can always sleep at my place." Amado smiled.

Isabella took him by the hand, led him to the door and kissed his cheek. "Good night, sweet prince."

Chapter 37

The quiet of early Sunday morning in downtown Santa Barbara was disturbed only by the scrubbing and scraping sound of the street cleaners' brushing and the hosing down of debris from Saturday night revelers.

Amado stood behind his desk and extended his hand to John Gruenwald, who managed a smile on a face unaccustomed to smiling. "Thank you for coming in on your day off, John. Our offices, as you can see, are quiet on Sunday morning. There should be few interruptions. Can I get you a cup of coffee?"

"No, thank you." Gruenwald stood until Amado pointed to a chair on the other side of his desk.

Amado offered him a cigarette, but Gruenwald shook his head. "I hope this meeting didn't keep you from attending Sunday mass."

Gruenwald grunted. "Religion is not a priority with me. The preachers I've known have been hypocrites. I have no faith in those who preach what others ought to do while they live in sin."

"Sorry, I didn't mean to pry."

"No need to apologize. I should not express my dislike for organized religion. Did I offend you?"

"Hardly, my religion, if one can call it that, is based on a modified proverb: Do unto others before they do unto you." Both men laughed, and Gruenwald seemed to relax. Amado continued, "I asked you to meet me here because you gave me the impression that you had something important to tell me."

"I remember. You asked about that concealed opening in Colonel Montenegro's den and the stairs leading to and from it."

"That's right. What was the reason for that?"

Gruenwald looked around before speaking. "Please, do not make a record of this meeting."

"Don't worry. There are no hidden microphones or cameras, and no one is near this room. However, I must warn you: any information you give me can be used to incriminate a guilty party—you, or anyone else. Is that understood?"

Gruenwald bit his lower lip and lowered his head, then nodded. "All right, I trust you." He took a deep breath. "I don't know what you have been told about the colonel."

"Not very much, only that he and the señora did not get on well."

"Hah! That's for sure. Everyone knew the señora and General Franco were lovers. The señora would not allow her husband in her bedroom."

"How did you know?"

"Years ago, when I was hired by the Montenegros as a mechanic and chauffeur in Madrid, I knew they did not get along well. All the hired hands knew of their odd relationship."

Amado nodded and jotted a few notes on his pad. "How would you describe the colonel? What did he do around the property?" Amado sat back, inhaled deeply on his cigarette.

Gruenwald sitting stiffly on his chair, said, "He strutted around the estate like a peacock, trying to give the impression of a well-bred aristocrat, somebody with class. But it was all show, I assure you. Truth is, he was an evil man, a puppet with strings manipulated by Franco, who cuckolded him. In this country, his wife, the señora, controlled him and made sure he did nothing to diminish her standing in the community. She told him how to dress and kept him sober when meeting dignitaries."

"Why did the Montenegros leave Spain? If she was

Franco's mistress, why would she have left him and come to the States?"

"I can only speculate," Gruenwald said. "After the Spanish Civil War there was demobilization, and Franco no longer needed all his officers, especially those who did nothing and posed like mannequins in a store window."

"That doesn't answer the reason for the Montenegros leaving Spain."

Gruenwald paused to phrase his answer carefully. "I believe several factors played a part: number one, Franco came under the church's disapproving eye because of his association with the married señora : number two, the public, mostly Catholic, regarded Franco with a jaundiced eye at a time when he needed more loyalty and less criticism, and number three: the señora was—well, losing the blush of youth, although she was still attractive. As to why the Montenegros came to the United States, I'm not sure."

"That answers one of my questions, but before we get too far afield, I want to know about the concealed passageway from the colonel's den. What was the reason for it?"

Gruenwald regarded Amado sharply and paused before answering: "If this information becomes part of any record, I will deny being the source." Amado raised his right hand in silent consent. Gruenwald continued, "The colonel confided in me alone; he trusted no one else. His secrets weigh heavy on my heart. He made me take an oath of silence, but now that he's gone, I can tell you his sordid secrets."

Gruenwald cleared his throat and requested some water. Amado left the room thinking the guy was using delaying tactics. He hurried back and handed a glass of water to the chauffeur, then sat and leaned forward on his desk.

Gruenwald drank slowly, staring into the glass he held with both hands. "Eleven years ago, one year after the Montenegros settled into their home in Montecito, the colonel hired a contractor to open a doorway in a wall of the den which you found. The colonel was fearful that old enemies from Spain would seek him out to murder him. He made many enemies during the war and wanted a secret escape route from would-be assassins. That was his supposed reason for the concealed opening in the den. At least that is what he told me."

"What do you mean by his *supposed reason*? There's more to this?"

"Sadly, much more." Gruenwald closed his eyes and shook his head, obviously revolted by the evil he remembered, perhaps wondering if the telling itself would summon the devil. "That man was evil to the core, guilty of the basest sins known to mankind."

Amado's brow furrowed. "What do you mean?"

"You already know that the colonel and señora did not share the same bed, yet both had strong sexual appetites. The señora satisfied her needs by cavorting with various men."

"Did she come on to you?" Amado's question caught the chauffeur off guard.

Grunewald hesitated. "I would prefer not to answer that."

"Fine. Let's continue. We know that the señora filled her dance card with obliging gigolos. What was her husband doing during those times?"

"The colonel's sexual appetite was shameful, depraved—bestial. I would not mention this, but he is no longer with us, thank God, and the señora, of course, is also dead."

Amado persisted. "Tell me about the colonel's need for the secret passageway."

"He was a disgusting pervert who forced young boys into his den. That was the main purpose for the secret passage. He had the crazy notion that if his victims were not seen entering or leaving, then no outsiders would know."

"Where did the young boys come from?"

"They were the sons of the workers—illegal immigrants. The young boys were forced into unnatural acts by that devil." Gruenwald hesitated and shook his head. "He threatened their parents with deportation if they refused his demands or reported him to the authorities."

"So, any one of the workers might have killed him," Amado said.

"That, Mr. Detective, is probably how he met his death."

"But he was killed in an auto accident."

"So it appeared," Gruenwald said.

Amado's phone rang; he put up his hand to interrupt the conversation, then listened to the caller for several seconds. Speaking into the phone, he said, "I'm on my way," and hung up. As he moved toward the door, he shook Grunewald's hand. "I've got an emergency. We'll continue talking about this again, soon."

Chapter 38

As he drove up to the entrance of the Goleta warehouse, Amado saw two cars and an unmarked van. He recognized Isabella's pink Cadillac convertible with its gaudy tail fins, but he could not identify the owner of the black boxy Chrysler sedan.

As soon as he stepped into the warehouse, he heard Isabella's voice shouting over a deeper male voice. Amado walked farther into the irregularly-shaped aisle to see Isabella shaking her finger at the deformed Spingarn who leaned on a cane and craned his neck to look up at her. Two burly thugs with arms folded flanked him.

Seeing Amado approach, Isabella sighed, "Thank God you're here."

Spingarn turned his twisted torso to stare at Amado. "What are *you* doing here?"

"I have the same question for you, counselor."

Spingarn waved his cane dismissively at Amado. "My business here does not concern you."

"Right now, unless I hear differently, you're trespassing—unauthorized entry with intent to illegally remove valuable items…"

"Stop your idiotic blathering. You haven't the foggiest notion why I'm here." Spingarn's pinched face grew dark, the corners of his mouth drooped. "If you must know, I'm here to remove some of these relics to a safer environment."

"By whose authority?"

"I don't have to answer to you. I'm the family attorney. I'm exercising my duties by overseeing the safe disposition of items belonging to the estate." He waved his cane at the concealed items about him. "All this must be protected against..."

"Save the palaver, Spingarn. Nothing gets moved from here without a court order, and what's more, you damn well know that. Now, if you have that legal document, I'd like to see it. If you don't, I suggest you leave, pronto."

Spingarn, enraged, rocked from side to side and shook his cane at Amado. "Why are you poking your nose into this? Why does any of this concern you? You're a homicide detective, aren't you?" The gnarled diminutive figure croaked. "Go solve a murder. Don't interfere with matters that don't concern you."

As Spingarn sputtered, Amado cut him off: "But *this* does concern me, counselor, and what's more, these treasures, I believe, could relate to the murder of Señora Montenegro and possibly the Spanish priest."

"What? Nonsense! That's ridiculous. I see no connection..."

"Better leave these premises and take your muscle men with you. If you're not out of here..." Amado looked at his watch... "In ten minutes, you could be hauled in for trespassing."

"Oh, be quiet, you fool!" Spingarn snapped and screwed up his face as though sucking on a lemon. "You don't even know how to phrase that properly. I'll leave only because you'll call your uniformed cretins to carry me out. And I don't want them touching me. He motioned to the two brutes, and the three walked toward the door.

Amado called after him, "Would you care to put your attempted robbery in proper legal wording?" Spingarn made no reply.

Isabella hurried to Amado and threw her arms around him. "Oh, Fred, I'm so grateful to you." She gave him a lingering kiss and he made no attempt to curtail the pleasure. Then, she backed away but held onto his arms. "I phoned you right after Spingarn called to tell me he was going to the warehouse with a moving van."

"You did the right thing, baby. That wily old sonofabitch knows things we don't. More than that, he probably wants this loot for himself."

"I'm still terribly confused by all of this." Isabella turned to look at the covered objects. "These treasures... who collected them, and why are they here? And who owns them? Were they stolen? When I hear you mention the prices of some of these paintings my head swims. I have a gnawing suspicion that one day some agency will swoop down with an army of movers, clear this place out, and put me in jail for the rest of my life."

Amado laughed and embraced Isabella more firmly. "Don't hang the crepe just yet." He held her chin and lifted it to look into her sorrowful eyes. "You're probably right in thinking these pieces came from various sources. The paintings and furniture in the mansions of the Rothschild, Schloss, and Rosenberg families in Germany and France could have filled this old warehouse. But as for you being guilty of owning stolen property—the authorities would have to go a long way before pointing an accusing finger at you. Truth is, so far we don't know a damn thing about the provenance of any one of those paintings or those pieces of furniture."

"Do you think any of those paintings might not be real?—maybe forgeries?"

"From the brief viewing I've had, those paintings look original enough. Rabino had several paintings analyzed by an expert from the university. He said they were bona fide and worth a bloody fortune. I can tell you that the furniture is real as well as the china, urns and the ancient kraters. They're rare and costly ... Sevres, Dresden, Capo di Monte...magnificent stuff. I've seen the likes of them in my father's store. Some of these things might have passed through his place."

As Amado and Isabella walked toward a coffee shop after leaving the warehouse, she said, "Fred, can you explain how those paintings and furniture might have gotten there."

"I can only speculate. The European cultured class, those anti-Nazi liberals throughout Germany, Poland, France, the Netherlands...any who owned paintings of value lost them to Göring's vicious art thieves who formed roaming units called *kunstchutz*. The paintings they appropriated came from so-called enemies of the Third Reich, which meant all occupied countries and particularly their Jewish citizens.

"After the war, when a UN international body was established to find the rightful owners of those paintings, they ran into a number of difficulties. One problem, for example, occurred when the thieves were caught. They, of course, denied stealing the paintings. When they couldn't deny the theft, they might have had some art student reproduce the paintings, then they kept the originals and surrendered the forgeries.

"Making matters worse, many of the rightful owners died or were killed in concentration camps, and heirs had problems making claims.

"One art dealer in Munich, a Herr Kurt Meisser, had been one of Göring's experts on paintings; he helped in the selection of the Masters and the Impressionists. Some post WWI paintings were rejected as decadent and lacking in true German values. Those paintings were supposedly destroyed— at least orders were given by der Führer to have them destroyed. However, Meisser, the art expert, a real double-dealing greedy sonofabitch did not destroy those paintings but hid them, then sold them secretly to collectors for cold cash."

"You think some of those paintings are here?"

"I wouldn't be at all surprised."

Chapter 39

Lieutenant Rabino scanned several documents on his desk, initialed them and shoved them to one side. He flicked ash off his cigar, then looked at the two homicide detectives sitting opposite him. Reaching down into a desk drawer, he pulled out a thick folder marked: *Montenegro.*

"Okay, men, let's go over what we've got so far: two murders, number one, the rich Spanish dame with a .22 bullet in the back of her noggin, number two, a visiting padre from Madrid with a stoved-in skull and a crucifix carved on his chest and belly. Further mutilation consisted of a hacked off nose and his severed cock stuck in his mouth." He looked at Connors then at Amado who responded with a nod. "Okay, is that it for the mayhem?"

"Don't forget some sonofabitch winged me," Amado said.

"Right. There are treasures in a warehouse presumably owned by the deceased Colonel Montenegro, the murdered seῆora's husband. He died in a car accident two years ago. Let's go on. Amado, you told me about a dealer in east L.A., a Mr. Periera who deals in art treasures and fine furnishings. He knew Seῆora Montenegro well—at least well enough to attend her memorial service in Montecito. "

Amado cut in. "But he denies knowing anything about the warehouse in Goleta. And now we have that shyster Spingarn who attempted to remove paintings and furniture from that warehouse."

Rabino grabbed the smoldering cigar from the ashtray

and stuck it in the corner of his mouth. "How about bringing in Periera for a chat? Would he respond to an invitation?"

"If I ask Miss Chavez to invite him, he might come. He's fond of her," Amado said.

"Really? That old guy has to come in from L.A....a long ride. What pretext would she use?" Rabino asked.

"She could say she's thinking about dismantling the big house, getting rid of the fine furnishings and ask him to handle the sale."

Shaking his head, Rabino said, "I don't want her around when we're asking him questions."

"You're the boss, but first, let's get him out here. We'll find a way to sequester him long enough," Amado said.

"You've got the green light. Talk to that señorita, convince her to extend an invitation...maybe a nice dinner too, something like that."

"I'll see what I can do," Amado said. "You don't know old man Periera?"

"I know of him. My daughter dated his nephew's son. There was a time when I knew every Sephardic Jew from here to Ventura County."

"You bragging or complaining?"

Rabino ignored Amado's question and continued, "The older folks died off and the youngsters located elsewhere. Not many are left. In some families, the Sephardic would not marry the Ashkenazi."

"Marv, I don't know what you're talking about. Sephardic, Ashkenazi—what's the difference?"

"It's not important now, but historically, the Sephardic Jews were largely from Spain and Portugal before the Inquisition. They were learned and skilled. The Ashkenazi were located in Central Europe, mainly Germany after the Diaspora. They became merchants, itinerants at first, since they could not own land. Much later in the nineteenth century, when they were permitted to attend universities, many became professionals, scholars, scientists..."

Amado interrupted. "What about the Sephardic?"

"They had to leave Spain on Isabella and Ferdinand's edicts or convert to Catholicism—or suffer tortures by the Inquisition. Then there were the Marranos. Jesus, don't get me started on all that."

"It isn't as though I don't appreciate this refresher course in human misery, Marv, but what point are you trying to make?"

"Only that some businesses and trades were handed down from generation to generation: diamond merchants, art dealers and bankers for example. Those people closely guarded their professions, their trades, their guilds. For instance, the Rothschilds, bankers to kings and emperors, had iron-clad rules about operating within strict religious constraints, until some of the women married outside the faith..."

Amado nodded. "Where are you going with this? Why is this important?"

"Bear with me. There are three men in L.A. with Sephardic names who are dealing in valuable art treasures. A check of their backgrounds shows that they come from a long line of European art dealers."

"Meaning?"

"People regarded them..."

Rabino grabbed the ringing phone and placed his hand over the mouthpiece. He looked at Amado and whispered, "It's the chief; he's got a burr up his ass—about you."

Rabino gazed at the ceiling, rolled his eyes and spoke into the phone. "Yes, chief, I understand. Our men have been working on it constantly...chasing down leads...no, nothing substantial...no sir, I'm not challenging your decision. I'll get right on it." He replaced the phone and sighed.

"Guys, I think the shit has really hit the fan. The Spanish consul out of D.C. landed with his entourage in Sacramento yesterday. He spoke to Governor Warren about the murders of Señora Montenegro and the Spanish priest. The *Sacramento Bee* picked up the story, and put it on page one. They're calling the murder of the priest a "Crucifixion". They're appalled that the killer or killers haven't been apprehended, and they're playing it up as a gruesome, ritual cult murder. In the meantime, the Spaniards want permission to do their own investigating. I questioned the chief about the wisdom of that. He got pissed off and told me to give them complete cooperation."

"Fine," Amado said. "I'll lisp like a Castilian and try not to sound like a Mexican."

"Hold it, Fred. That was another part of the chief's order. As of now, you're no longer on this case."

Amado reared back. "Excuse me? What the hell does that mean?"

"The Attorney General's Office wants you on administrative leave until they can sort out complaints filed against you by Spingarn and Periera. They claim you're officious and violated their civil rights. Both those upstanding citizens have friends in high places."

"What the hell am I supposed to do in the meantime, twiddle my thumbs?"

"Don't complain. Your pay check will continue."

"It was never about a pay check, and you damn well know it."

"One more thing, Fred, no more romancing the señorita while these *carabineros* are snooping around."

"You can tell each and every one of those pricks to go fuck himself." Amado slammed the door when he left.

Chapter 41

"Alicia, the cook, prepared a wonderful meal for us." Isabella reached for Amado's hand and escorted him to the dining room. "*Comarones y arroz* just for you. I think she's quite fond of you. Even prepared your favorite desert—flan. Well, aren't you happy about that? Be sure to say something nice to her."

The table was bedecked with the estate's finest china, ornate silverware and crystal goblets. Marie bustled around straightening the tablecloth, lighting the candles, then dimming the overhead lights. Amado helped Isabella into her chair, then poured the Sangria. His toast was perfunctory and without his usual bonhomie.

The candlelight cast a warm glow on Isabella's face making her appear more radiant and lovelier than ever. She leaned forward and gazed at Amado. "All right, Mr. Detective, tell me what's on your mind, and don't say it's nothing at all. You've been glum, much too quiet. It's not like you."

Amado, demurred, but at Isabella's insistence, began to unfold the events of the afternoon. "The Spanish consul spoke with the governor about the murders, and the stories made the front pages of the *Sacramento Bee* and the *San Francisco Examiner*. The implication is that the two-month-old murders haven't been solved because we're an inept bunch of small-town rookies. To top it off, the sheriff wants a shake-up after getting a notice of an impending lawsuit by Spingarn— because of me."

Isabella sat back and squared her shoulders. "Ridiculous! That's not fair. They don't know how hard you work or how clever you really are."

Amado smiled weakly and reached across the table to hold her hand. "Good to know you're in my corner, baby." He remained less talkative while Isabella attempted cheerful banter. After dessert, he reached for a cigarette in his jacket pocket. Isabella walked around the table to light it, then bent over to kiss his cheek. He stood and gazed into her large turquoise eyes. "I forgot to mention how lovely you look tonight. You're like a delicate rose in full bloom."

"How poetic, my love." She caressed his cheek.

"Here I am sulking like a spoiled kid, and you've been doing your best to cheer me up." He stood and placed his arms around her. "I love you more than ever, baby."

Isabella's smile widened. She placed her hands gently on his chest. "I think you're entitled to some good news."

"Good news? Tell me someone has confessed to the murders."

"No. Something much more wonderful."

Amado watched as her eyes danced with excitement.

"I'm pregnant."

Chapter 42

The flashing red light coming off the rearview mirror and the piercing siren jarred Amado out of his dream-like state. He pulled over to the curb on the 5500 block of North Hollister and waited for the officer to approach. After rolling down the window, he looked at the broad-shouldered deputy who smiled easily.

The officer leaned on the window sill. "Hey, Fred, I've been following you for three blocks. You went through that last stop sign like it wasn't there. You're not snockered, are you?"

"Hi, Buzz, sorry. No, I'm sober. I just wasn't paying attention. Got some news tonight that kinda shocked me."

"Something serious, eh? Well, better be careful. You could have collected your pass to the pearly gates, back there."

"Thanks Buzz. I'll try to stay focused. Do me a favor, don't mention this to anyone." The officer assured him the incident was their secret, then waved him on.

Amado slipped into the stream of traffic but remained introspective. For him, the last twelve hours were an emotional rollercoaster. He thought it had been one hell of a day... told to get my ass out of the department in the afternoon and learned that I'm going to be a father in the evening...crazy damned world. I don't know whether to celebrate or go into depression. Hell, I'll celebrate, why not?... finally a father at age 42. Just wait a minute, stupido, you're not even married. If I marry her, the sheriff is going to kick my ass off the force for good. He still thinks of her as a prime suspect and that isn't going to sit well with him. Did Isabella think she could trap me by having a kid? There I go again, dammit. Why do I always think like a goddamned cynic? What the hell, I really love her, and she seems happy enough with me.

If I get thrown out of the department, I'll lose retirement benefits. Of course, that won't worry her. She'd like me to manage that estate full time—be the big honcho—hire, fire, watch over the workers, maintain that crumbling pile of bricks. Hell, I just can't do that. I'm not cut out for that sort of thing. And what about taking on the responsibilities of being a father?

Could I be a good father to a little girl? She'll probably be as beautiful as her mother, and when she's grown up, I'd have to protect her from galoots like me. If it's a boy, he'll be able to take care of himself. Wait a minute: I didn't do such a great job on myself, but I'll be able to guide him to do better. Listen, wise guy, you need to marry the girl first, and soon, remember? Isabella's not going to walk down the aisle with a belly full of baby. You'd better get your ass in gear and plan to marry soon. Yeah, I'll go to Churchill's tomorrow morning and choose a ring.

She can buy any ring or bauble she wants at ten times the price of anything I can afford. Hell, it's the gesture that counts, I suppose. With her money and her looks she can have any guy she wants... easy as snapping her fingers. Why does she want me? There I go again, doubting. Stop asking, dummy, and just be grateful... can't wait to tell Mom...the shock might kill her.

Chapter 43

Amado decided that he would pursue the investigation without sanction from the sheriff or the state's attorney. He had only to avoid any appearance of official detective work.

He pushed the doorbell at the servants' entrance. He knew Isabella was attending a community meeting at the Westmont College auditorium this morning. Maria opened the door and smiled as she asked him to come inside.

"Is John in?" Amado asked.

"No. He is driving the limousine for Señorita Chavez. Can I help you?"

"Maybe you can."

Maria led him into the kitchen. She hand-wiped the table oilcloth with its bright Mexican floral pattern and invited him to have coffee. He thanked her and sat at the table. Maria, a woman in her late forties, moved quickly, like one accustomed to getting things done. Although still moderately attractive, aging had produced fine lines radiating around her eyes and mouth and her dark hair pulled back into a tight bun showed streaks of gray. Her figure had begun a matronly transition to middle-age spread.

She poured coffee into two mugs and said, "How can I help you, detective?"

Amado explained that he had learned from her husband about the late colonel's disgusting abuse of some of the young sons of the braceros. Maria nodded and lowered her head. Amado leaned toward her. "Maria, would one of the braceros have killed the colonel for molesting his child?"

Maria expressionless, remained silent.

"Maria, you must tell me. That person might have killed the señora and the priest. Give me his name. I must know who he is."

She shook her head, then looked aside signifying that she no longer wished to participate in the conversation.

"If you withhold information, Maria, you could be fined and arrested for aiding and abetting a criminal—a murderer. That's a very serious charge." Amado was not above exaggerating and fabricating facts to create apprehension and fear.

Maria sat with her chin tilted upward in defiance. He took another approach. "Maria, tell me about yourself." She looked at him suspiciously, but Amado continued, "How long have you and John been married?"

"Why is that important, Mr. Detective?"

"I need data on all people who came in contact with the murdered victims." Amado stared at her. "Let me warn you, if you refuse to give truthful information, I'll regard you as a hostile witness, and I'll review every year of your background as well as your family's." Leaning back in his chair, he knew he had her complete attention.

He continued, "Most people have something to hide, something they wouldn't want their employers or neighbors to know. Now, let's start again. How long have you and John been married?"

"Twelve—twelve and a half years."

"Where did you meet?"

Maria seemed to resent the intrusion. Her neck stiffened and her lips pursed; she said curtly, "We met here—and we married here."

"Children?"

"We have a son and daughter, born here like me. I am a fifth-generation Guerrero from Santa Barbara."

"But your husband is not from here."

Maria took several seconds before responding. "John

came here from Spain with the Montenegros in 1939. We married soon after he arrived. We were both married before and eager to make a new beginning together." Maria left the table abruptly and returned with a framed black and white photograph of her and John embracing in a garden setting. She handed the picture to Amado. "That's our wedding picture taken here, near the fountain on this estate."

Amado studied the photo, then looked at Maria. "You and John were a good-looking couple. You're still attractive, Maria." She smiled politely but said nothing. Amado returned the picture and asked, "You were not married in the church?"

"No. John is not Catholic...he does not believe in any religion, so I did not insist on a church wedding." Maria looked around, then spoke softly. "I tell you this in confidence. I, too, have no love for the church with its money-hungry, so-called servants of the Lord."

Amado did not pursue the subject. "Who do you think might have murdered the señora?"

"I do not know." Maria sipped her coffee, then looked aside.

"All right. Why do you think someone wanted her dead? Surely, you must have thought about that."

Maria hesitated, then nodded. "Many times. The señora was fickle and selfish. She had plenty suitors. She flirted shamelessly." Maria became excited and spoke rapidly. "She would go to bed with married men—even caused divorces. For her whoring, she..." Maria stopped and put her hand to her mouth, then said, "She had many enemies."

"Well, she obviously loved Isabella and gave generously to charities and donated land for a park..."

Maria nodded. "That is all true, yet..."

"Who would be her enemies? Can you give me names?"

Maria, about to say something, stopped. "I do not know." She started to rise from her chair when Amado said, "I have one more question. What did you think about the murder of the Spanish priest?"

She answered slowly. "I did not know the man, but someone must have thought he was terribly bad to have murdered and mutilated him like that."

"Yeah, that's for sure." Amado stood, looked around and said, "Where are your children now?"

"In a private school. Señora Montenegro paid for their tuition. Now that she is gone, Señorita Isabella continues to pay, and we are grateful to her."

Amado thanked Maria for the coffee and said he hoped he had not upset her.

As he drove past the gates onto the street, a black Lincoln sedan moved slowly in front of him, blocking his passage.

"Hey, what the hell is this?" Amado shouted and sounded his horn. When the vehicle did not move, he charged out of his car. Two men in dark, double- breasted suits emerged from their car to confront him. In appearance, they were strictly European: wide-brim dark fedoras and suit jackets pinched at the waists. Their thin-line mustaches reminded Amado of the movie stars, John Barrymore and Ronald Coleman. One of them started speaking Spanish rapidly.

"Hold on, señor, my Spanish is elementary. Do you speak or understand English?"

One of the Spaniards smiled broadly. "Yes, of course, I trained at Scotland Yard for one year and worked at the Interpol for several years." He displayed a shield-shaped badge similar to Amado's. *These guys had to be the Spanish detectives Rabino referred to.* Cordial greetings were exchanged and Amado showed the men his own badge. The Spaniards quickly confirmed that they were seeking answers to the murder of the Spanish priest.

"We are hoping you will cooperate with us," the talkative one said.

"Fellas, you might not have heard, but I'm off this case, so theoretically, I can't discuss it with you."

The lead detective laughed, then nodded. "Yes, yes, I know about these things. Bureaucratic nonsense, it is the same everywhere, but we will ignore it. I must learn what you know about this murder. What you tell me will be off the record." He held up his right hand in affirmation. "In exchange for your information, I will tell you what we know."

"Fair enough. Let's get our cars out of the driveway and go where we can talk. There's a café in the village center. Park your car here and ride with me."

Chapter 45

"Hello, handsome," Sally, the waitress, greeted Amado. She escorted him and the two Spanish detectives to a booth at the rear of the café.

"Three javas, doll face, and leave the carafe here." All three watched Sally's backside as she ambled away with exaggerated hip shifts.

Amado explained that Señorita Chavez and her chauffeur, John Gruenwald, were not at the estate at this time, and that he had just spent time with Maria, the head of the household staff. Amado decided he was going to offer just enough information to get these foreigners to tell him what he needed to know, but he also knew they were going to be playing the same game. Sally returned with three cups and a carafe of coffee, then began to pour.

She looked at Amado. "Been a long time since you entertained this poor working girl. Did you lose my phone number, honey?"

"I was afraid to call after I saw you with that muscle beach Adonis."

"Oh, that twit? He used me to get at other guys." She sashayed off.

"I love this country, there is so much freedom of expression," the talkative Spaniard Inspector Escobar said with a broad grin. He was trim, a distinguished-looking man, more like a diplomat than a police officer. The other detective, Inspector Rivera, was squat and taciturn. "You treat waitresses and domestics as equals. You have no social caste system as we do," Escobar said.

"We respect all people of good faith," Amado said, not sure what he meant, but feeling the need to say something. "Generally speaking, ours is not an inhibited culture. We share our thoughts and information easily, and we expect others to do the same." *Was this Psychology 101 ploy going to be effective?*

"Tell me again about this Father Allende," Amado said to Escobar. "I'm having difficulty understanding how he went from being a Nazi officer to a priest and advisor in Franco's cabinet."

The Spanish detective poured more coffee in his cup, then sat back. "The priest, whose original name was Fritz Gruber, an Austrian from Vienna, joined the Nazi party as a college student while studying accounting about the time Hitler emerged. Gruber came from a long line of civil servants, bourgeoisie who were quiet, unassuming people. Like most middle class folk, they were law-abiding and fiercely patriotic."

"You seem to know a great deal about this Gruber and his family," Amado said.

"We've done a good deal of research to uncover facts that I believe will interest you."

"Go on."

"When Hitler came to power, young Fritz thought he found a hero he could follow to the ends of the earth. He wore his brown uniform and waved the Nazi flag like a boy scout marching in his first parade. He idolized that monster and his hooligans and swallowed their poisonous propaganda against Jews, gypsies, Slavs and other so-called *untermenschen, subhuman beings.* Gruber's rise to power in the party was meteoric since he had a zeal, a passion, for military life. In a short time, he became a subordinate to Adolph Eichmann and Reinhard Heydrich, the architects of the Final Solution.

"At Dachau he assumed the reins of camp commandant long enough to oversee the systematic murder and butchery of thousands. There he selected women to be raped and beaten. He entertained himself by bayoneting humans and using them for rifle practice. He entered into a life of unimaginable evil and debauchery."

"Tell me how in the hell he got from Dachau to Spain as a pious priest?"

"Hardly pious. He had a special skill for organizing raw recruits and firing them up with a passion for serving the Führer. Eichmann submitted his name for a higher command post. Göring took notice and transferred him to Spain. His assignment was to assess the number of German soldiers needed to train and augment Franco's Nationalists and the amount of armaments and the number of planes needed for Spain's Civil War. Gruber's training as an accountant enabled him to apply numbers to the most hideous situations.

"In a rare moment of sober reflection, Gruber, ever calculating, confessed to another officer that he was fearful of Germany's defeat, and his own death sentence by the Allies for crimes against humanity. If any one of his crimes had been committed in a country with a civil government, he would have faced a death sentence. Though he assumed this role and put on a Roman collar, he did not acquire a conscience. He gave no indication of remorse for his prior salacious behavior—ravaging and raping young girls and women and forcing them to satisfy his sexual perversions. His crimes against pubescent boys were scandalous. Sadly, none of his victims could testify against him. He killed every last one of them, but to him those unspeakable acts were acceptable...a Nazi officer's privilege."

Escobar studied Amado. "What do *you* know about the priest?"

"Very little. In fact, the Spanish Bureau of Passports and Travel Documents in Madrid was reluctant to disclose any information other than to verify his name and age. We received shipping instructions for the corpse, and that was all. Shortly before his death, I tried to engage him in conversation at Señora Montenegro's memorial service, but we were interrupted. Within two hours, or so, he was murdered."

"Did you know he was on General Franco's advisory staff?"

"Someone mentioned that. I figure he must have had some importance if you fellas and the consul came all the way here to investigate. By the same token, the señora's murder must have been important to bring that sham priest here."

The Spanish detective nodded. "We both know now that the priest had a powerful enemy or enemies right here. The question is, who and why?" He sat back, then reached into his inner jacket pocket and pulled out an envelope. "I'd like you to look at the photo in this envelope. It's old and a little grainy. Tell me what you see."

Amado reached for the black and white photo that was creased and yellowed. He squinted at it closely, then at a distance. "The picture shows a Nazi officer in dress uniform...can't make out his facial features too well...looks vaguely familiar."

"Look again closely and try to subtract eighteen years."

Amado realized the image was that of the murdered priest as he appeared as a young Nazi army officer. Intrigued, he leaned across the table eager to learn more. "Tell me more about him. How did he go from being a Nazi officer to a priest serving as a religious adviser to Franco?"

The lead detective took one of Amado's cigarettes and held it between his thumb, index and middle fingers, in the European manner. He lit it, inhaled deeply, then exhaled a long stream of smoke upward. "Before the start of the Spanish Civil War, Hitler sent a cadre of officers to Spain to inspect the possible battle sites and to estimate the needs and types of armaments including the number of planes necessary to win battles against the Republicans, who were the Communist-backed forces.

"One of Hitler's military experts became a favorite of General Franco who wanted him to stay on as a permanent member of his war cabinet. That man, the one in the photo, was Captain Fritz Gruber. He was eager to defect and to assume a new identity as Father Julio Allende."

"That's a real leap of faith. Why a priest?"

"Presumably, he wanted to hide behind an untouchable disguise."

"So, he was able to defect and become a high-ranking clergyman? That, my friend, sounds too easy."

"Not easy, but the German high command was in no position to argue. They were eager to test their Blitzkrieg techniques and catered to the requests of Franco. Meanwhile, Franco, aided and abetted the captain's conversion to the priesthood since Franco and the church hierarchy were bed fellows. Once Gruber took the vows, he was exempt from Nazi military service and given Spanish citizenship." The detective snapped his fingers. "It was as easy as that.

"With his new identity as Father Allende, he assumed the role of the privileged. He attended official gatherings, banquets and indulged himself in every kind of perversion—this time with all the trappings of a sanctimonious holy man. All the while he helped the Nationalists by advising the Luftwaffe where to drop bombs. He developed a vicious reputation for ferreting out and condemning Communists and the relatively few Jews and Muslims who remained in the country. Among old-line Spanish military, he was regarded as an arrogant bootlicker—despised by many."

"What could have been the purpose of his trip to California—the señora's memorial service?" Amado asked. "That hardly seems likely."

"For the present we do not have a satisfactory explanation," the Spaniard said.

Escobar pushed his coffee cup aside and leaned forward on the table. In a half-whisper he said to Amado, "Franco doesn't dismiss the murder of a staff member easily: he himself lives in fear of retribution. He admitted recently to an underling that the long arm of revenge knows no time limits. He's been lucky in avoiding assassination—so far."

"Would your assignment be to identify the killer or killers, and destroy them to make the world a safer place for assholes like Franco?"

A knowing smile crossed Escobar's lips. "Perhaps, my friend—perhaps."

Amado pushed his tongue against his inner cheek as he studied Escobar. "I don't mind telling you, amigo, if we find the murderer before you do, you're going home empty-handed."

"So you say, Amado. Just remember, we have our methods and a much longer history of treachery and cunning than you Americans have." Escobar laughed too loud and too long at his own remark that Amado did not find amusing.

Amado stood, shook hands with the Spanish detectives and thanked them for their time and information. He walked toward the waitress to pay for the coffee but was blocked by Escobar who insisted on paying. "Please, Sergeant Amado, allow me to pay. It is a small gesture, but it gives me pleasure. Since I have no intention of permitting you to capture the priest's murderer before I do, this might be the last favor I can extend to you." The smirk on Escobar's face annoyed Amado.

Chapter 46

The late afternoon sunrays that scattered through the leaves of the tall sycamores created a dappled effect on the lawn as the ladies of the Montecito Women's Club filed out of the college auditorium.

Nancy Peabody, chairwoman of the group, hurried to Isabella's side with giddy excitement. "I just loved your presentation. It was so informative, and the details of those murders were so vivid and gory. I got goose bumps listening. Golly, two murders in our own little community, and here you are in the middle of it all. Frankly, I don't know how you can live in that awful old place." She hardly paused to breathe. "I've seen newspaper photos of the detective in charge. What's his name?"

"Sergeant Fred Amado."

"That's it. Listen, I'd commit murder just to have him come out to my place—that is, when my husband isn't around. He's absolutely gorgeous. I don't know whether he looks more like Errol Flynn or Clark Gable. Did he ever make a pass at you?"

"Make a pass at me? Nancy, dear, I'm going to have his baby."

Nancy's eyes widened, she threw her arms up and laughed aloud. "Oh, Isabella, you're a riot. That's the funniest thing I ever heard." She opened her purse, pushed things around until she found a personal card. "When you see him again, would you give him this and have him call me? Thanks, hon."

Isabella accepted the card, then walked toward the

parking lot where the chauffeur waited. She tore the card into pieces and tossed them into a trash receptacle.

The chauffeur opened the rear door for her, but Isabella walked to the front passenger side. "John, I'd rather sit up front and talk with you. That silly passenger-to-driver phone works so poorly. You don't mind, do you?"

"Not at all, ma'am. I am honored."

Isabella sat back in the shiny leather seat softened and creased with age. She smiled with her own private secret. Her appetite had increased; she felt robust without symptoms of morning sickness.

"Are you comfortable, ma'am?"

"More wonderfully comfortable than you can imagine." She turned in her seat to look at the chauffeur. "John, you're such a gentleman and so talented. You managed to repair and keep this relic running. I've been meaning to tell you: there is no need to continue patching up this old thing. As far as I'm concerned, we can get rid of it. Besides, this was Señora Montenegro's vehicle. She enjoyed the attention of being paraded around in it—I do not."

The chauffeur nodded but made no immediate comment, then said, "Will I be turned out with the car as well, ma'am?"

"Oh, of course not, John. You and Maria are like family— my only family now. Who else can I tell my troubles to?"

The chauffeur smiled. "Thank you, ma'am. I hope you don't mind my saying this, and I apologize beforehand, but I think of you as my own daughter." He bit his lower lip, then with his handkerchief dabbed his eyes and brushed his nose.

"John, that's so sweet. In all the years we practically lived under the same roof with the Montenegros, I've never really known much about you. Did you have children, that is, before you married Maria?"

"Yes, ma'am. I had a daughter. She would have been your age."

"Really? Oh John, tell me about her. What was she like? What happened to her?"

Contorting his mouth and blinking, to keep from tearing, he said softly, "Forgive me, I cannot talk about her now."

Chapter 47

Amado ignored the order for his administrative leave and went to work without reporting in. In the deputies' lounge, he sat smoking and reading the *Santa Barbara News Press* while Connors used the men's room. Amado glanced through the sport section, then the world news when an article caught his eye. *More art treasures uncovered at Bavarian Castle.* The column reported that several paintings attributed to Raphael and Rembrandt as well as sketches by Leonardo da Vinci were found in a previously undiscovered room in the Neuschwanstein Castle, a fairy-tale castle in appearance that served as a so-called salvage depot for stolen Jewish "cultural properties." Those properties consisted of paintings, furniture, Gobelin tapestries, vases and collections of precious gems and jewelry.

Amado read how the Nazis had plundered the homes of wealthy owners and kept records of the owners' names. In an irony characteristic of Nazi compulsiveness for order, they had labeled as "ownerless" the stolen items. Meticulous record-keepers they named the places where the paintings had been stolen. Unfortunately, not every item was so labeled. The article went on to say that the problem of returning unlisted property had no immediate solution. In many instances the owners had died and no known heirs existed or had come forward.

Amado set the newspaper aside when Connors appeared. He didn't acknowledge Connors' presence and seemed to look through him.

"Fred, you got that far away look in your eyes. What're you thinking?"

Shaking his head as though coming out of a trance, Amado told Connors about the newspaper article. "I'm trying to make some kind of connection between the stolen treasures in the Goleta warehouse, but I'm coming up with zilch." He looked at Connors. "You got any ideas?"

"Fred, I don't see any connection, but then I don't have your smarts. As I recall, the Nazis stole every worthwhile thing in every country they conquered—France, Poland, Belgium, the Netherlands, then shipped it all to Germany."

"I know, I know." Amado interrupted. "But the valuables in the Goleta warehouse have Spanish and Portuguese shipping labels."

Sergeant Sorenson rushed into the lounge. "Hey! Fellas there's been one hell of an accident. A car drove off the cliff on the Mesa. Rabino wants to rule out a homicide. You gotta get there before the cleanup crew screws everything up."

"Why would Rabino think the accident was a homicide?" Connors asked as he drove toward the Mesa. "He didn't say anything about gunshots, did he? Is he thinking maybe suicide?"

"Sorenson said the car might have been slammed off the cliff by another vehicle. Six months ago a homicide occurred there, just like this one."

"Homicide will be hard to determine, don't you think? If the car fell a hundred or more feet, there'll be more damage than…"

Amado interrupted. "The guys at the wrecking yard are pretty good at figuring out whether a car's been rammed before it flies off a cliff. Most accidents happen at night when a drunk fails to negotiate the turn. Did Sorenson say whether the victims were men or women?"

"He didn't say." Connors craned his neck over the steering wheel. "Traffic's been held up—must be thirty cars lined up in both directions. I'll put the flashers on and drive around."

"Every sheriff's car in the county must have responded," Amado said.

"Crooks could be robbing three banks in town and there'd be no deputy around."

Amado muscled several onlookers aside and walked toward the crumpled mass of metal. He looked up at the steep embankment and saw the ruptured guardrail hanging over the side. He moved closer to the wreck. The remains of the distinctive grill identified the car for Amado. *Christ, this is the Lincoln sedan that Escobar and his partner were in.* He approached the deputy in charge. "Where are the bodies?"

"Coroner's wagon hauled them off to the Ventura morgue. Two males, late thirties or early forties, I'd say. One guy's just about decapitated, head went through the windshield—blood all over the damn place. Other guy's body just a bag of broken bones, I swear. Never saw such a savage sight. Had to pry them out with a crowbar."

"No signs of life?" Connors ask.

"Uh-uh. Total carnage. Instant death, for damn sure."

Amado looked into the twisted wreckage. The stink of spilled gasoline and the organic smell of blood, urine and feces pervaded the mangled front passenger area. "Any personal items? I.D.s?"

"Yeah. I'll get their wallets for you," and their Spanish passports." the deputy in charge said.

<hr/>

"What're you thinking, Fred?" Connors asked.

"Let's go up on the Mesa to the turn in the road where the car plunged down. Radio headquarters. Tell them to keep the road blocked until we get there."

"Amado scrutinized the severed guardrail hanging over the precipice and the sheared-off wooden post. He walked slowly along the road for about fifty feet from where the car struck the guardrail. A pattern of dark comet-shaped fluid drops caught his attention. He reached down to rub the fluid between his fingers. His nose wrinkled as he smelled it. "Brake fluid. Probably had no brakes. Poor bastards hit the rail full bore."

"Think the hoses were cut?"

Amado shrugged. "It's possible, or they were punctured." Amado wondered who might have wanted the two detectives dead. Ostensibly, they had come here to apprehend Father Allende's killer. They were a threat to whoever it was. Again he sniffed the brake fluid on his fingertips.

Chapter 48

Rabino clamped down on the cigar stub, then scowled when the bitter tobacco juice trickled down his gullet. He looked up from behind his desk and pointed at the apprehensive Connors who was sitting on the edge of his chair. "Connors, I want an inventory on all the paintings in that Goleta warehouse. Make an appointment with that snooty Professor Chadwick Grobstein at the Fine Arts Department at UCSB. The sheriff's department can manage his hourly fee of thirty-five dollars, but he has to give us the artist's name, the year of the painting, and most importantly, the value and authenticity. Have you got all that? Write it down, dammit. After that's done, get someone to evaluate the furnishings: those fancy urns, vases, settees, desks—things like that. If you have trouble, talk to Amado. He knows about those things. Any questions?"

Connors quizzical expression preceded his slow questioning. "Lieutenant Rabino, I don't know anything about international law or anything like that, but don't you think those art treasures should be handled by a federal agency? I mean they probably came from overseas. Could have been stolen and..."

Rabino cut him off. "Listen, Connors, I don't want any feds prancing around here like fairies hauling away those treasures, then stashing them in some vault at the Smithsonian or in the basement at the National Art Museum. We can keep those things in our own museum until we know for sure who owns them. What's more, I want an inventory, so I know what we have in case anyone decides that he's entitled to them, like that shriveled-up mouthpiece, Spingarn."

"Suppose someone shows a bill of sale as evidence of purchase," Connors asked.

A smile crossed Rabino's face, and he leaned forward on his desk. His eyes looked up from his lowered head as he spoke conspiratorially. "That's what I'd like to see. A bill of sale for more millions than I can count in a week." He leaned back in his chair and intertwined his fingers behind his head. "This is plundered stuff—loot—it's simply gotta be. I'll bet my car's pink slip against yours. How it got here, and who claims ownership is what we've got to find out."

Chapter 49

Amado opened the undersheriff's office door to find Rabino seated at his desk while two dark-blue suits sat across from him. Rabino signaled Amado to come in and sit in a chair beside him. They faced the two dour-faced men. Rabino with a cigar clenched on the side of his mouth grumbled from the other distorted side. "Sergeant Fred Amado, this is Bob Jones and Ralph Wilson, FBI agents, out of L.A." The three men shook hands. Rabino said, "They're here about Father Julio Allende, the murdered priest from Madrid. "

Amado nodded, then sat back and folded his arms across his chest. He was not favorably impressed by the men he faced. *I put in a lot of time on this case, and I'm not about to release my files to them unless they get on their knees and beg. Screw these hot shots.*

The older agent, Bob Jones, sensed Amado's hostility and said, "I realize you put a lot of effort into this case, and you might be close to reaching resolution, however, the Spanish consulate in Los Angeles is demanding..."

Rabino put up his hand. "We understand. You men will find Sergeant Amado, completely cooperative. He and his partner, Bill Connors, will tell you what they know, and maybe we can get these murders solved—with your cooperation, of course."

The FBI man gave Rabino a quizzical look. "Did you say murders with an 's'?"

"That's right, Señora Montenegro and the priest. And

there may have been two others related homicides as well." He went on to describe the deaths of the Spanish detectives. "It may have been an accident, but we're investigating to make sure that it was. The two detectives came here from Spain to find the priest's killer. They might have been victims as well."

While Rabino described the recent automobile deaths of the Spanish detectives, the younger FBI man made rapid notes. A call on the intercom interrupted the conversation and Rabino excused himself. "You fellas carry on. I'll be right back."

The senior agent focused on Amado. "You mean you've had two violent homicides and two possibly suspicious deaths and no clues?" His patronizing tone infuriated Amado whose jaw muscles alternately tensed and relaxed. The agent continued, "Look, I understand you might be understaffed here, and maybe you can't give these cases a solid effort, but c'mon..."

Amado exploded and pointed his finger at the Fed. "There's a hell of a lot you don't understand, mister! One thing for sure—you won't get any cooperation with your damned attitude and snide remarks. You're not talking to some rube who just fell off the manure spreader."

The FBI agent backed off. "Sorry, I had no intention of challenging your capability. Look, I know we can work together. We have certain information on the priest. With what you know, and what we know, we can probably put a case together and get to the bottom of this."

Not completely placated, Amado said, "How much *do* you know?"

The agent reached into his jacket pocket for several type-written pages. "Let's do this, I'll give you details compiled from our Washington bureau. It's information you probably don't have. If that turns out to be true, then you can tell me what you know."

Still smarting from the confrontation but acting more calmly, Amado said, "All right, tell me what you have."

Chapter 50

After sunset that evening, Amado sat next to Rabino at the Sabbath dinner and held up his wine glass again while Rabino poured. Rabino said, "If the amount of kosher food you're eating and the amount of kosher wine you're drinking could result in conversion, you'd make one fine Jew, Amado."

Amado raised his glass and faced Rachel seated at the other end of the table. "L'chaim, darling. If you weren't married to this galoot," he turned to look at Rabino, "I'd grab you up in a minute."

Rachel nodded with a weary smile. "Thanks. Would you adopt the children also?"

"Let me think about that. Too much goodness at one time is kind of overwhelming." Amado smiled at fifteen-year-old Monte seated at his other side. "Monte, you're a handsome dude...must take after your mother, because you sure don't look like your old man."

Monte squirmed with the attention. The twin daughters rose from the table and began gathering the empty dishes and dinnerware.

Rachel said, "Girls, leave everything and go! Get yourselves ready for your dates. Your father and I will clean up."

The twins hurried to give Rabino a peck on the cheek, then turned to Amado who smiled in anticipation as each twin bussed his cheek. They hugged their mother who hollered as they ran off. "Be home no later than 12:00!"

Rachel looked at Amado. "See what you're missing? I'll

be up worrying until they come home. Their father, Mr. Legal Correctness, will sleep through it all."

Rabino looked at Rachel. "It's enough that one of us worries."

Rachel walked toward the seated Amado and placed her hand on his shoulder. "Fred, darling, if you're thinking about becoming a papa, you'd better get started. Wait much longer, and you won't have the strength to woo a young girl, much less chase a toddler around."

Amado patted the back of Rachel's hand and winked. "I'm thinking I could become a father within a year."

"Really? I've got news for you, Freddie dear, just thinking about it won't make it happen." Rachel returned Amado's wink and walked back to the kitchen.

Facing Monte again, Amado said, "What are you learning in school, dude? If you tell me you want to be a cop, I'll box your ears."

"No, Sir, I'm not going to be a cop. I don't want a wife who'll worry like Mom does every time Dad steps out of the house."

Amado nodded. "I've heard that song before. So, what interests you?"

"If you promise not to laugh, I'll tell you."

"You've got my word on it."

Monte's eyes widened in anticipation of the telling. "I want to be in charge of a big city art museum. Last week we went on a field trip to the Santa Barbara Art Museum, and we met the curator. He's a real neat guy who gets to choose paintings that are super, and he knows all about artists, and he gets to travel and lecture...things like that."

"What paintings impressed you?"

"There was this copy of a big painting showing a weird-looking guy in a long robe. He had a long face and kind of sorrowful eyes that looked up. The curator told us the painting was by El Greco. The original painting is at the Prado Museum in Madrid. Do you know anything about El Greco?"

"Oh, yeah. So happens when I was a student at the university I took a course in art appreciation. I wrote a paper on him."

"Wow! That's nifty. The curator said the original painting at the Prado was removed before the Spanish Civil War in 1936. During the war, bombs blew out the windows at the museum. The people were afraid the paintings would get damaged."

"Did the curator say where those paintings were taken?" With increasing interest, Rabino leaned toward his son.

Monte continued, "One of the girls in our group asked him that same question. He said they were taken to the countryside and were hidden in cellars of farm houses and churches. After the Civil War all the paintings were returned." Monte looked at his wristwatch and asked his father to excuse him, he had a radio program to listen to in his room.

Rachel cleared the rest of the table and asked the men to retire to the living room to continue visiting and smoking. As they left the dining room, she called out, "Don't drop ashes on my rug."

Sitting, Rabino put a cigar in his mouth and extended his arms along the back of the sofa. Amado dropped into a club chair and lit a cigarette.

"What did you learn about the two Spanish agents from those FBI professors?" Rabino asked.

"Not a friggin' thing. They said they were waiting for a response from the Madrid police and the Interpol. Sounded like a lotta crap. They were hoping I'd give them something. I gave them what we know which isn't very much."

Rabino nodded but was preoccupied. "Fred, I've been thinking about something Monte said."

"The kid's smart. He doesn't want to be a cop. That puts him way ahead of us."

Rabino shook his head. "It's not that. It's what he said about the Nazis looting paintings from European museums and the homes of Jews. Is it possible these paintings belong to Jews?"

Entering the room, Rachel carried a tray with two glasses and bottles of Napoleon brandy and Portuguese sherry. She placed the tray on the coffee table and told the men to help themselves, then she walked out. Rabino picked up the sherry and asked Amado if he wanted some. Amado shook his head and reached for the brandy.

Holding the glass of sherry to the light, Rabino said, "Probably the best in the world, and they managed to produce it without the help of Jews."

"What Jews?" Amado asked. "Spain and Portugal had too few to do anything significant since the Inquisition..."

Rabino cut him off. "I know, I know." He jabbed the air with his unlit cigar. "Those paintings, that fine old furniture and those furnishings in the Goleta warehouse—they came from the Iberia America Trading Company. Isn't that right?"

"Pereira denies any knowledge of that Goleta warehouse."

"Forget his bullshit, Fred. I'll bet Pereira and his partners had that stuff shipped to the Montenegros who put all that in storage."

"Marv, you might bed right, but that doesn't answer the question of why. There's got to be reasons, and you can be sure it has to do with money."

"Suppose those art treasures belong to Jews living in Spain and Portugal..."

Amado interrupted. "Why? The Jews in Spain and Portugal had no fear of being thrown into Nazi concentration camps..."

"Are you crazy, Amado? Think about this: that bastard Franco was kissing Hitler's ass. Franco could have allowed that fucking madman to round up all the Spanish Jews and toss them into a furnace."

"So you're saying all those art treasures in the warehouse belong to Spanish and Portuguese Jews who anticipated Hitler's looting?" Amado did not wait for Rabino's response. "Explain this to me, it's five years since the war ended. Why haven't those people claimed their treasures?"

A moment of silence followed. Rabino turned and stepped away. His voice became distant and soft. He said, "I just don't know. I just don't know."

"Maybe Periera will provide some answers when we meet him for dinner at the Montenegro estate next week," Amado said.

Chapter 51

Amado looked at his watch as he eased into the passenger seat of Rabino's Buick sedan. "Six-ten, right on time. I talked to Isabella, I mean Miss Chavez, told her we wanted time alone with Pereira after dinner."

"Was she all right with that?"

"Yeah, she said she'd make herself scarce. Pereira should have been at the estate at about five o'clock to give her an estimate on the value of the estate furnishings."

"Is he alone?" Rabino asked.

"As far as I know, he is. Does that make a difference?"

"We want this visit to be personal. You know, kinda intimate. We don't need unnecessary, polite conversation with anyone else. After a few glasses of wine or whisky, Periera could become talkative. That's the whole idea."

The Buick entered one of the dark narrow roads in Montecito already obscured by overhanging foliage and made more difficult with sudden turns. Rabino, frustrated, looked to either side and slowed down. "Where the hell are we? Tell me where to turn on these damn twisting roads. I get lost every time I come here."

Amado's instructions were exact ... "fifty yards right... quick turn left... forward one hundred yards..."

"Fred, you could probably find your way around here blindfolded."

"Since I'm on administrative leave, I've taken time to come out here to gather bits of information."

"Sure. I'll tell you what you've been gathering—a little nooky, a little poontang, if you remember what we called it in the Pacific. If you don't use good judgment, you're going to screw yourself into big trouble. That gal's got you wrapped around her pinky. What the hell are you going to do when we find her guilty or complicit in these murders?"

"I'll invite you to the wedding."

"Go ahead, laugh—jerk."

After dinner, Pereira walked out of the dining room, kissed Isabella, then with a broad smile patted his protuberant abdomen. "My dear child, you have accomplished that which I thought impossible. You have surpassed the gracious hospitality of your wonderful mentor—God rest her soul. That dinner was more delicious than any I've had in years, including those at Chasen's."

The three men walked to the far end of the spacious living room. Rabino offered Pereira a White Owl cigar, but he wrinkled his nose and refused. Instead, Pereira removed a silver Dunham cigar case from an inner pocket of his jacket and offered Rabino and Amado Cuban panatelas. "Treat yourself to something good, gentlemen. I have these made for me in Havana. Examine the labels, my names on them." Amado refused and lit his own cigarette.

Rabino lifted the cigar from the case, placed it next to his ear, rolled it between his thumb, index and middle finger, then put it under his nose before lighting it. After two puffs, he leaned his head back, removed the cigar from his mouth and looked at the burning end. "That's about as fine a smoke as I've ever had. Sir, you have excellent taste."

"I know I do."

Rabino filled Pereira's glass with Portuguese sherry for the fourth time. The three men chatted amiably while the older man, sitting in a wing-back leather chair, held court. Amado and Rabino sat on a sofa facing him. They asked questions on unrelated matters before asking about the L.A. warehouse.

Pereira loosened his tie and unbuttoned his collar while he slumped in the commodious chair. He flicked the ash off his cigar, but his coordination became impaired and his speech began to slur.

"Mr. Pereira, the furniture and paintings in your L. A. warehouse are magnificent. Where did they come from?" Rabino asked.

Pereira puffed on his cigar, his eyelids drooped, and he spoke slowly. "Wealthy people sold their possessions to us."

Amado sat forward on the sofa. "What wealthy people?"

Pereira turned his head unsteadily to look at Amado. "Why is that of interest to you, detective?"

Rabino's elbow nudged Amado, warning him to back off.

"Just curious, sir, that's all. Such elegant things aren't seen around here very often," Amado said.

"Some of the finest paintings in all of Europe are in that warehouse," Pereira said. He closed his eyes momentarily.

Rabino whispered to Amado, "Don't interrupt. He's on a roll. Let him do the talking."

"...and that furniture..." Pereira spoke haltingly. "Have you ever seen such magnificent pieces? Gorgeous bombe' dressers... ormolu accents...exotic wood finished like a mirror—not like American furniture with its dull finish. Yes, we got the finest."

Amado nodded and leaned forward, hoping the old man had sufficient sherry to answer incisive questions but not so much as to shut down. "Were your art pieces sent to the Goleta warehouse?"

Slouched in the club chair, Pereira's brow wrinkled; he stared with difficulty at Amado, then drew himself into a more upright position. "Listen, detective, I'm not so drunk or stupid as to tell you all that stuff in the Goleta warehouse is ours."

"No sir, I don't think you have to tell us that...not at all."

"Where the hell is my chauffeur? I've got to get home."

When Pereira made an attempt to stand, Rabino hurried to his side to offer support. Amado left the room to summon the chauffeur who had taken his meal in the kitchen and was flirting with the help.

"Your boss is ready to leave," Amado said. "Where is his home?"

"Beverly Hills, Roxbury Drive, about a two-hour drive. He'll sleep most of the way."

"Have you ever been to the warehouse in Goleta?" Amado asked.

"You mean that big barn crammed with all that old junk? Oh, yeah, many times. My bosses have a big investment there. Didn't Mr. Pereira tell you?"

"He did—he did, indeed."

Chapter 52

"Oh, Fred, I love it!" Isabella held the back of her left hand in front of her, smiled, then brought her hand to her chest and covered it with her right hand. "It's the most beautiful ring I've ever seen."

"C'mon, baby. Who are you kidding? It's okay for now, but one day..."

"It's lovely, and the fact that you chose it makes it all the more precious." She sat next to Amado on the settee and snuggled against him. "Darling, we'll have to make wedding plans soon."

"That's your department, baby."

"We'll plan on having a small wedding. I have no one except Maria and John Gruenwald, and your mother, of course. I really don't want any others. Do you object?"

"Not at all. We could go to Reno, as far as I'm concerned, or go before a judge here and be done with it."

"I'd like Mr. Gruenwald to give me away. I think of him as the father I've lost. Did you know he had a daughter my age?"

"You mentioned that previously. Did you ever learn what happened to her?"

"No, but I am eager to find out. When I had asked him earlier, he became teary and didn't want to talk about her."

Chapter 53

A mixture of stale kerosene, gasoline and grease created the distinctive stink and the smudges on the white block walls of the auto wrecking yard office. Amado enjoyed the atmosphere. It was a place for virile and bawdy men. Calendar pictures of luscious nudes in poses inviting male companionship shared the walls with Indy 500 racing vehicles. A poster ad showed a cowboy holding up a pack of Big Guy condoms and declaring, "I use these whenever I ride a filly."

"I'll get that report on the wreck off Cliff Drive," Jack Touey, the portly owner of Harbor Wrecking Yard said, as Amado watched him open a file cabinet drawer." The report's listed under *Spanish Detectives*." Touey placed the report on the counter, then moved his finger down the hand-written statements. "Here it is: 'perforations in the brake line hoses...'"

Amado nodded. "That's what I thought. Tell me how anyone could predict where the vehicle would be when it ran out of brake juice?"

Touey shrugged. "Good question. I'd say it was a matter of happenstance. Wouldn't make much difference if the car was speeding on the highway or in downtown traffic...no braking power could cause one hell of an accident...maybe not as bad as what actually happened to those two guys on that hillside curve, but bad enough."

"I'd like a copy of that report. Anything else to indicate tampering with that car?"

"Yeah, you bet! There's something else, all right. The

Pitman arm was loose. Steering could have gone out at any time, too."

"That's more than just coincidental," Amado said. He folded the copy of the wreckage report and placed it in his jacket pocket. "Thanks for your trouble, Jack. If you think of anything else, let me know." Amado handed him his card. "I'll have the photographer come by to take photos of those parts."

"What d'ya mean take photos? Those parts are gone. They were picked up by the police department last week. A guy came in and said he needed them for further analysis."

"Was he in uniform?"

"No. Plain clothes, like you."

"And you let him have them?"

"No reason not to. We can't save every piece of junk that comes in. Besides, the guy paid cash, and he looked honest enough."

"Did he give his name or leave a card?"

Touey scratched his head and shrugged. "I think he said his name was Wood. No, that's not it. It was Forest, yeah, G. Forest."

<hr />

Amado hopped into his coupe and headed for the Montenegro estate. At the gate he sounded the horn and waited until Lobo charged forward, barking to warn of an enemy approaching the castle. He was followed by a gardener who ran over to push the enter button on the gatepost. Amado leaned out the car window. "Amigo, is Miss Chavez in?"

"No. She go to store with John and Maria—maybe ten minutes ago." Amado parked the car beside the garage, out of sight of those approaching the estate. He reached into the glove compartment for a flashlight and walked to the servants' entrance. He pulled out his master key but found the door unlocked.

In the large kitchen, he looked around and called out, "Hello!" No response. He walked into a hallway just beyond the kitchen area and opened a side door. He was struck by the pungent odor of onions, hanging garlic, clusters of chili peppers and an assortment of herbs and spices. The shelves were filled with canned goods, sacks of flour, sugar and salt. Using a small stepladder, he reached the top shelf, pushed some cans aside to look for weapons and ammo. Nothing.

He moved further into the hallway to discover another side door. It opened on to a dark stairwell where he noted the offensive stink of sewer gas he and Isabella smelled near the chauffeur's workshop. He turned on his flashlight, closed the door behind him, and began the slow descent.

The creaking stairs caused some anxiety. Scanning the area, he saw rows of old furniture, discarded sinks, washtubs, picture frames and mirrors, some uncovered, others covered with dusty bed sheets. Amado thought some nut could stalk and attack him, then toss his dead body into the rubble. His corpse would only add to the existing stink.

He held his S & W .38, at his side and listened for strange sounds. Reaching the concrete floor, he walked toward the right until he saw the door to the workshop. The door was locked. He placed the gun in his holster and put the flashlight on the floor while he jiggled the master key in the lock.

"Dammit!" He pushed, pulled and turned the key clockwise, then counterclockwise with no success. As he started to withdraw the key, the door opened. He picked up the flashlight and located the wall switch. The shop lit up and the simultaneous whirring of an exhaust fan startled him. The smell of solvents and fresh-cut wood permeated the room.

He opened several bench drawers, moved tools aside but saw nothing unusual. The top drawer of a three-tier file cabinet revealed the names of suppliers, paid and unpaid bills. The second drawer held similar contents. He did not bother with the bottom drawer, but as he stepped away, he berated himself for doing an incomplete search. He would rail at any junior officer who made such a half-ass attempt at inspection. He walked back and opened the bottom drawer.

This is interesting. A stash of photographs bulged out of two manila folders. He carried the folders to the workbench and turned on a lamp. Some of the photographs were yellow with age, creased and bent or torn at the corners. A few revealed a handsome young officer in a Nazi naval uniform seated with a beautiful woman and a pretty child on her lap. Another photo showed the officer with a laughing child astride his shoulders. A studio photograph with a painted tropical background of a sandy beach and palm fronds showed the officer seated with the same attractive woman standing next to him, her hand resting on his shoulder.

Amado brought the photo closer to the light and squinted to study the features of the man's face. *Yes, it was a young John Gruenwald, but who were the others in the photos? He remembered Isabella saying Gruenwald told her he had a daughter her age.*

Amado stopped and stiffened with the sound of muffled voices from above. He gathered the photos quickly and shoved them into the manila folders, then closed the file cabinet door. He listened for approaching sounds and wondered where he could hide and what excuse he could give if Gruenwald came into the workshop. *There's a good chance he won't come down here. Relax, you're investigating a murder—no, two murders, and it's your responsibility to explore every detail.* He held his breath. *Jesus, the stairs are creaking...someone is coming.*

He turned the light switch off, reached for his gun and held it at his side, then opened the door to a supply room filled with old car parts: boxes of sparkplugs, hoses, brake shoes, nuts, bolts, all neatly stacked on shelves. In one corner a tarp covered something. Amado lifted the tarp and stared at mud-encrusted parts: steering components, a Pitman arm and drag link... he knew they were parts missing from that vehicle in which the two Spanish detectives were killed. Amado remembered Jack Touey saying the parts were purchased by a G. Forest. *G. Forest, hell, yes, that's it...G for Gruen, and the word "forest" translates into German as "wald". Gruenwald, of course.*

He froze with the sudden whirring sound of the exhaust fan and the appearance of light below the storage room door.

He held his gun at his side, applying light tactile pressure on the trigger. His senses became brittle, keenly acute to any noise just beyond the closed door. He waited.

The sound of a drawer opening, the rattling of metal, then the closing of the drawer, diminishing footsteps and the disappearance of light and sound from the exhaust fan meant the person left. In the dark, Amado waited several seconds before opening the stockroom door. Using his flashlight, he found his way out of the workshop. Reassured by the distant creaking of stairs and the muffled sound of voices from above, Amado's tension subsided.

He tip-toed hoping the squeaking stairs would not be heard. At the top of the stairs, he opened the door partially and looked to either side. No one in sight. He stepped briskly into the hallway, then walked nonchalantly into the kitchen.

Gruenwald, seated at the kitchen table, had clock parts spread out on newspaper sheets. Maria and Alicia, the cook, preparing vegetables for the evening meal gasped as Amado appeared. Gruenwald looked up and stared.

"Didn't mean to startle you folks. I'm looking for Miss Chavez. I didn't find her in the main building. Is she around here?"

Gruenwald gave him an icy response, "The señorita is probably resting in her room. She's tired from shopping, exhausted from worry."

"Yeah, that's understandable. Will you tell her I was here? Nothing important. I'll get in touch with her later."

Amado walked through the kitchen and pushed the door to the outside when Gruenwald called out, "Just a minute, sergeant, I'd like to talk with you."

Amado stepped back into the kitchen. Gruenwald said, "I'd prefer to talk outside."

"Have it your way."

Gruenwald walked with Amado as he headed for his car in the sheltered area. "I see you discovered how to conceal your auto from casual onlookers."

Gruenwald's ingratiating smile irritated Amado. "Okay,

John, let's have it, what's on your mind?"

Gruenwald stopped walking, a signal for Amado to stop and listen. "I know you are trying to solve the murders of the señora and the priest, but I resent you invading our privacy. You threatened my wife with prison unless she told you things you wanted to hear. Well, let me tell you, detective, she knows nothing about those murders, and I want you to stop snooping, looking for only God knows what. You won't find anything connecting us to those murders." He glared at Amado. "Do I make myself clear?"

Without responding, Amado started to walk away, but Gruenwald, red-faced and grim, hurried after him. "Detective, I want to know—do you understand?"

With the car keys in his hand, ready to open the door, Amado stopped and turned to face Gruenwald. "Yeah, I understand. Me thinks thou protesteth too much."

Gruenwald blinked. "I don't know what you are saying."

Amado hiked his shoulders. "Look Mister, I don't know how innocent you are. I, too, have a few questions for you. To begin, why did you buy that steering equipment from the wrecking yard? Those pieces came from the vehicle that crashed through the barrier off Cliff Drive. That's right, the car those two Spanish detectives were killed in. You paid cash for those parts and gave the guy a false name. Why?" Amado studied Gruenwald's expression. "I'd say you have some explaining to do."

The chauffeur's aggressive expression disappeared. His face turned ashen; he swallowed hard, remained quiet for a moment, then struck a challenging posture. "I know nothing about the deaths of two Spanish detectives. I go to the wrecking yard to find parts for the old Hispano-Suissa since I can no longer buy parts from the factory. I use the name Forest, because it is easier to spell and pronounce for most Americans."

"Why did you say you were from the police department? That's a punishable offense."

"I never said that. That is ridiculous. I would deny that in any court."

Amado turned his back on Gruenwald and slid into his car. He lowered the window and looked up at Gruenwald who stood staring at him. "I gotta hand it to you, Gruenwald. You think pretty fast on your feet. You accounted for everything neatly. Trouble is, I'm cynical enough to think you're handing me a lot of bullshit." He pointed his finger at Gruenwald. "As for me not snooping around and asking more questions—forget it. You just joined my circle of prime suspects."

Gruenwald watched as Amado put the car in reverse, then turned and spun his wheels heading toward the gate.

Chapter 54

Rabino looked up from a stack of papers on his desk and glowered at Amado. "Goddamit, Fred, you're not supposed to be in this building and for damn sure, not in my office. What is there in that restraining order that you don't understand? You're on administrative leave. Remember? Go to Reno. Go to Miami. Go to Hawaii. Get lost!" Rabino chewed the stub of a stogie clamped between his teeth while Amado sat expressionless on the other side of Rabino's desk.

"Do you want to hear what I've learned or not?" Amado said.

"Yeah, yeah." Rabino reached for his jacket draped over the back of his chair. "Let's head out for the Maxwell House Coffee Shop on State Street. Take a table near the rear. I'll leave here five minutes after you. On your way out of the building, don't stop to talk to anyone."

Hunched over the two-person table, Rabino's middle fingers made slow circular movements over his right temple as he listened to Amado's clandestine experience in Gruenwald's workshop and then his discussion with the chauffeur.

"Want me to bring him in for questioning?" Amado asked.

"Are you out of your mind? You're on leave, remember? The sheriff would snatch both our badges. Besides, what are you going to ask him that you haven't already asked? He's given you every slick excuse for what he did."

"He's lying."

Rabino nodded and rubbed his eyes. "Okay, so he's lying. Let's say he jimmied the Spaniards' car to make it dive over the cliff. Prove it. And what was his motive?"

"Maybe those Spanish cops knew something about Gruenwald and were about to ask for his extradition, or maybe they wanted to kidnap him or kill him..."

"That's a lot of maybes, Amado."

"Hell, Gruenwald knows. We've just gotta get him to talk."

"All right. When the chief says you can resume duty, you can go after him. In the meantime, I want to know about those paintings in the Goleta warehouse as well as those in the basement of the Montecito estate. The questions remain, where did they come from and who owns them?"

Amado said, "Spingarn, the lawyer, said they're part of the Montenegro estate. I told you he attempted to move some of those paintings out of the warehouse with the excuse that they had to be placed in a safer environment. That twisted bastard can't be trusted, either."

Rabino was about to light another cigar when Amado said, "Jeezuz, Marv, do me a favor. Don't smoke that stink bomb in here. It changes the flavor of the coffee. What I was about to say was that, thousands of paintings, statues, furnishings stolen by the Nazis were recovered by guys designated as Monuments Men in the American armies. When possible, those treasures were returned to their countries of origin. Articles stolen from individuals, were returned when proper claims were made."

"Not true, Amado," Rabino said. "Jewish families are still trying to claim art treasures held by state museums. Many of the legal owners are dead, but their families are attempting to recover the items. The Austrians, for instance, are not about to acknowledge private pre-war ownership, and for damn sure, the Russians will never return the stuff they confiscated. The Russkies retrieved treasures from underground tunnels, salt mines, castles, churches, anywhere the Nazis thought they could be concealed. Of course the Americans did the same— difference is, we gave it all back."

"Okay, I understand that," Amado said, "so where did these

paintings and all that ephemera that's here come from?" Before Rabino could respond, Amado continued, "There are enough paintings, statuary, china, and tapestries in that warehouse to fill a fleet of twenty trucks. I'm willing to bet that stuff is worth more than the gold in Fort Knox. As soon as word gets out that the stuff is located in some unsecured building, somewhere in the boonies of Santa Barbara County and in an old Montecito casa, the newspapers are going to blow the whole thing up. They'll go for scandal...tie everything to the murders and ..."

"Amado, hold on. I'm not so sure they wouldn't be right. I'm thinking there could be a link between the paintings and the murders. It all comes down to who owns what. I don't understand why there've been no claims made on those items."

"Are you putting an extra watch on the warehouse?" Amado asked.

"We don't have that kind of manpower. Our black and whites are stretched to the limit, and the county is tightening its budget on our backs." Rabino's eyes made a quick pass around the coffee shop, then he leaned toward Amado. "Fred, keep a watch on that Goleta warehouse, will ya?"

"I'm on administrative leave, remember?"

"Yeah, but you're still drawing a paycheck. When you think about it, you can phone me and give me a progress report, but disguise your voice." Rabino picked up the bill of sixty cents, gave the waitress a dollar and told her to keep the change.

"Walk out ahead of me. I'll follow in three minutes," Rabino said.

Amado glared at the undersheriff. "Marv, cut the chicken shit. So what if we're seen walking together? They're not going to *can* you. If anyone says anything to me, I'll tell 'em to kiss my ass."

Rabino scowled. "Watch you language and keep you voice down. Don't bring any attention to yourself or to me. Why are you going back to the station, anyway?"

"My car is in the lot, and besides, I left my fedora in your office."

Rabino gave him a side glance and mumbled, "Great, that's just great."

Walking through the city hall toward Rabieino's office, the men were met by the department secretary who approached Amado to tell him he had received a phone call. She handed the memo to Amado who read the message to Rabino. *Back in town. Will be happy to talk with you. Signed, Uncle Ben.*

"Good." Amado smiled and stuck the memo in his pocket. "Now, maybe we can get some answers."

Chapter 55

Ben Goldberg, a short stocky man with an old Trappist monk's baldness played a portion of the Grieg Piano Concerto with more determination than accuracy and finesse, omitting a few notes and striking a few wrong ones.

He ended his abbreviated concerto with a flourishing glissando, then stood, smiled and bowed as Amado, leaning on the Steinway grand, shouted, "Bravo, Uncle Ben, bravo. *Uncle* was the title Amado had bestowed on Goldberg for as long as he could remember. Mrs. Goldberg, seated across the spacious formal living room, applauded enthusiastically.

"Thank you, my charitable music lovers. Fortunately for me, you enjoy the schmaltz and can forgive the missed chords and passages. But, after all, much of art is like that. It's often glitz that determines acceptability. And with that little philosophical nugget, we can retire to the library for coffee and Mrs. Goldberg's delicious homemade strudel."

Ben Goldberg, at age seventy-eight, a head shorter than Amado, looked up at his guest and said, "I look at you and see your father of blessed memory. How I loved that man. Oh, we had our disagreements, but they were few and unimportant. We enjoyed many years as business partners and just being good friends. We furnished the very finest homes in Santa Barbara and Montecito. Hah, did I say homes? I should have said mansions, castles, palaces," he rhapsodized. "And the genteel clientele never argued about our prices. But we never gouged them, and we catered to them as though they were royalty. Those were wonderful years." Ben turned silent for a moment and sighed.

"Uncle Ben, I want to hear about your trip to Europe. Did you buy any art?"

"Freddie, I'll tell you all about that, but I'm eager to hear about you. Tell me, are you married? Any *niños?* No? What are you waiting for? You know you can't remain a happy bachelor forever. Get married and suffer a little."

They chuckled, Fred placed his arm around Mr. Goldberg's shoulders while they walked into the library. "It's been a long time, Uncle Ben, but I remember that wonderful home furnishings store in the village center. Tell me again, why did the store close? You say, business flourished, and you and Dad both enjoyed what you did. Did a rift develop between you two? I was never quite sure."

"No, no. It was never anything like that. Your dad had several episodes of chest pain, but nothing serious showed on the EKG according to the doctors. Your dad took medicine and watched his diet...drank less booze and smoked fewer cigarettes. I encouraged him to take more time off, play more golf, go fishing—things like that, but he never did. He worried constantly while you were in the service, especially when he didn't hear from you for days. He would say, if anything happened to you, he'd kill himself. After the war, when you came home, he was better for a while, then the old ticker acted up again."

Amado said, "So it was his heart that gave out."

"Yes, but there were other problems."

"Such as?"

At that moment, Mrs. Goldberg arrived with a tray of coffee and strudel and joined the two.

"We never discussed this with others, but your father and I faced a dilemma...nothing bad between us, of course, but there were problems with others. Freddie, I would be obliged if you said nothing about this conversation to anyone else."

"Of course not, although let me give you fair warning:

if you tell me anything illegal or something of a serious criminal nature, I'll obey my conscience. I'm not a priest at a confessional. Now, if you want to tell me, go ahead." They both laughed.

"At this time, I think you should know exactly what happened twenty years ago. I'll start at the beginning. Your father and I opened a small home furnishings store in Montecito after WWI. The year was 1919. We borrowed money and put what little savings we had together. Your father had a large family in Santa Barbara and was able to sell furniture and home appliances to them. That kept us afloat in the beginning. I went door-to-door selling furniture out of catalogues from Chicago and Los Angeles wholesale dealers. We developed a reputation for service and low prices that made our business grow. We could hardly keep up with the demand.

"We had commissions to furnish enormous places— places the size of palaces. We expanded our sales force, decorators, fabric experts, delivery and repair men. Our success was wild. We thought it would never end." Ben paused and shook his head slowly. "Then the good-times bubble burst after ten years of rapid growth. Your father took the loss very hard. I wasn't exactly happy either, but I figured, how long could the downturn last? One year...two years...three years at the most. We had some financial reserves and curtailed our operation to a third of its size. But the depression deepened, and by 1932 we were on the ropes. I mean we were talking seriously about bankruptcy."

"But you managed somehow," Amado said. "Business must have picked up. That's when I came to the store during summer breaks from the university."

"We were not completely out of the woods. Your father and I subsidized your wages, meager as they were. With the election of Roosevelt, there was a feeling of optimism. We figured things had to get better...they couldn't get worse. Business didn't respond immediately to the promise of *Happy*

Days Are Here Again, but we remained hopeful. Then slowly our fortunes began to change." Ben sat back, a smile crossed his lips.

"What changed your fortunes, Uncle Ben?"

Goldberg sat forward and placed his elbows on the table. "One day, during the early part of 1936, two strangers came into our store. They were dressed well, like dandies, had an air of superiority as they walked around examining our merchandise. One of them handed me a fancy business card that read, *M. Periera, Importer and Exporter of Antiques and Fine Furnishings.* I thought he was trying to sell us something we really didn't need. I was about to hand the card back to him when he pushed my hand back and told me to keep it. He said he was about to offer me an opportunity to become quite wealthy with no investment on my part.

"Freddie, I don't have to tell you, I've been around long enough to know there are no free lunches, but I listened to this smooth-talker with a continental accent. I told him about our lines of American-made furniture. I bragged about stuff made in North Carolina, Michigan, Iowa...all the best. He pooh-poohed and said, 'I'm talking about exquisite, fine, old English, French and Italian pieces...not only furniture but magnificent accessories like lamps, vases and oil paintings.'

"He continued, 'I mean masterpieces by famous artists like Corot, Monet, Pissarro.' Quite honestly, I didn't know the difference between an Impressionist and a cartoonist, but I listened. Meanwhile, his partner was measuring the area of our store by walking its length and breadth. Your father came into the store at that point, and this dandy went through his whole spiel with him.

"We had a lot of questions for this guy. To begin, your father who always had a healthy skepticism, drilled Periera and his side-kick, Mr. Beneveniste, about the ownership of these fancy-shmancy European art treasures."

Amado was captivated by every word he was hearing. He scrutinized Goldberg's expression and hung on every syllable and nuance. Amado had questions but did not dare interrupt. "Periera said he needed space to display his paintings and furnishings," Goldberg said.

Amado, unable to hold back further questioning, said, "Uncle Ben, I've got to ask now: why did Periera choose Dad's and your store? There had to be any number of first-rate furniture outlets in L.A and..."

Goldberg interrupted. "Aha, you're as astute as your father was. In fact, I remember him asking the same question. The answer we got from Periera was that the Montecito community had the kind of wealth necessary to acquire such treasures. New estates were rising like mushrooms and had to be furnished while the older ones had to be refurbished. American manufactures took orders but could not deliver for three to six months. The fine European pieces Periera had in storage, he said, could be delivered at once."

"I understand, but why was this community selected? Why not the east coast, like the Hamptons in New York, Bloomfield Hills in Michigan, Beverly Hills...?"

Goldberg anticipated the question. "Because, dear boy, this is the area Periera selected. His closest relatives lived in Santa Barbara, and besides, he said he loved *the American Riviera.* Logistically, the location was good for him. He could run his trucks up from L.A. and keep close control of shipments."

Mrs. Goldberg apologized as she interrupted. "Ben dear, it's time for your evening medication and your bedtime."

"In a moment, darling." Mr. Goldberg continued, "When your father and I went to the east L.A. warehouse to look at Periera's furniture and paintings, we were struck dumb. We had never seen such fine workmanship, such quality. I thought those things existed only in the pictures of the *Architectural Digest* and English antique auction brochures.

"Periera said his trucks could be loaded and rolled out to our place in twenty-four hours. We had only to select our pieces and sign for them. However, there was a caveat: we were not to pursue the origin of a single item. Everything would be delivered on consignment with a suggested retail price. We would get fifty percent of the sale price. All we had to do was display the items and touch up any scratches or blemishes.

"I saw that as a win-win situation, at least on the surface. Truth is, I didn't want to delve too deeply into the deal. I was secretly fearful that it was somehow illegitimate, crooked and something would happen to make it all disappear."

"What did my father think?"

"Your father—well, that's another story."

Mrs. Goldberg, in a robe, appeared at the library entrance. "Ben, please say goodnight. Fred will forgive you. He'll be happy to hear about your travels another time."

"Yes, dear. Be right with you." He turned to Amado. "Freddie, call me. We'll have lunch at the Montecito Inn. I know the manager; he'll give us a free round, and then we can talk. I have so much more to tell you."

Chapter 56

Isabella hummed as she and Amado strolled hand in hand in the estate garden profuse with roses and their fragrances. Amado stopped, pulled out his pocketknife and cut the stem of a deep red rose. He handed it to Isabella who inhaled its perfume, smiled, then kissed him.

"Thank you, sweetheart. You're so kind and thoughtful. I'm hoping you've been as thoughtful about setting a wedding date."

"Uh-uh, that's your domain."

"Fred, I've been thinking, a large wedding will take several months of planning. We would have to send out formal invitations, provide bridesmaids' wear, ushers' suits, decorations..."

"Whoa! I thought we agreed on a quickie...you, me, the dog and a justice of the peace. What's this craziness about a royal wedding?"

"That's my point exactly. We could elope. Go to city hall for a license, then go somewhere quiet for a week. We can have our marriage bash sometime later...a lovely garden party here among the flowers and the fountain...maybe a mariachi band, a barbeque, cocktails. Does that appeal to you?"

"You appeal to me, baby. Having you to myself all day and all night..."

Isabella put her finger to his lips. "Fred, there's more to marriage than sex."

"Yeah, but the next thing comes in at a distant second."

Isabella raised one eyebrow. "Maybe I ought to rethink this whole thing."

"Too late, dearie. That baby you're growing will need a mommy and a daddy, and I've got a legitimate claim on him—or her."

Isabella, tilting her head with a mischievous glance, said, "What makes you so sure you're the daddy?"

John Gruenwald interrupted the playful banter. "Excuse me, Señorita, Maria and I are going to Solvang to buy lily bulbs and grass seed. Is there anything we can get for you?"

"No thank you, John." Isabella looked at her watch. "You'll be back in two to three hours or so?"

"Yes, ma'am."

Amado watched as the couple drove off in the Chevy pickup. "They come and go as they please and decide what is needed for the estate?" Amado asked.

"Yes, of course. John gets food supplies and takes requests from the head gardener. He doesn't bother me about every purchase, and I'm grateful for that."

Amado looked around before saying, "Would you mind if I, or rather we, scrounged around John's workshop?"

Isabella glared at him, placed her hands on her hips and said, "I certainly would. Why in the world would you invade his privacy?"

"Princess, you've got to know that Gruenwald, to me, is a prime suspect in the murders."

"What? That's ridiculous! Of all the idiotic ideas you Keystone Kops have come up with, this is the craziest. I can't imagine what you're thinking. I'd trust this man with my life. He's thoughtful, kind and gentle. Oh, you can make me so angry. The very idea..."

Amado waited for a break in Isabella's tirade, then said, "If you're convinced of his innocence, then you shouldn't object to a peek around his workshop."

"Absolutely not and don't ask again." Isabella hurried off to avoid further conversation.

Amado caught up to her and reached for her elbow. "Would you like to see some old photos of Gruenwald and his family in Germany—pictures of his little daughter?"

Isabella stopped. With a quizzical expression, she said, "Yes, but..."

"Look, love, I promise we'll take him off our suspects' list if I find nothing incriminating. If you don't consent, he'll remain a prime suspect, and we'll tail and hound him until we're satisfied that he's innocent or not. Gruenwald will never know we were there. Again, if we find nothing, we'll call the dogs off. Is that reasonable?" *This guy will stay on my list, no matter what she says.*

Isabella said nothing immediately, then responded. "You've created a terrible dilemma for me. How much time are you planning to spend down there?"

"As long as it takes."

"That's not good enough. They could be returning soon, and I don't want them to know..."

"Okay. Twenty minutes—thirty at the most." He hurried toward the basement before she changed her mind.

<hr />

Amado jiggled his master key until he could feel the lock tumblers lining up. He opened the shop door and turned on the light switch. The exhaust fan went on automatically creating a muffled high-pitched sound. As soon as Isabella entered, he closed the door, then reached into his pocket and pulled out two pairs of latex gloves. He handed her one pair. "These will be too large, but wear them anyway."

"What you're doing is entirely illegal, you know that," she whispered.

"Tell me something I don't know," Amado said quietly. He surveyed the room, then walked to the file cabinet and pulled out the bottom drawer. "There are photos here that'll interest you. Try to keep everything neat. We don't want him to know we were here."

Isabella said, "Really, tell me something I don't know."

"Touché."

Amado returned to the storage room while Isabella placed two manila folders full of snapshots as well as an album on the workbench.

After several minutes, she called out, "Fred, come here, look at these photos!"

"I've seen them," he yelled back. "I'm looking for something else."

Isabella continued talking loudly to him. "If this little girl is John's daughter, what happened to her and the pretty woman who was probably her mother?"

Fred answered, "Probably victims of war."

"Do you think he lost his family?" Without waiting for Amado's answer, she said, "That would be terrible."

"Yeah, but he's got another family to take care of now. That reminds me— how long are you going to pay the tuition for his kids?"

"Just until they enter junior high. For the girl, that will be the end of this semester and for the boy another two years. After that they'll go to public schools. Why do you ask?"

"If we marry, I'll want to know where all the money goes..."

"What do you mean, if we marry? This baby better be able to claim a father with no ifs, ands or buts."

"Yes, ma'am." Amado remained in the storage room and pushed several boxes of ignition points aside on the top shelf, then yelled, "Hey! Pay dirt!"

Isabella hurried to Amado's side. "What is it?"

He held something in his hand covered with a yellow chamois, then he walked into the workshop and placed it on the workbench. Isabella was right behind him as he peeled back the folds of the chamois cloth. She gasped at the sight of the revolver.

"I think we might have discovered the long-lost gun from the colonel's collection," he said.

Isabella's brow knitted. "Now wait Fred, that doesn't prove

anything. Besides, it's just not possible that John could have..."

"Hold on, sweetheart. No one is condemning him. It's just that we can't ignore something like this."

"Fred, you can't take that gun, run fingerprint tests and accuse..."

"All right, how about ballistics? We still have the bullet found in the señora's skull."

"That won't be admissible, will it? We're here on unlawful entry and seizure. Some smart attorney will..."

"No, no, sweetheart. This property belongs to you. Our entry is not unlawful, and if the gun is the murder weapon, we have every right to seize it. Do me a favor, baby, don't make excuses or try to defend this guy. I'm not accusing him of anything—yet. By the same token, I'd like you to be less protective and just a tad more realistic. I've seen too many guilty jerks get a free ride because some dick or state's attorney was too lazy to pursue all the evidence. Right now, I don't know why Gruenwald would want to kill Señora Montenegro—if in fact, he did. Do you know any reason why he would?"

"Of course not. That's ridiculous, and furthermore..."

"Uh-huh. You're still responding blindly to his defense. Let it go, baby." Amado moved the album toward the gooseneck lamp. Black and white photos were held in place by triangular corner holders. The pictures had shown people at a country inn with signs printed in German.

"Who are these people?" Isabella asked while she shared the album with Amado. She pointed to two images: a German sailor and a young woman who held the handle of a baby carriage. "Both of them are squinting into the sunlight, so it's difficult to make out their features distinctly."

She turned another page to view a professional studio photograph with clear detailing that revealed a young mother with a child on her lap. A young man stood next to her. "The child looks to be about two years old. The mother is beautiful—a pretty smile, lovely eyes and lustrous dark hair." Isabella brought the album close to her face and stared at the man's image. She pulled the photo out of its retaining tabs, looked at the backside and read aloud: "Schmidt Fotos, Berlin, 1926." She looked at Amado and pointed to the young man in the photo. "I bet that's young John Gruenwald and his little child. He told me he had a daughter who would have been my age."

Amado took the photograph from her and studied it. "Did he say what happened to her?"

"When I asked him, he became teary and told me he couldn't talk about her."

"Did he say anything about his wife?"

"No, I didn't ask him."

"Didn't ask him? Don't ever apply for a detective's job." Amado put the photo back into the album.

"His wife could have divorced him and got custody of the child," Isabella said.

Amado, returning the album to the file cabinet, felt a box at the far end of the drawer. He reached in and pulled it out. Beautifully crafted in rosewood with a mother-of-pearl inlay design, it measured approximately 5"x 8"x 2." Amado placed it on the workbench and opened the lid. Isabella looked over his shoulder then reached in to pull out a woman's fine tortoise shell comb. Next to the comb, a stack of letters tied with a faded pink silk ribbon retained the faintest hint of lavender essence.

Below the stack of letters lay a dark purple velvet sack with gold stitching. Isabella picked it up and reached inside to pull out a delicate gold chain necklace. An attached pendant had a finely crafted Star of David set with tiny diamonds. Isabella looked at Amado. "I don't understand, Fred. What does all this mean?"

Amado shrugged. "The letters are addressed to Kapt. Johann Gruenwald. Do you read or understand German?" Amado asked.

"From my schooling in Switzerland, I can read only

the most basic words. We spoke mostly French and English there." Isabella slipped one of the envelopes out of the tied pack and pulled out a letter. "Do I dare read this?"

"Sweetheart, if you don't, all this is wasted effort. Hell, yes, read it!"

Isabella unfolded the letter and scanned the page before attempting a translation. "It's written in endearing terms." Isabella's translation was halting. "She tells how much she misses him and how desperately she wants to be in his arms once again. The letter is signed, 'Yours is my heart alone, Gisele.' A post-script says, 'Analise wants her daddy home.'" Isabella folded the letter and placed it carefully in the envelope and replaced it in the stack. Her eyes glistened with tears as she put her hand to her mouth and turned away. "Fred, I think I violated something sacred, and it makes me terribly sad."

She looked at the necklace and said, "What about this Star of David? John is not Jewish. He was in the German Navy. Do you think his wife was Jewish?"

"I haven't the foggiest, but I'd like to ask him some questions." Amado reached out and held Isabella's arm. He became rigid, then put his finger to his lips and whispered, "Quick! Put everything back." Pulling Isabella by the hand, he shut the light and hurried out of the workshop. His flashlight lit the cluttered path. Isabella whispered, "Not that way—give me your flashlight and watch your step." She took his hand and led him through a narrow, twisted passageway with occasional steps going up, then down. Breathless, after three to four minutes of hurrying, they approached a closed door.

With a nervous hand, Isabella turned the knob. "We're safe now." Inside a hallway, she breathed a sigh of relief and leaned against the closed door.

"How did you find your way around this house of horrors with all its damned secret passageways?"

"The estate was built over a number of years with different levels of construction and connecting passages. It seems confusing at first, but after you've been through it a few times, it really isn't."

She opened another door and led Amado into the main kitchen. "What did you hear that made you want to leave so suddenly?"

"A car door slammed, or so I thought." He looked through a window onto the front of the estate. "Strange, I don't see anything."

"Could have been one of the workers at the servants' entrance." She walked ahead, through the long living room, then turned to say, "I've worked up a nervous sweat. I'm going to freshen up. Why don't you relax? Pour yourself a drink, turn on the TV, stretch out on the sofa..."

"Mind if I watch you freshen up? I haven't seen that sexy body of yours since..."

She interrupted. "You're incorrigible. I know what you have in mind. Tell me what plans you've made for our honeymoon, and then I'll consider allowing you to help me out of my undies."

"That's the best offer I've had in a week."

Isabella hurried up the circular stairway to her bedroom. Amado followed, removing his tie and unbuttoning his shirt.

With the climax of complete sexual fulfillment, Isabella sighed as she lay nude, physically exhausted but emotionally invigorated. She turned her head to gaze at Amado who lay next to her, spread-eagle.

"That was wonderful," she murmured as her fingers walked along his abdomen, then down his thigh to make small circular movements in the pubic area.

Amado gripped her hand. "Better not try to stimulate old Pete just yet. He's needing time out."

"Did you enjoy it?" she asked. "The doctor said intercourse may not be safe after the second trimester."

"We have a long way to go, baby. We'll do the best we can until then." Amado turned to face Isabella who seemed more voluptuous than ever. He got on his knees and straddled her to suckle her enlarging breasts.

"Haven't you had enough?" Giggling, she held his head in her hands.

He looked up at her. "I've got to get this in now. Once the kid arrives, these luscious boobs become his or her property, but I'll have the rest of you."

Isabella sat up. "All right, enough play. I've got to get some work done."

Amado watched the symmetry of her exquisite hourglass figure as she walked toward the shower. He called out, "Can I treat you to dinner tonight?"

Without stopping or turning, she said, "You've already treated me, darling. Nothing else could possibly taste as good. Another time—soon."

Chapter 57

"This is something you guys should know." Rabino held a memorandum in his left hand, a smoking cigar in the other. Amado held his nose and shook his head. "Before you start, Marv, open the damn door and windows. Why in the hell must you smoke that five-cent rope of camel dung in here?"

Rabino looked at the burning tip of his cigar. "This elegant White Owl is smoked by some of the most discriminating..."

Amado cut him off. "Hobos passing through Santa Barbara."

"Okay, wise guy, I just thought you'd like to know you were suckered by two former Gestapo agents from Argentina who posed as Spanish secret service men. We called Madrid to verify their status. They didn't know what the hell we were talking about. We got further information from the C.I.A. Unfortunately, or otherwise, those birds were killed when their vehicle flew off the cliff."

Amado nodded. "Well, I'll be damned. I thought that sonofabitch's accent was kinda queer. The other guy was smart; he didn't talk. They didn't get much out of me—not that it would have made any difference now. What the hell did they want? Wonder if the guy or guys they were after got to them first?" Amado walked behind Rabino's desk and raised the window. "Let's get some of the smog and stink out of this room."

"Sit down, Fred!" Rabino barked, "Let's try to put a few facts together before we see the chief tomorrow."

"Hey! Just a goddamned minute. I'm on administrative

leave, remember?"

"The hell you are. As of now, you're back full time. A report came in this morning on the teletype from Sheriff Black's office."

"Was anything said about a promotion for me?"

Rabino gave Amado a caustic glance as he extinguished his soggy cigar stub in the ashtray with a downward twist. "I've never had a case with so many deaths and no goddamned solid clues." He banged his desk. "This crap is embarrassing. Who in this shitty fiasco is laughing at us as though we were a bunch of rookies?" Pointing at Amado, he said, "Tell me why we shouldn't haul in that Chavez dame and make her squirm until she gives us some answers. She's too damned cool, too damned uppity. Don't shake your head, Fred. Tell me why we shouldn't bring her in."

Amado looked at the ceiling, then rolled his eyes. "Because she's innocent, that's why."

"What makes you so damned sure?"

"I just know, that's all. Besides, there's no history of hatred between her and the señora. And she didn't even know that phony Spanish priest."

"She came into a mighty hefty inheritance," Rabino said.

Amado threw up his arms. "So what? You're wasting your time— but if you want me to bring her in, I'll bring her in."

Rabino, frustrated by Amado's reluctance said, "All right, forget about her, but give me another suspect, dammit."

"We've got several. Think about this: those paintings could make any sonofabitch a murderer. Any one of those could bring in a mill or more."

Rabino looked out the window. "There are at least two *goniffs* who know more about those paintings and furnishings than they've told us. Bring in that old cocker from L.A., Periera."

"We had him come out to Montecito once, remember? Isabella invited him for dinner. We didn't get anything out of him then. Supposing he doesn't want to come in?"

"We'll issue a warrant for his arrest." Rabino shook his

head, grumbled and argued with himself. "No, no. That's not smart. On the other hand, maybe it is. Next week we'll go out to his place, kiss his ass. We'll make him think he's wonderful."

"He already thinks that," Amado said.

Chapter 58

Amado, eager to hear more from Ben Goldberg, invited him to the Montecito Inn for lunch. He knew Goldberg had more information to give him about those paintings. Amado picked Ben up at his home and drove him to the inn.

"The last time I was here, I had a pretty girl at my side," Amado said as he opened the door for Goldberg.

"Well, I'm not a pretty girl," Goldberg replied. "In fact, I'm an ugly, played-out old fool who can barely remember what my youth was like. Some things, however, I remember as though they happened yesterday."

The two walked to a table far from the window facing the street. "The light bothers my eyes," Goldberg said. "Besides, I like a little schnapps without the whole world looking in on me."

Joey, the bartender, with a smile like an Ipana toothpaste ad, came by to shake Goldberg's hand, then Amado's.

"That's the wonderful and annoying part of living in a small community," Goldberg said. "Everyone knows you and what you do. So you better be good." He ordered a BLT and insisted that Amado order anything on the menu. "Have something expensive, Freddie. I'll put it on my expense account and list this as a security conference. Besides, I'm having remorse for those poor wages I paid you a lifetime ago."

"Uncle Ben, I remember only the good things about you. The last time I saw you at your home, you were telling me about Periera and his partners offering you and Dad a deal some time back in the mid-thirties. You said they had exquisite European art treasures and wanted you and Dad to sell them in your store. A proviso went with those deals. You were not to ask about their prior ownership. Did I understand that correctly?"

"You did, my boy, you understood perfectly. Now, when I think about it, that was all so foolish."

"You were about to tell me that my dad thought differently about selling that stuff."

"Your father was suspicious. Rightfully so. He didn't understand why we couldn't know where those fine pieces came from. He wanted nothing in the store that didn't have a factory invoice. As you know, he was that kind of man—honest, straightforward and not inclined to take chances. I, on the other hand, have always been just a bit more adventurous, more trusting and enterprising."

Amado nodded. "But you did nothing illegal. The merchandise came from an established wholesaler who provided you with bona fide bills of sale."

"Yes, Freddie, what you say is true, but your father suspected that the merchandise might have had—how shall I say?—questionable origins? Suffice it to say, he felt uneasy." Ben made small circles with his finger on the rim of the glass, then looked up. "Your father continued to worry even as the profits were adding up. We both managed to buy a few luxuries and build comfortable homes.

"One afternoon, two men from the sheriff's department came into the store. Your father might have thought they were coming after him. According to the deputies, he clutched his chest, gave an eerie moan and fell to the floor... probably dying as he went down." Ben took a long swallow, turned his head aside and dabbed his eyes with a cocktail napkin.

Amado reached across the table and patted Ben's forearm.

The older man looked up. "Like I said before, the whole thing was so stupid. Those deputies came in to offer your father tickets to their annual benefit ball. They were giving him a gift because we always supported them." After a moment of silence, Goldberg continued, "Now you've heard the whole sad story again. I think about him every day of my life."

Eager to change the topic, Amado said, "Tell me about your recent trip to Europe. Where did you go and what did you do?"

"The trip was fine, but quite frankly, I'm getting too old to hop from London to Paris to Rome looking for *tschotskies* for designer studios ...a vase, a lamp , a painting...you know, the pieces that are supposed to complete a home. If a piece comes from Europe it has a certain cachet. It's all a lot of nonsense, but I get paid well."

"Uncle Ben, I saw a Mary Cassatt painting in that Goleta warehouse. I know that painting was in my father's and your store years ago. Do you remember it, and do you know who bought it?"

"Yes, of course, I remember it, a Mary Cassatt, who could forget it?"

Amado leaned across the table. "Where did it come from and who bought it?"

"It came from Periera—IAT, Iberia America Trading. All our best paintings came from his company."

"Who bought it and why is it in the warehouse?"

Goldberg scratched his bald spot and shook his head. "Freddie, I'll have to pass on that. I can't remember."

"Think hard, Uncle Ben. Does the name Montenegro come to mind?"

Goldberg's brow knitted, then he waved his finger at Amado excitedly. "Yes, that's it! Colonel and Mrs., or rather, Señora Montenegro. They bought a number of paintings from us. She was a class act, had discriminating taste; he couldn't have cared less... a boorish ass, as I recall. Why it's in the warehouse, I don't know."

"Why wouldn't the Montenegros make purchases directly from Periera?"

"In the trade, a wholesaler must sell only to a retail outlet. That has to do with taxes, business codes and ethics.

However, I suspect many sales are made to private buyers on the Q T, and at a higher price."

"Uncle Ben, tell me about old man Periera. What is he like? Do you know from whom he acquired those paintings and those fancy home furnishings?"

"I've known Moses Periera for years. The man brags about coming from a long line of Spanish Jews who managed to survive the Inquisition. Whether they became *Conversos* or *Marranos* pretending to be Christians, I don't know. He's been in this country from the early thirties and lives quite comfortably in a large home in Beverly Hills. I've been there and met his housekeeper."

"Is there a Mrs. Periera?"

"No. He lives with his housekeeper, who sees to all his needs. As for him personally? He can be a gracious host but a curmudgeon when it comes to business. He would set a price on a painting or other item and never waver. He knew what the market would bear and expected to get the last cent out of everything sold."

"But what he delivered to you was on a consignment basis, wasn't it?"

"Yes, and we had a markup of at least 100%, which isn't unusual for the furniture business. Pricing on paintings—now that follows no sensible rules and is determined by bidding at an auction and what art critics say. It's a strange, unpredictable market."

"Where did those paintings and furnishings come from—I mean before Periera got them?" Amado studied Ben's facial expression closely and waited for the answer he'd been seeking for too many weeks.

Ben took another sip of his drink before answering. "Freddie, you're asking the same question I asked Periera long ago."

"And his answer was...?"

"He really didn't give me one. That wily old bird insisted he was committed to secrecy and would not elaborate further.

If you expect to question him, you better get to him soon. He's not well... might take his secrets to the grave."

"Doesn't he have business partners?" Amado asked.

"You mean Perez and Beneveniste? They're partners in name only. He bought them out long ago. He drags them out to funerals and dedications of former acquaintances and associates. You told me you saw them at Señora Montenegro's burial service...three old buzzards riding in an ancient Pierce Arrow that looked like a hearse."

"So, you really don't know where Periera got his paintings and furniture." When Ben just shook his head, Amado turned to get the bartender's attention to refill Ben's drink. Another martini was brought to the table and Ben protested. "Freddie, you're going to get me drunk, and I won't know what the hell I'm talking about."

"Don't worry. I'm enjoying your company and I'll get you home safely."

They continued chatting for another hour, without Ben recalling more substantive details. He told Amado that the paintings came from Paris art salons mainly, but some had also come from galleries in London, Rome and Berlin.

Chapter 59

Amado drove the department's new unmarked '51 Ford sedan while Rabino sat beside him. They traveled south on the 101, exited onto 10 for El Monte, and located Periera's office and warehouse in east L.A. Amado glanced at Rabino who sat with an unlit cigar in his mouth. "Marv, you look like a real mensch in your JC Penny civvies. I could spot you anywhere as a flatfoot out of uniform. Too bad that bump on your hip spoils your sartorial splendor."

"Sartorial splendor? You throw those fancy words around to let me know you went to Berkeley? We didn't learn such high-falutin' language at U.C. Santa Barbara."

"Of course not, you were too busy partying, surfing and getting laid. What did you get your degree in—social studies or dance and dating techniques? You attended the world's most laid back school that coddles sun-tanned jocks and long- legged blonde air heads. All of that funded by unsuspecting taxpayers."

Rabino smiled. "Yeah, it was wonderful, even if what you say is less than half true. I was a diligent student. Leaned everything I could about the criminal justice system—then found I could apply almost none of it when I joined the force." Both men laughed then fell silent for a few minutes.

"How are you going to approach Periera?" Amado asked.

"It's time to stop farting around and being polite."

"I think the two are mutually exclusive, Marv."

"You know what I mean. He's got to tell us everything

about all those goddamn art treasures. Where did they come from? Who owned them? How are they linked to the murders of the Montenegro dame and that phony dress-wearing priest from Madrid? And where does that weasel Spingarn, fit into all of this?"

"That's a long agenda, Marv, and you haven't even mentioned the two birds that flew off the cliff. Suppose Periera refuses to give you answers."

"I'll ask him if he'd like the F.B.I. to investigate and tie up his operation for a year or two...maybe haul his ass into a Federal Court for investigation of importing illegal wartime loot."

"That sounds impressive. Do you really know what you're talking about?"

Rabino opened his window, bit off the cigar tip, spat it out, then lit it and puffed twice. He turned to look at Amado. "Hell no! But that never stopped me before."

The deputy's car pulled up alongside the old sedan as Periera, leaning on his chauffer's arm, was about to mount the running board and climb into the rear seat. Rabino called out, "Mr. Periera, can we have a word with you?"

Annoyed, Periera stepped down to the pavement, pulled out a gold pocket watch, looked at the time and said, "I'm going home now to take care of some personal matters—sorry." He turned, then continued to climb into the rear seat.

Rabino said, "Can you give us just a moment or two of your time? This is an important matter." He turned and muttered to Amado, "After driving for two hours in that damned traffic, I'm not going back empty handed."

Periera leaned out of the sedan window and said, "If you insist on talking to me, you can follow me to my home."

Amado looked at Rabino. "What d'ya think? Should we follow him?"

"Hell, we've come this far. Let's do it."

"West Sunset Boulevard is one of my favorite drives," Amado said. "Expensive real estate hidden among those hills." He scanned the landscape from side to side. "Creeping along at thirty miles an hour behind that old slug gives us a chance to see this area. Years ago I took a tour of the movie stars' homes with my parents. We rode in a bus with some guy sounding off with a megaphone. He pointed out the homes of stars like Clara Bow, Harold Lloyd, Buster Keaton and some whose names I didn't know. Hell, he could have made up any film actor's name to impress us.

"When I dreamed about some of those film queens, I'd get an erection...then I'd help it along with a little message." He gave Rabino a side glance. "Don't look at me like that. I was a kid with a fertile imagination."

Rabino shook his head. "Make your confessions to the priest, Amado—not to this rabbi. I've got my own problems."

The Pierce Arrow stopped at the driveway entrance of a two story brown brick mansion with a tiled mansard roof and lattice-type windows. An atrium with a tall splashing fountain in which two marble cherubs frolicked divided the path leading to the heavily carved wooden door entrance.

With the chauffeur at his side, Periera walked slowly with a cane toward the mansion. He stopped, then motioned for the detectives to follow him. At the vestibule his house-keeper, a middle aged woman, greeted him, took his hat and helped him remove his suit jacket. "Your medication is on the library table. The doctor phoned to say he had an emergency and would be detained for perhaps an hour or so. He requested that you not take any food or alcoholic beverages before he sees you."

"What?" Periera fumed. "For what I pay him, he should be seeing me first. He tells me his injections keep me alive, then he makes me wait. I'm surrounded by incompetents and bullshitters."

The housekeeper accompanying him and the detectives to the library gave no emotional response as she said, "Moses, another hour or so is not going to shorten your life. Now please take your pills and try to relax."

"When did you get your medical degree?" Periera grumbled as he sat heavily in a large leather wing-back chair. "Here I am almost ninety with a weak heart, poor circulation, almost blind—is living this way worth the damned inconveniences?" The question prompted no response from the detectives, who were alone with him in the room. Periera continued, "I don't know how much more I can do for anyone." He spoke as in a soliloquy. "I've treated all those wretched souls the best way I could. I have enough money to live. I can leave the rest to my one relative, my nephew in Santa Barbara, but he doesn't need it, and his wife doesn't even care for my taste in furnishings."

Rabino looked at Amado sideways, raised his eyebrows and shrugged.

Periera sat forward holding his cane with both hands and looked at the two detectives. "Sit down, both of you. Now tell me what is so important that you had to follow me and spend half a day in travel at taxpayers' expense?"

Rabino cleared his throat, then said, "Mr. Periera, we believe the paintings and fine furnishings in the Goleta warehouse and those hidden or stored in the Montenegro estate came from your trading company."

"I won't admit anything, but suppose they had. Why is that important to you?"

"Only this, have all those properties been acquired legally? Were they stolen, and if so, by whom and from whom?"

Periera sat back in his chair, and said, "Every item sold by us was obtained honestly. A receipt was given to the owner of every item and a copy of that receipt can be found in our files."

Amado said, "Can we examine those files?"

Periera leaned forward, his eyes squeezed to narrow slits, and the corners of his mouth drooped. "No, sir. Not unless you have a court order."

"If you conducted business legally, why wouldn't you show us your files?"

"These matters should be of no concern to you." Periera sat back in his chair, his fingers interlaced over his abdominal paunch.

Amado noted that Periera's breathing had become labored and his color paled. "Mr. Periera, there could have been other reasons why Señora Montenegro was murdered and that Spanish priest butchered, but we think their deaths were somehow related to those paintings. We suspect that the paintings you sold were looted properties, and we think we can prove it. Why not confess now?"

Periera sneered and turned his head. "I don't know what you're talking about."

Amado stared at Periera, who avoided eye contact with either detective. "Let's try this scenario," Amado said. "You and your partners obtained valuable artwork in Europe, shipped it to Spain and Portugal where it was crated then sent by ocean freighters to the States. When the shipments reached the east coast or Houston they were sent to your warehouse in L.A." Amado paused momentarily to assess Periera's reaction. His breathing appeared more labored.

Amado continued, "Your own warehouse could not handle all the large shipments, and you had to dispose of those properties to get a return on your investment."

Periera's disdain did not change; he slid his tie knot down and opened his collar. He stared at Amado, then at Rabino. "Nothing you've said indicates unlawful activity on my part."

"Not yet, not until you confess that the paintings you sold were looted properties," Rabino said.

"I'm not confessing to any such foolishness. You haven't a shred of evidence that what you're saying is based on facts, and you know it." Periera reached for a handkerchief from his back pocket to wipe his brow.

"I'll suggest this scenario to make the picture more complete," Amado said. "The priest who came to the señora's

funeral also had a financial interest in those cultural arti-
facts, or he represented those who did. When the señora was
murdered, he came to California under the pretext of repre-
senting Franco. His true mission was to determine who was
going to be making payments on those art treasures. You were
in charge of that merchandise, and your payments were in
arrears. The priest made a personal visit to advise or threaten
you to make payments on an outstanding bill." Amado
watched Periera closely. "Am I getting close to the truth?"

"Copper, you don't know what you're talking about. You're
like a kid throwing mud against a wall and hoping some will
stick. Are you saying I killed the señora and the priest?"

"No, not personally, you could have hired thugs," Amado
said.

Periera's color took on an ominous hue, his voice lost
volume as he said, "Thugs—where would I find thugs?"

"They're about as scarce as Mexican restaurants in Santa
Barbara," Rabino said.

"Tell us where those paintings came from...the statuary...the fine furnishings," Amado said as he walked back
and forth in front of Periera.

Periera slumped in his chair, his eyes glazed over. Both
detectives knelt on either side of him. Amado reached for
the glass of water on the table and moistened Periera's lips.
Rabino ran to the door and called for the housekeeper. At
that moment the doctor entered the mansion. With Rabino's
excited message, he rushed to the moribund Periera. The
housekeeper followed closely. Within seconds the doctor
pulled out a loaded syringe from his medical bag, reached
for the back of Periera's hand, slapped it twice, then injected
the syringe contents.

Periera took a deep and audible breath, his eyes flickered
in confusion as he looked about and attempted to sit upright.
The doctor and housekeeper assisted him. Looking at the
pledget of cotton and the strip of tape on his hand Periera
said, "Where the hell've you been, Doc? I thought sure I was

leaving this crazy damned world."

The doctor placed his stethoscope on Periera's chest, asked him to remain quiet as he listened. He listened to the back of the chest and had Periera breathe deeply then exhale slowly. Pulling up Periera's pant leg, the doctor pushed his finger into the front of the leg. The depression made in the skin formed a small crater.

"Well, what d'ya think, Doc? Am I going to live?"

The doctor folded his stethoscope and placed it in his bag. "You'll live long enough to continue complaining about my medical bills, but for now I'm putting you in Cedars again for evaluation and treatment. I'll phone for an ambulance."

"Ambulance?" Periera's voice strained. "I can have my chauffeur...save me a pile of money."

"We'll do it my way," the doctor said. "For your information you were about to meet your maker. I'll see you on the ward."

Rabino approached the doctor out of Periera's hearing range. "Doc, can we ask him a few questions before the ambulance arrives?"

"Sure, but knowing Periera, I'd say he won't give you any straight answers."

Periera, drawn and exhausted, looked at Amado then at Rabino. "The doc said I almost died. I didn't want to die with a cop on either side of me. It would look bad on my resume." He attempted a brief smile.

Rabino leaned close to Periera's ear and Amado did the same on the opposite side. "Mr. Periera, where did those paintings come from?" Amado asked again.

Periera said nothing and turned his head to the other side, but he faced Rabino who asked the same question. "Both of you—get the hell away from me."

Amado speaking gently, said, "Mr. Periera you almost died a few minutes ago. If that happened some grave questions would remain unanswered. Tell us about the paintings. Who did they belong to originally? What arrangements did you make with the Montenegros and attorney Spingarn?"

Rabino cut in. "Were the murders of Señora Montenegro and Father Allende related to those...?"

Periera grimaced but remained silent. Rabino walked toward the door and motioned for Amado to follow. Rabino, in a last desperate attempt turned and gave Periera a baleful look, saying, "Periera, both of our Sephardic families have endured suffering, torture and death from those who would have tried to rid the world of our kind. Your silence plays into their hands. In the name of all that's decent and honorable, Periera, help us find those who are murderers. You know the art treasures are related to those killings. You are our last chance for solving those crimes. If you die before telling us, you'll leave us with nothing, and the murderers go free."

Still silent, Periera sat motionless looking at his fingers intertwined in his lap.

Rabino and Amado turned to leave when Periera murmured, "Wait."

Both men hurried to kneel beside the ashen-faced Periera, who spoke hesitantly, wheezing just above a whisper. "Those paintings and furnishings came from wealthy Jewish Spaniards and Portuguese, Frenchmen too, who wanted to flee their homes fearing persecutions and Nazi lootings. Those people wanted whatever money they could get... money for transportation and bribing officials."

Periera's speech became slow and less audible. His breathing was interrupted by wheezing. "Many desperate people trusted me to give them the most for their art treasures. My family had been in the business of buying and selling art for many years... yes, they trusted me."

"And, of course, you paid them well," Amado said with more than a hint of sarcasm. Rabino poked him, a signal to stop needling.

Periera continued, "They had many things to sell—heirlooms, jewels, rugs, paintings—they were frightened. I paid them as well as I could."

"Ten cents on the dollar?" Amado asked.

Periera did not respond.

"How did that phony priest figure in all of this?" Rabino asked.

"In Madrid, he insisted on buying paintings from me—masterpieces—a Monet, a Rubens, others. I was hardly in a position to refuse him." He added quickly, "But he never paid me."

"He never paid you for paintings worth thousands of dollars?" Amado said.

"Hundreds of thousands. And he wanted even more. I told him most of the paintings had been sent to the United States. He became furious and was about to attack me when I reminded him that my family knew Franco well."

"So, that's why the priest came to California, ostensibly on behalf of Franco to make a condolence call on the señora's death," Amado said. "In reality he wanted to acquire more paintings. The priest owed you a great deal of money and threatened to take even more paintings you had stored in the Santa Barbara area. That was enough to make someone sufficiently angry to want him dead—in the worst way."

Periera shook his head slowly, his eyelids flickered; he mumbled, "I never killed him."

His hands fell away from his lap, his head drooped on his chest, his jaw opened and mucous spilled onto his shirt.

Amado reached for Periera's wrist, then he placed his fingers on Periera's neck. "He's gone."

The housekeeper wailed in inconsolable grief as she fell to her knees in front of Pereira. She laid her head in his lap and sobbed as she held and kissed his cold hands.

Chapter 60

Amado climbed into the driver's seat of the sheriff's car, while Rabino slid onto the passenger's seat.

Rabino stuck an unlit half-smoked cigar into the corner of his mouth and began chewing it. "What I don't get is why the priest was butchered. Hell, killing in itself is bad enough. Periera could have been mad at not getting paid by that fraud in a cassock, but I can't see why he would carve him up."

"I go along with that," Amado said. "It had to be some perverse whacko who chopped off that priest's cock and shoved it in his mouth. Man, that's mean, really mean."

Rabino nodded. "Another thing that bothers me are the murders of those two pseudo dicks who ran off the cliff. Where do they fit in?"

"Hey, don't stop there. We still don't have a damned clue as to who killed the señora. For that matter, who in the hell winged me? If that sonofabitch had better aim, my mother would be collecting death benefits now."

"Don't remind me," Rabino said, laughing. "Our insurance rates would go up."

"You've got a shitty sense of humor, Rabino."

"You inspire me. All right, let's get serious. We've gone over the details more times than...okay, you want to review what we learned? Fine." Rabino removed the cigar stub from the corner of his mouth. He grimaced and ran the back of his hand over the cigar juice that dribbled on his chin. "We agreed that most probably the murderer was someone the señora knew, right?"

"Probably, but not necessarily. Some armed thief could have sneaked up, and told her not to move. When he got close enough, he put a gun to the back of her head and—bang! The trouble with that is, nothing was stolen, not a damn thing. Secondly, the victim was sitting in front of a mirror—she would have seen him approaching and could have yelled, but no one heard any yelling. I say the killing was *not* robbery related."

"I think you're right, but you keep referring to the killer as *he*. Maybe it was a *she*. Regardless, the question remains: who wanted her dead? We've asked that a thousand times. She didn't keep a diary; none of the laborers on the estate, as far as we know, held a grudge."

Rabino waited for a response.

Amado anticipated Rabino's next probe. "Marv, if you mention Isabella Chavez's name as a suspect again..."

Rabino cut him off. "Relax, lover boy. I know damn well you've broken the cardinal rule about relationships between investigating deputies and suspects. There's no damned good reason why we shouldn't have fried your hide. I just hope I don't have to go before the board again to defend you. We might not be as lucky next time. Can't you stay away from her until we...?"

"No!"

"Jeez, that was quick. At least give me a chance to finish what I wanted to say."

"I know what you're thinking. Listen, if she's guilty, you can fry my ass... take my badge and shove it. This bullshit about telling me who I can and can't see has got to stop. You better know now that I intend to marry her."

Rabino turned slowly in his seat to look at Amado. "You what?"

"That's right, and I was thinking you'd be my best man, but if..."

"Hold on, Amado. Give me a chance to think. Why do you make things so damn difficult?" Rabino pressed his middle fingers against his temple, rubbing it in a circular motion. He looked out the side window, then turned to look at Amado. "Forget our conversation of the last five minutes. Do me a favor, concentrate on the murders. What have we overlooked? What was said or done that we didn't follow up on? You're always taking notes. Is there anything in that notebook of yours to connect the señora with anyone? Who was she involved with after her husband was killed?"

Amado kept one hand on the steering wheel; with his other he reached into his jacket pocket, then gave Rabino a notebook. "Here, try reading this."

Rabino moistened his index finger on his lip and flipped through several pages. "Fortunately, I can read your handwriting. Here's a note about Spingarn... says he's trying to date her... she wouldn't go out with that ugly little man. He became furious when she dated his former associate, Mark Anderson." Rabino looked at Amado. "Make arrangements to talk with this Anderson guy."

Chapter 61

Just east of Cliff Drive, a rambling white ranch-style house perched on the crest of a hill, overlooked the Santa Barbara channel to the west and the city nestled beneath the mountains to the east. Amado, in the front passenger seat, directed Connors to turn into the narrow street leading up to the home.

Amado looked upward. "Jeezuz, another house in the stratosphere. These people don't want to live below like the rest of us peons."

"I'm gonna park right next to the entrance. I'm not climbing up anymore hills," Connors said. He drove into the driveway and parked in front of a walkway that led to a massive double-door entrance.

The door chimes prompted a dog to begin a high-pitched yapping, then a male voice called out, "Be right with you!" The door opened showing a handsome, trim man about forty-five dressed in a flowery Hawaiian shirt, shorts and sandals, cradling an English bulldog puppy in one arm. He extended his free hand to shake Amado's, then Connors'. "Come in fellows. You'll have to excuse the appearance of the place. Today is my day away from the office, but as you can see, my work is all around me. I'll remove some of these folders so you can sit down."

Mark Anderson's affable manner set the tone for a comfortable meeting. "I'll put Winston in his room and we can talk without interruption."

When Anderson walked away with the dog, Amado surveyed the collection of portraits and photos, mostly of women, on the mantle. He leaned toward Connors and whispered, "There's a picture of the señora. Think he carries a torch for her?"

Anderson returned. "Can I offer you fellas a drink: coffee, Coke, sparkling water?"

Connors was about to accept when Amado said, "No thanks. We have a few questions, then we'll be on our way. We'd like to know about your relationship with the late Señora Montenegro. What can you tell us about her? Did she ever say anything about having enemies, that is, people who might have wanted her out of the way?"

Anderson shook his head slowly, pursed his lips, then said, "I really don't recall any..."

Amado interrupted, "Mr. Anderson, I know you're not going to reveal any privileged client-attorney information, and I respect that, but we're trying to solve a murder, and we need all the help we can get. A person usually doesn't see an attorney unless there is a problem."

The smile on Anderson's face disappeared. "You understand that I worked as a junior partner to Mr. Spingarn who handled legal matters for the Montenegros..."

"We understand, and as a junior partner you must have been privy to problems that arose affecting the firm. Surely, Spingarn would have discussed them with you."

"One of the reasons I left that office, Mr. Amado, was that Spingarn did not take me into his complete confidence."

Amado nodded. "I see. You said that was one of the reasons. Were there other reasons?"

"I don't intend to discuss my personal problems, since I don't believe they're germane to your investigation."

"Anything you can remember may be relevant and helpful to us. We're asking that you don't spare details. We know you dated Señora Montenegro—a fact that caused old man Spingarn to burn, since he wanted a relationship with her, but she rejected him. Isn't that right?"

Anderson folded his arms across his chest and squared his shoulders. "I think you know everything I can tell you about Señora Montenegro, so if you have no further questions, I'll..."

"Hold on, Mr. Anderson, with all due respect, sir, we've learned nothing about your relationship with the señora."

Anderson walked to the mantel, picked up the framed 8x10 photo of the dark-haired beauty, a picture taken at least ten years earlier. He had a wistful smile. "She was an outstanding beauty, perfect in every way—except one." Anderson replaced the picture on the mantle and sat down.

"What do you mean she was perfect in every way, except one?" Amado asked.

Anderson hesitated before responding. "You're asking me to reveal confidential, highly personal matters that could be construed to demean the character of the deceased. I'm sorry. I find that difficult if not impossible to do. Accept the fact that we had a loving relationship until..." Anderson stopped and cast his eyes downward.

"Look, Mr. Anderson, we know you're having difficulty explaining this to us. If this weren't a murder case, we wouldn't insist on your telling us. Some detail, no matter how small or bizarre, could be the key to unlocking this case."

Anderson glared at Amado. "I don't see how this matter could help you at all."

"Try us," Amado said. "Sometimes the oddest item can trigger a new line of thinking. What you tell us, of course, will remain strictly confidential."

Finally Anderson gave in and opted to be open with them. He cleared his throat and said, "She had a strange medical or psychological condition. Perhaps not strange to the endocrinologists but strange nevertheless. She went to the Mayo Clinic in Rochester, Minnesota for consultation. After many tests, she was advised that she could be treated at home, that is, at a Santa Barbara facility. Truth is, after several months, she couldn't find effective treatment here or in L.A.

"At first her condition just inflamed our passions. We couldn't wait until we were in each other's arms. We dated frequently and enjoyed wonderful experiences, full of thrilling discoveries, and," he hesitated... "complete sexual abandonment."

"That doesn't sound all that bad to me," Connors said.

Anderson continued, "Well, I won't say I didn't enjoy liaisons, at least initially. The problem started when she insisted that we meet two or three times a week—my place, her place, a hotel—location made no difference. Her needs or rather her wants became insatiable. She proposed marriage a number of times and with it the promise of luxury living. I didn't need her wealth. As you can see, I live quite comfortably."

Amado leaned forward. "Mr. Anderson, you referred to her *condition* and mentioned that she went to Mayo for consultation. What was that condition?"

"That's what I was about to tell you. I accompanied her to Rochester where she underwent a battery of tests over a five-day period. She had adrenal function and pituitary evaluations. All her tests were normal except for the psychological evaluation. The results were forwarded to her doctor, a friend of mine, here in Santa Barbara. Against usual medical ethics, he confided in me that her condition, really an illness, was termed *sexual impulsivity,* a fancy term for a person suffering from nymphomania. Hah, we could have saved a lot of time and effort, because I could have made *that* diagnosis."

Anderson walked to the window. With his back to the detectives, he continued, "After a while, our meetings evolved into a kind of mechanical sameness, a brief physical encounter and then detachment. A chasm developed between us that couldn't be bridged. We had little or no intellectual common ground. Her world was physical, sexual, one interlaced with the business matters of her estate.

"Quite frankly, I could no longer endure the sameness of our liaisons and her driving desire for sex only. I'm almost ashamed to say that the constant repetition of our meetings began to bore me and were wearing me down. I could have masturbated and fantasized to a more interesting companion." Amado looked at Connors, who raised his brow.

Anderson continued, "After I insisted that we see one another less often, I learned that she was getting sexual fulfillment with others. One evening, she had too many whiskey sours and laughingly told me she had taken to forcing her chauffeur to have sex with her in the back seat of that old limousine. Then she invited him to her boudoir. She became disgustingly explicit. I packed her off and drove her home. I haven't seen her since—that was about one month before she was murdered." Anderson became quiet, lit a cigarette and inhaled deeply. "I don't think there is any more I can tell you about our relationship."

Connors said, "Wow, that kinda gives me a different take on the señora. I thought..."

Amado interrupted. "Once again, Mr. Anderson, did she ever discuss anyone she detested? Were there any labor problems on the estate? Do you know if anyone owed her a lot of money?"

Anderson shook his head after each question.

"You must have given some thought as to why she was murdered, "Amado said.

"Of course, I gave it a lot of thought. The only person she said she disliked was old man Spingarn, and that was because he has a nasty disposition and quite frankly, is physically repulsive. He became angry by her rejection and even more so when he learned that she was seeing me. But I have difficulty believing that Spingarn would have murdered her. She was, after all, an important and wealthy client."

The detectives were about to leave when Connors said, "Can you account for your time on the night the señora was murdered?"

Anderson laughed. "You can't be serious. Give me the date, the exact time, and I'll tell you. I keep a social calendar that is complete and correct."

Connors felt uneasy and looked at Amado for help.

"We'll look at your social calendar some other time,

counselor," Amado said. "Thanks again."

As they approached the car, Amado said, "Billy Boy, don't ask questions just to be asking questions."

"Sorry, Fred. You're the one who tells me never to take anything for granted. We can't assume that Anderson is innocent, can we?"

"After you've been on the force for a while and have a few gray hairs, you'll be able to tell a bullshitter from an honest John. There's nothing remotely suspicious about this guy, even though he is a lawyer. He's a guy who can fuck'em and leave 'em, a real cocksmith. Didn't you see the photos of all those dames on the mantle? They weren't his sisters or his aunts."

Amado looked at his watch. "It's 3:10. Swing by the Montecito Inn, Mr. Goldberg might be having a cocktail. I want to ask him a few more questions."

Chapter 62

The bar at the Montecito Inn had about twenty patrons seated at the bar and at the cocktail tables. The chatter was subdued, several couples appeared to be exchanging intimate comments. Amado looked at Connors. "Don't these people have better things to do in the middle of the day?" Amado answered his own question. "I guess not." He looked at the far end of the room and saw Ben Goldberg who had already seen the detectives and waved them over.

Amado introduced Connors and the three sat at a small table. The detectives refused Ben's offer to buy them drinks, but they nibbled on the assorted nuts in a dish.

"I was sorry to hear about Moses Periera's death," Goldberg said, "but now I can talk more freely about what he did and why he did it."

Amado took out his pad to make notes.

"Freddie, what I'm about to tell you falls under the heading of hearsay or gossip. Take notes if you must, but I doubt if any of this will help solve the murders."

"Uncle Ben, let me be the judge of that. Take your time and tell us whatever comes to your mind. We'll sort it all out later. What do you know about the paintings that came from the IAT Company? Were they stolen from wealthy people or art dealers or museums?"

Goldberg shook his head. "No, no. Let me start from the beginning. Moses Periera was proud of his heritage. He would brag about his ancestors who came from an old line of

Sephardim who inhabited Spain and Portugal from the time of the Diaspora when Jews were expelled from Babylon by Nebuchadnezzar. Is that name familiar?" Goldberg sipped his drink and smiled. "How Periera knew all that, I don't know, but he was always full of details. He said his people were skilled artisans, makers of regal jewelry, weavers of fine cloth and tanners of soft leather. In his family there were also prestigious scholars in the institutions of higher learning. They and the Moors flourished side-by-side until the reign of Isabella and Ferdinand—but you know all that.

"By declaring themselves to be *Conversos*, that is adopting the Christian faith, they were permitted to survive—even to prosper as dealers in the fine arts. This went on for centuries until Hitler came to power. There were several thousand avowed and practicing Jews in Spain—their religious freedom had returned over the centuries, in a manner of speaking.

"The Periera family had been well respected as art dealers for over a century. They sponsored artists and bought and sold museum-quality paintings.

"When Franco accepted Hitler's soldiers and armaments in the Civil War of 1936, fear arose among the Jews in the principal cities of Spain. They feared Hitler's doctrine of hatred would consume the country, and its Jews would be treated like the German Jews. Many Spanish and Portuguese Jews wanted to leave in the early 30s and began to liquidate their properties for whatever they could get. Fine silverware, jewelry, paintings, gold coins were exchanged for money to buy air fares and ocean voyages to England or North and South America. Naturally, many tried to sell their paintings to Periera."

"Did he deal with them fairly?" Amado asked.

Ben Goldberg paused. "I can't give you an unqualified yes or no answer. Obviously, Periera did not give them market value. In his defense, if I can be charitable, I'd say he took a gamble, not knowing whether he could peddle those paintings profitably in a distant market. To buy those paintings, he needed hard cash, and he could have been strapped for money. In addition the Spanish government limited the amount of pesetas or their equivalent value in belongings that could be taken out of the country. One has to assume that politicians were paid off, to get the paintings to a seaport. That alone, carried considerable risk.

"All things considered, I believe Periera rendered a humanitarian service. Of course, he was well compensated." Ben Goldberg stood, and said, "You boys will have to excuse me while I relieve a weak bladder, one of the drawbacks of aging. I'll be back in a few minutes. Think about any questions you want to ask me."

Amado looked at Connors. "I've heard much of this story from Periera himself, but I didn't want to stop Ben because he's on a roll, and I do have questions for him. Is there anything you want to ask him?"

"I was wondering why Periera didn't unload those paintings on the east coast, Boston or New York." Connors asked.

"During my conversation with Periera, I asked him the same question. He said that he did leave some paintings with east coast dealers but only a few because they decided what they thought the paintings were worth. Their figures were much lower than his estimates. Periera wanted to set his own prices on those paintings. Another problem was the necessity of going through an agency that would have cut further into his profit margin. When I asked him about placing the paintings in auctions, he said that was out of the question. He believed too many were rigged."

Ben returned. "All right. What questions do you have for me?"

"Uncle Ben, what relationship, if any, existed between those paintings and Señora Montenegro's murder and the murder of the priest?"

Ben raised his hand and snapped his fingers to get the attention of a nearby waitress. "Darling, refresh my drink, and bring something for my young friends here."

The waitress looked at the detectives, until Amado said, "Coke will be fine."

"Ditto," said Connors who watched the shapely waitress hurry away.

"Anything I tell you is mere speculation," Goldberg said. "Their deaths might not be related at all to the paintings. But if you want to allow your imaginations to work overtime, try this scenario: paintings had been sent to the Montenegros over a period of several years. Those paintings were delivered under the auspices of the Spanish Government, the Office of the Secretary of National Arts and Treasures."

Amado leaned forward. "You mean the paintings in the estate's basement belonged to Franco's government?"

Goldberg nodded. "As you know, the Montenegros lived lavishly—servants, gardeners, fancy automobiles—all the accoutrements of wealthy gentry. The money to support that lifestyle, I believe, came from the sales of several of those paintings. I know because they were offered to me. Now, it's quite possible that the money from those paintings was never sent to the agency in Spain. The Spanish government might have lost patience and decided on a solution, a hired assassin to...well, you can imagine the rest."

"What can you tell us about the priest who was butchered?"

Goldberg sat back in his chair; his eyes roamed the ceiling, he pursed his lips, sucked in his breath and exhaled audibly. "Freddie, that remains a puzzle. I know the priest had a monetary interest in those paintings. Whether he came to threaten the estate into paying him, or..."

Amado bolted upright. "Wait a minute, Uncle Ben. The owners of the estate were gone, remember? The señora was being buried and the colonel had been killed in a car accident two years before. There is only Miss Chavez who has inherited...you can't be thinking that she..."

Ben interrupted. "Freddie, I told you, I am only speculating. I am not accusing Miss Chavez of murdering anyone. However, it's possible that..."

"No, no!" Amado said. "We're not going to run with that possibility—not for a damn second." He stood, pushed back his chair and said, "Thanks, Uncle Ben. We'll stay in touch."

Chapter 63

Walking to the unmarked sedan, Connors avoided conversation or looking directly at Amado who remained uncharacteristically quiet. Amado yanked the door open, then slid into the passenger seat. "Everybody's an expert, a criminologist," he snarled. "Old Ben sure as hell pissed me off, suggesting that Isabella could be implicated..."

"I don't think he did, Fred. He was only doing what we always do: consider all suspects, then eliminate them one-by-one."

"I've already eliminated her as a suspect long ago." Amado crossed his arms over his chest, took a deep breath, then exhaled with a sustained, "Shi--it!"

"One thing your Uncle did do, he cleared up the mystery of why nobody's made a claim for those paintings or that other fancy stuff in the warehouse."

"What d'ya mean?"

"He said Periera paid for those things with cold cash. They were a kind of 'all-sales-are-final transaction' with those people who were high-tailing it out of Spain...getting out as fast as they could with as much money as they could carry. They had no legitimate claim on any of those things after they sold them. It ain't like those paintings or valuables were stolen from them or anything like that."

Amado looked at Connors. "Billy Boy, your perspicacity at times simply confounds me."

"Is that good?" Connors asked.

"Since you're so perceptive, tell me, who in the hell killed the señora, butchered the priest and caused the accident that killed those fake Spanish detectives."

"Aw c'mon, Fred, don't ask me. You're smarter than I am. I think you already suspect that the chauffeur, Gruenwald, queered that Lincoln steering gear and brake line. Frankly, I don't see why we can't haul him in and charge him. You got any reason for not doing it?"

Amado looked out the side window and seemed to direct his remarks to an imaginary third person. "What we've got is circumstantial—nothing more. We can get him for impersonating an officer when he went after those car parts... I've got bigger plans for him. The guy is shrewd... clever enough to have conned the Nazis to hook up with the Montenegros in Spain. But there's still too much we don't know about him. He's like a friggin' onion whose layers have to be peeled away."

"Think Isabella—er, I mean—Miss Chavez would object to your suspicions about Gruenwald?"

"She already knows what I think of him, and she's not happy about it."

Chapter 64

In a sleepy stupor, Amado reached for the jangling phone at his bedside. He blinked to focus at the Big Ben next to the phone. *Jeezus, 6:48. Who the hell is calling on a Sunday morning?* He grabbed the phone. "Yeah, who's there?"

He wriggled his upper body to rest against the headboard, smacked his tongue against a dry palate, then smiled as he recognized the caller's voice. "Sweetheart, you can call me anytime. Can't imagine a sweeter wake-up call...what's that?... go to mass? ...a parking lot bake sale afterwards. I see. Look, sweetheart, I don't do church services...no, not since I was a kid. Tell you what I'll do, I'll come by afterward, pick you up and take you to that nice beachside restaurant. Tell your chauffeur not to wait for you. I'll bring you home."

Card tables and chairs in the parking lot were being cleared and folded by the ladies of the church's auxiliary when Amado saw Isabella placing trash into a receptacle. She failed to see him when he came from behind and kissed her neck. Startled, she pirouetted rapidly, smiled broadly, placed her arms around him and kissed him in full view of the other volunteers. Among them, Nancy Peabody stared at Isabella and the handsome detective whose picture had appeared in the newspaper several weeks earlier. Nancy did a half curtsy when Isabella introduced her to Amado.

She looked at Isabella, then at Amado and said, "My dear,

now I really wonder if what you said about having his baby..."

Isabella interrupted, "Oh, for heaven's sake, Nancy, I was just kidding. Sergeant Amado, is a very good friend, that's all."

"Well, I for one, would certainly like to become his very good friend." Nancy Peabody ran the tip of her tongue around her lips and touched Amado's arm.

Isabella pulled Amado out of the parking lot and hurried him toward his car parked on the street. "The nerve of that hussy. Can you imagine that over-blown dame with three kids carrying on a shameless flirtation?"

"I've known some very nice married women with whom I shared an intimate moment or two."

"I don't want to hear about that. The only woman you're to get intimate with from now on is sitting beside you."

Amado's right hand came off the gear shift knob after he put the car in third gear. His hand moved to Isabella's left thigh and stroked it gently.

She looked at him out of the corner of her eye and said, "Two can play at this game." She put her left hand on his right thigh and moved it seductively upward.

"Whoa, girl! This is no time for foreplay—but don't let me discourage you." They both laughed. "I never dreamed I'd enjoy a gal's company as much as I enjoy yours. I'm sorry we had to meet the way we did, two months ago, but I'm grateful for the way things turned out between us."

She leaned over and put her head on his shoulder. "Fred, I want to spend a lifetime loving, laughing and having babies with you."

"My sentiments exactly. But before we get all dreamy and starry eyed, I want you to promise to do something for me."

She sat upright. "Oh boy, here it comes, I might have known the romance wouldn't last. What is it now?"

"Don't think I'm devious—maybe a little opportunistic. Could you spend time with Gruenwald and get him to tell you about his first wife and child. I have a hunch that'll lead to something... I don't know what, but something."

"How do you suggest I broach the subject? Should I just confront him and ask point blank about his former wife and child? Really, Fred, how gauche!"

"Not gauche at all. You may have forgotten, but you're the mistress, the *dueña*, of that old fortress. You have a right to know about your employees' backgrounds."

"Oh, stop that. I'm not going to stick my nose into anyone's painful past."

"You stuck your nose in mine, and I stuck mine in yours. Most people enjoy talking about the past. It's cathartic."

"Spare me the Psych 101 details. Are you always going to assign the crud work to me after we're married?"

"Your only obligation will be to love me—on demand," Amado said with a knowing smile.

"Don't count on it. I'll let you know when you have my permission." She sighed and looked out the side window. A moment of silence passed.

Amado said, "Will you give it a go? Please? Ask Gruenwald?"

"I will, but only because I'm foolish enough to love you, and you happen to be the father of our unborn child." She snuggled against Amado, held his right arm with both her hands and again placed her head on his shoulder.

Chapter 65

Isabella picked up the in-house phone and dialed Gruenwald's number. "John, I want to shop at the Fashion Store...yes, on State Street...no, I won't need Maria's help. Bring the Packard around to the front in thirty minutes."

Gruenwald drove her to the store, and after an hour and a half of selecting outerwear, trying on dresses, rejecting most and keeping a few, Isabella became weary. To the chauffeur who had accompanied her, she said, "Please put these boxes in the car, then meet me at Ernie's Café. I fatigue so easily these days. A strong cup of French roast should pick me up. I want you to join me."

"Thank you, ma'am."

Isabella found a table near the back wall. She sighed with relief as she eased out of her high-heeled pumps. "John, get me a croissant with black coffee and get something for yourself. I don't want to eat alone, and I don't want you looking at me while I'm eating."

"Yes, ma'am."

Isabella pulled the croissant apart, buttered it quickly, then stopped as though remembering the lady-like manners she learned at some finishing school. She handled the roll more delicately and held the coffee cup with her pinky extended—another sign of acquired etiquette. After finishing half the croissant, she sat back and dabbed the corners of her mouth with a napkin.

The chauffeur finished his hard roll and sat squarely in

his chair.

Isabella leaned forward on the table. "John, some time ago, you told me you had a daughter my age. Tell me about her."

The chauffeur coughed and turned his head aside before facing Isabella. "I have difficulty talking about her—it is very painful for me."

"John, we have all suffered terribly from the horrors of war. Both of my parents were murdered, shot to death while I looked on as a ten year old."

The chauffeur looked down and shook his head, then looked up and said, "Have you forgiven the murderers?"

"I will never forget them. As far as forgiving them..." Isabella hesitated. "No, I can never forgive them, even though my father confessor says I must."

He gave her a hard look and nodded, as if to say, I know how you feel. Then, as all the bitterness and rage welled up in him, he blurted out, "What do those stupid pigs hidden behind a curtain know about the deaths of innocent men, women and children? What did they ever do to prevent filthy scum from raping, murdering..." His voice rose in a bitter crescendo.

Several patrons looked his way while Isabella reached out and touched his arm. "Sh-sh." The intensity of his rancor frightened her. She had never seen this side of him. She searched his eyes. "John, are you all right?"

Hesitating, he nodded slowly. The redness in his face subsided; he lowered his head. "Forgive me, ma'am. Some things bring back terrible pain..."

"I understand, John. Would you like to leave?"

He looked at her plate and cup. Then like a parent, he chided gently. "You haven't finished eating. You are always running. Take your time." He continued, "I would feel better if you ate and relaxed. You work too hard and worry too much. If you were my child, I would insist that you take more leisure time. Enjoy life. It is too precious..." Gruenwald's voice tapered off and he looked away. In a matter of seconds, his emotions had switched from bitter hostility to caring tenderness.

Isabella hoped this might be the moment when he would talk about his first daughter and wife. "John, tell me about your daughter, is she alive?"

He shook his head.

"I'm sorry. Can you talk at all about her? Perhaps some of your grief would be more bearable if you shared her story with me."

Gruenwald, cleared his throat and took a moment before continuing. "I have never discussed this with anyone, other than Maria. In 1927, my wife, Gisele, gave birth to the most beautiful girl in all of Germany. She was a perfect doll-like copy of my wife...lovely in every way. We named her Analise, after my mother. We had a small apartment in Bremerhaven because I was a merchant sailor. I would be gone for weeks at a time, so I could not be with my little girl or my wonderful wife as I would have wanted. In spite of that, we lived happily. My wages as an officer were reasonably good and our wants were few. We were optimistic about the future. We hoped for more children, but Analise, was our only one.

"In 1932, everything changed. It was like a frightening nightmare. I never could have imagined what a terrible turn our lives would take when that wretched ex-convict came to power."

Isabella listened intently and urged him to continue, "John, please go on."

He took a deep breath. "That ranting psychotic and his stupid henchmen grabbed power and squeezed everything good out of a civilized nation. They tore our little family apart. Gisele begged me to leave the country when the Nazis started their dirty work. She tried to convince me that we could start life over in England, Canada or America. I argued against her. I thought that mad puffed-up Austrian was going to be driven out by reasonable people. He could not possibly last, I told her. How could I have been so terribly wrong?" He lowered his head. "I will never forgive myself."

"John, I still don't know what happened to your wife and child."

He shook his head and said he did not want to recall any more bad memories.

Isabella persisted with her questions, wanting to hear the rest of his story. "John, I want so much to learn about your past. Tell me about your wife."

Reluctantly, he began again, slowly. "Gisele and I were sweethearts from the moment we met at a gymnasium dance in Berlin two years after the Armistice of WWI. She was a dark-haired beauty with large black eyes and skin like snow. At age seventeen she moved with the grace of a ballerina. When she smiled at me, I knew I had found the girl of my dreams. Her chaperone watched us closely—me especially. At age eighteen, I thought I was quite a man and mature enough to know what I wanted. We dated as frequently as we could... sneaking out of our homes to meet in a theatre or a park. We took long walks and talked for hours. I was devastated when she was sent to a finishing school in Lausanne, Switzerland. Her folks did not want her to see me."

"Why, John?"

"The family was well-to-do. Her father owned a fabric dyeing plant, and they had hoped that she would marry one of her own kind."

"Her own kind?"

"Yes, they were Jewish. Although I was raised as a Lutheran, I was quite willing to convert. In fact, I started the conversion process with a rabbi, but my obligations at sea... well, it was too difficult. Gisele's family came around eventually. They made no unreasonable demands since they were Reform Jews and liberal in their thinking."

"What about your family? Did they object?"

"My parents were divorced. I lived with my mother who was totally charmed by Gisele. My mother encouraged the marriage thinking it would bring stability into my life and with the wealth of Gisele's family, we would never want. In 1933, an appeal went out for the training of submariners. Being an officer on a U-boat appealed to me. It meant an increase in salary and a promotion. I should have foreseen the madness that was behind the call for U-boat operations, but I didn't. Later I regretted the days, the weeks, the months I would be away from my little family." Gruenwald's eyes moistened.

He continued, "A condition of the Versailles Treaty prevented Germany from building submarines, but that didn't prevent the Germans from building them in other countries, like Portugal, Spain and Finland. In October of 1939, I was in Spain on one of those secretive submarine-building missions when radio reports from Oslo said that hundreds of Jews had been rounded up and placed in Polish camps ostensibly to protect and keep them from marauding hooligans. I knew those were filthy lies and they made me sick. My wife's parents no longer responded to calls or letters. Their whereabouts were unknown to us. We never heard from them again.

"I feared that..." Gruenwald stopped. His peripheral vision caught movement. He looked up to see Amado standing next to him. Gruenwald stiffened. He turned his glance away from Amado.

Isabella, annoyed, said, "Fred, what are you doing here?"

Gruenwald stood, pushed his chair back and still ignoring Amado said, "Ma'am, I'll bring the car to the front of the building. Excuse me, please." His bearing appeared almost militaristic as he left.

Isabella looked at Amado. She said, "I'm surprised to see you. How did you know I was here?"

"Your chauffeur is under surveillance. Don't want him out of our range." Amado sat in Gruenwald's chair and reached out to hold Isabella's hands. "How's my little mother-to-be?"

"Darling, I'm developing a voracious appetite. This baby and I are going to be enormous in another several weeks."

She stood and pressed her hands against her abdomen, then reached for Amado's hand. "Come, walk with me to the car... and Fred, darling, please be civil toward John. I still think your suspicions about him are misplaced."

Chapter 66

Gruenwald opened the front passenger door of the '51 Packard as Isabella slid in. She thanked Gruenwald and blew a kiss to Amado who stood beside the chauffeur. Gruenwald started the engine, put on the turn signal and slipped into traffic. After traveling for about two miles, he glanced in the rearview mirror to discover the two detectives in their unmarked car. Gruenwald's jaw muscles alternately tightened and relaxed.

"John, you're driving too fast, aren't you?" Isabella's concern increased as she watched the chauffeur's frequent glances at the rearview mirror. The car was speeding in excess of twenty miles over the speed limit.

"Sorry ma'am." He remained quiet for several minutes, then said, "I don't know why Detective Amado is following us...that upsets me."

Isabella noticed beads of perspiration on Gruenwald's forehead, although the outside temperature was sixty-one degrees. His sudden jerking responses in traffic were troubling. He took one hand off the wheel and tugged at his tie and unbuttoned his shirt collar. His head began to droop and the car veered off the road.

Isabella grabbed the steering wheel and kicked Gruenwald's foot off the accelerator, but the vehicle did not stop until it plowed into a roadside utility pole.

Just seconds before, Amado had said to Connors, "Is the Packard weaving?" Amado sat upright. "Oh, Christ. It just went off the road, it's going to hit a post." Connors sped toward the accident. Amado flew out of the moving car and ran toward the passenger side of the Packard, yelling, "Isabella!" He grabbed the door handle. It did not open. With the butt of his gun he smashed the window, reached inside and opened the door.

Her body was wedged between the seat and the confined space below the dashboard.

Connors moved in to help extricate her. Amado shoved him aside. "Call an ambulance, now!"

A scalp wound dripped blood over her face and blouse. She whimpered as Amado placed his arms around her waist and thighs, moved her out and placed her carefully on the ground. He removed his jacket, folded it and placed it under her head. She touched her deformed shoulder. "This really hurts." She looked at Amado. "How is John? Please take care of him."

Connors ran back. "They're on their way."

Amado said, "Check out Gruenwald. Is he alive?" Without looking away, Amado placed his handkerchief on Isabella's head wound and maintained pressure.

"He's barely got a pulse, Fred...it's slow...man, he doesn't look good... pale and sweaty." Gruenwald's head lay on the steering wheel, his mouth gaped and bloody sputum dripped. He barely responded to Connors's voice. "What should I do about him, Fred?"

"The ambulance guys will know what to do."

The approaching siren sounds did not discourage drivers from slowing down on Highway 92 to gape at the smashed vehicle, the injured person on the ground and the flashing lights on the unmarked police car.

The young doctor dispatched with the ambulance out of Cottage Hospital made a rapid clinical assessment of both injured people. He injected an ampule of morphine into Gruenwald's arm after he was removed from the vehicle with its crumpled hood, its smashed grill and shattered windshield. Two attendants placed Gruenwald on a gurney. The doctor told Amado, "Guy's blood pressure and pulses indicate profound shock. Probably suffered a myocardial infarct."

He looked at Isabella, who was alert but grimacing with pain and gave her an injection of morphine also. Amado removed his handkerchief from her scalp. The doctor looked at the laceration and said, "That could be sutured with no problem unless there's glass in the wound." He looked at her shoulder. "Anterior dislocation, most likely. If she didn't lose consciousness, I see no lasting problems." He looked at her pupils with a pen light and tested her knee reflexes, then compressed her ribs and gently moved her hip and knee joints.

"Okay, we've got two to go for observation and treatment." The doctor helped the attendants place the patients into the ambulance then took his place between them.

Amado said, "Doc, will I be able to take Miss Chavez home later?"

"Give us about two hours. As for the driver, he'll require an extensive workup. Whatever he has, it doesn't look good."

In the hospital Amado approached the woman at the reception desk and asked if Mr. Grunewald's wife had been notified. She said she had phoned but was told that the wife and children were in Mexico. Amado waited in the sparsely decorated reception room with its smell of aseptic solution. He picked up a three month old *Field and Stream* Magazine, but didn't really concentrate on what he was reading. The thought of Isabella aborting made him terribly anxious. He chain-smoked, paced the floor, and asked the receptionist a number of times to check on Isabella's condition.

Two and a half hours later an orderly pushed Isabella in a wheelchair into the waiting room. Her face was clean and smiling, and her right arm supported in a muslin sling. She wore a hospital gown with a brown bag on her lap. She held out her left hand to Amado who bent over to kiss it. "Doctor said, I'll be good as new in a few days." Motioning for Amado to bring his ear to her mouth, she whispered, "I can still hold a bridal bouquet in my left arm—any day now."

Amado smiled briefly. In a hushed tone, he said, "What about -you know—down there?"

She nodded just as Dr. Krantz came though the swinging doors behind her. He introduced himself and told Amado that Isabella's scalp laceration was superficial and needed only eight sutures. No debris had been found in the wound, although she was given tetanus antitoxin and an injection of penicillin. He continued, "The right shoulder dislocation was reduced with a light anesthetic and then immobilized with a sling."

Amado shook his hand, thanked him, then said, "Doc, how is the driver, Mr. Gruenwald?"

"I wanted to talk to you about him. While I was treating Miss Chavez, Dr. Richards, a cardiologist, was examining him. I talked briefly with Dr. Richards who is quite concerned about the patient. In fact, he called in a general surgeon for consultation. Some critical decisions on his care will have to be made soon. Dr. Richards, I believe, is in the patient's room now. I can take you to him."

Amado started to follow Dr. Krantz when Isabella grabbed Amado's jacket with her left hand, "Don't you dare leave me here alone. I'm going with you." Dr. Krantz dismissed the attendant pushing Isabella's wheelchair and told him he would take over.

In the critical care ward, Gruenwald lay propped up in bed with IVs running, EKG leads on his chest, arms and legs and an oxygen mask covering his nose and mouth. A urinary catheter was attached to a bag on the bed frame.

Dr. Richards in a white coat stood next to the patient and held a chart. When Amado and Isabella came into the room, he smiled and said to Isabella, "I see you're all patched up and ready to leave."

Amado standing close to Dr. Richards said softly, "How bad is he, doc?"

Dr. Richards signaled him to step out of the room. In the hallway the doctor said there was little question about Gruenwald having had a severe heart attack. "There are typical EKG changes: the ST-segment shows depression, and the T-wave is inverted..."

"Hold it, doc. I don't know anything about that. Can you tell me simply what his chances are? Is he going to make it?"

Dr. Richards hesitated. "There's a complication here that is ominous."

"What d'ya mean?" Amado asked.

"His hematocrit is dropping. He's losing blood from somewhere in the abdomen."

"The blood can be replaced, can't it?"

"Not indefinitely and not if he loses it faster than it can be replaced. Besides, our local blood banks have just so much..."

"Why can't you operate and stop the bleeding?"

"The man is suffering from a heart attack, remember? I'm not about to sign his death warrant because of a hasty decision."

"Dr. Krantz said you called in a surgeon."

"It'll be just as much a problem for him. However, surgeons are much more likely to recommend operating."

"What are his chances for surviving an operation?"

Dr. Richards pursed his lips. "Probably fifty percent—or less."

"And if you don't operate?"

"Zero."

"Doc, I don't know anything about medicine, but I've got to ask, what choices do you have?"

"The situation is complicated by the fact that we're unable to contact his wife or next of kin."

"His employer, Miss Chavez, can decide for him..."

The doctor shook his head. "That's not legal. However, I could get an opinion from the hospital's lawyer."

"Why not get the patient's consent? Tell him what the odds are. Hell, it's his life."

"That may not hold up in court if the guy dies. Someone could say the patient was under the influence of narcotics and was unable…"

"Doc, what are we arguing about? A man's life is hanging by a thread, and you're talking lawsuits. Mind if I talk with him?"

"Not at all. Go to it and good luck."

Chapter 67

"John, can you hear me?" Amado leaned down next to Gruenwald's ear and spoke above the hissing sound of the oxygen. "They're going to operate on your belly—stop the bleeding. The doctor told me the surgery is risky, but it's got to be done. In case you don't make it, you're going to leave a lot of questions unanswered. Are you with me?" Gruenwald closed his eyes, his consenting nod barely perceptible. "Good. I'm going to ask some questions. You can answer with a few words or by nodding or shaking your head. Understand?"

Amado signaled Connors to start writing. He whispered, "Get the question and answer exactly as they're given."

"John, did you kill Señora Montenegro?"

Gruenwald made no attempt to respond.

Amado waited several seconds, then bent closer to Gruenwald's ear and repeated the question, louder. "Did you kill Señora Montenegro?"

Both detectives watched closely for Gruenwald's response. There was nothing.

"Damn!" Amado muttered. He cupped his hand around Gruenwald's ear and shouted, "John, did you kill the priest?"

Again they watched for a response. Gruenwald said nothing, but his mouth transformed slowly into what the detectives saw as a slight smile. Amado quickly pointed to Connor's notepad and whispered, "Make a note of that."

The circulating nurse from the operating room arrived with pre-operative medication. She pulled up the short sleeve of the patient's hospital gown and gave him an injection. "Sorry to interrupt, fellows, but it's time for surgery." She released the locks on the bed casters and pushed the patient into the operating room.

"Goddammit! I could swear he was going to tell us something," Amado said.

Doctor Miller, the operating surgeon, was about to enter the doctors' prep room when Amado approached him. "Doc, how long before I can talk to the patient?"

"Before you can talk to him? A better question would be: will he survive the operation to talk to you or anyone? He might have a tear in his liver or spleen, but he could be bleeding from anywhere like a major vessel or the diaphragm. The surgery can take anywhere from," he looked at his wristwatch, "one-and-a-half to three hours if all goes well. But don't expect him to talk to you soon post-operatively. Why don't you plan on returning in a day or two? Even then he may still be out of it; he'll be getting medicine for pain, and his head will be foggy."

"Doc, keep this guy alive, will ya? He has to answer a lot of questions."

"I'll do the best I can, but I don't know what plans The Man upstairs has for him."

Walking toward the deputy's car where the doctors and personnel parked, Connors said, "You're quiet, Amado. What're you thinking?"

Amado slid into the passenger seat, lit a cigarette, inhaled deeply, then opened the window to exhale. "We know certain facts about Gruenwald that are damn incriminating. How else can you explain the gun and the tampered steering parts in his workshop? Sure, he had an excuse for the old car parts, and we know he was married to a Jewish woman in Germany during the Holocaust. She and their daughter might have been murdered by the Nazis." Amado became quiet, then said, "That phony priest was driven to the cemetery by Gruenwald..."

"What about the murder of the Montenegro woman? Think Gruenwald figures in on that, too?"

"I don't know. I just don't know."

"If Gruenwald survives, can't the state's attorney bring him before a grand jury, or something?"

"I don't want to bring him in on speculation or circumstantial evidence, then have some hot-shot defense lawyer blow smoke and charm some fat-ass jury members into giving him a ride."

"You want more facts?" Connors asked.

"Yeah, like a complete confession."

"That would just about kill Miss Chavez," Connors said.

"Don't think I haven't thought about that."

Chapter 68

"Can I help you gentlemen?" the evening receptionist at the Cottage Hospital asked the detectives as they approached.

"What room is John Gruenwald in? He's post-surgery by three days."

She referred to a roster. "He's in room 227, but," she pointed to the clock on the wall, "it's 9:37, well past visiting hours."

Amado opened his jacket to flash his badge. "This is an urgent matter."

"Let me get in touch with the nursing supervisor."

While she tried phoning several nursing stations, Amado whispered in Connors's ear, "Tell her I went to the john. I'm feeling sick. Keep her busy. I'm going to Grunewald's room."

He hurried along the hall, opened a stairway door and ran up the stairs to the second floor. Walking along, he saw a door marked Doctors Lounge. He opened the door and looked around a room that had yet to be cleaned by the night crew. The pervasive odor of cigarettes lingered, ashtrays were filled with butts and ashes, while newspapers and magazines lay haphazardly on a sofa and chairs. In one corner, a clothes rack held white linen coats. Amado found a large-sized coat to fit over his jacket. Looking in a mirror, in an adjoining washroom, he straightened his collar and cinched up his tie.

Opening the door, he looked in both directions, then walked past a sign designating rooms 225-245. A voice called out, "Just a minute, please."

Christ! I've been discovered, now what?

Amado stopped and turned around to see a young nurse running toward him, holding on to her wing-like white hat with one hand and a patient's chart in the other. "Doctor, I hope you can help me." She opened the chart to the doctor's order sheet. "I can't read this doctor's writing, and I can't get in touch with him. Can you read this order?" She placed her finger on the words in question.

Amado brought the chart under a ceiling light. *Jeezus, I can't pull this off without disaster.* He strained his eyes at the almost undecipherable writing, then said, "Is the patient diabetic?"

"Yes, he is."

"This doctor has terrible handwriting. Heh, heh. Maybe we're all guilty of that. I think the words look like 'regular insulin.'" He handed the chart back to her.

"I was hoping it said that. Thank you, Doctor." She was effusive with gratitude.

"Glad to help," Amado said. *Hell, that wasn't so difficult. I probably could have been a good doctor.* He walked with confidence into room 227, a private room with a TV set and attached restroom. The type of room, only those as wealthy as Isabella could afford.

He looked at Gruenwald, pale but without the pre-operative expression of pain and anxiety. He lay in a semi-recumbent position, an IV in his left forearm, his hospital gown partially covered abdominal dressings. Gruenwald appeared to be sleeping, but when Amado bent over to study his face, the man squinted then scowled.

In a rasping voice, he said, "What do you want with me, detective? Are you here to give me more grief?"

"It's not about you completely, Gruenwald. You managed to almost kill Isabella. Is that what you wanted?"

Gruenwald turned to look directly at Amado. "No, no! I would never forgive myself if that happened. I lost one family..."

"Because you were careless?"

Gruenwald turned his face away.

"Don't worry. Isabella will live— maybe with a scar or

two," Amado said.

Gruenwald shut his eyes tightly to keep from crying.

"Listen to me, I don't have much time. We know enough about you to put you away for life or give you the death sentence. You killed that fake Spanish priest, Father Allende. Our information from Interpol tells us that he was acting as camp commandant at Dachau in 1940. We also know he was a sadistic sonofabitch who tortured and raped women and girls before killing them. Look at me, John, isn't that right?"

"Leave me alone."

"Sure, just as soon as you tell me you killed that priest." Amado spoke into Gruenwald's right ear. "With what we've got on you, we can fry your ass, make no mistake about that. We've got an iron-clad case against you. Any jury would buy a conviction of premeditated murder. Killing a man of the cloth will get you the chair, for sure—even if the priest was an unholy, shitty, reformed Nazi murderer. Give me some extenuating circumstances, and maybe I can convince the prosecutor to spare you."

Gruenwald turned to study Amado's face. "I don't understand. What do you mean 'convince the prosecutor?'"

"I can tell him you were cooperating with the sheriff. You killed the priest because you were outraged. You were overcome with uncontrollable hatred. You were insane with rage and were seeking revenge for terrible crimes..."

"Yes! That's all true."

"Tell me about it."

Gruenwald suddenly shook off his sleepiness and reluctance to speak. "I've held it all in for too long. I am ashamed to say I was in Hitler's submarine corps. We hunted in wolf packs for Allied ships in the North Atlantic...away from our home base for weeks at a time. During one of our missions in 1941, a super patriotic neighbor notified the S.S. that my wife and daughter were Jews who failed to wear the yellow Star of David. They were pulled out of our home and shipped off to Dachau. I learned too late from a guard stationed there that my loved ones were murdered after they had been raped and tortured by the camp commandant, Fritz Gruber also known as Father Julio Allende." Gruenwald turned his head aside to hide his tears.

Amado handed him a Kleenex.

Gruenwald regained his composure and continued, "I lost my mind. I thought of ending my own life by putting a gun to my head, but I decided to live long enough to take revenge. Revenge gave me a reason for living. I wanted to kill Gruber with my bare hands. I would make him suffer until he begged me to kill him. But I had to find him first.

"Gruber was as clever as he was evil. He knew the Allies would win eventually, and he would be held accountable for the murders...the atrocities he committed. That's when he decided to return to Spain, change his identity and masquerade as a priest. A priest, no less. What a terrible irony."

"How do you know all this?"

Gruenwald struggled to continue. "I had my informants. Gruber made enemies among his own men. He was despicable...completely rotten. He feared that other Nazi rats would turn him over to the Allies as a war criminal to save their own skins."

"How did *you* get to Spain?" Amado asked.

He coughed, then held his painful abdomen. "I despised Hitler and his murdering gangsters. I was obsessed. I could only think of revenge. Revenge consumed me. When my submarine stopped for refueling in Lisbon, I made plans to get to Madrid. I knew that Gruber wormed his way back into Franco's graces and became a member of his cabinet as a religious consultant."

"John, you're moving too fast for me. You deserted your vessel? What about your identity?"

"Of course I deserted the U-boat. I changed my name, got rid of my uniform and found a job as a mechanic and chauffeur for one of Franco's cabinet members, Colonel Hermano Hidalgo Montenegro. I figured that would provide an opportunity to get close to that phony priest,"

"Did you attempt to kill him then?"

"Twice he was in my gun sight, but I didn't want to get caught. I wanted to get him alone...face him, tell him who I was and then torture him as he tortured my..." He hesitated.

"Keep talking, John."

"I thought my opportunity to kill that bastard priest disappeared when the Montenegros moved to the United States and asked me to join them. I was torn between joining them or remaining in Madrid to wait for my next opportunity to kill Gruber. He changed his name to Father Julio Allende. But I had to go with the Montenegros because I had no life in Madrid without them. They were my family—at least the little girl, Isabella, and the señora. I vowed that I would return to Madrid one day and finish my business with Gruber, but I put it off, and when I met Maria, I all but gave it up."

"Did you ever think you'd see the priest again?"

"No, never. I can't even describe my excitement when Miss Isabella told me he was coming to pay his respects and officiate at the burial ceremony of the señora. I knew his real reason for coming to Montecito had to do with the art treasures he owned in partnership with Mr. Periera. The priest never gave a damn about anyone—dead or alive."

"How do you know about the art treasures?"

"Señora Montenegro confided in me."

"What role did the Montenegros play in the paintings?"

"They took a percentage of the sales price. The señora had complete control of the business end since the colonel would have nothing to do with it—except to spend money from the sale of the paintings."

"How do you know about these things?"

"As I said, the señora told me during—how shall I say? Intimate moments."

"Intimate moments? Explain that." Amado listened carefully.

"Her husband was not a good sex partner— he wasn't even a bad sex partner. The señora needed frequent male companionship. I was convenient, that's all." He looked away before continuing, "When we came to this country she thought we should have no further intimacies. That was all right with me. I was happy to have met Maria here. We were both lonely. As you know, we have two wonderful children, Roberto and Linda."

"The children go to a private school?" Amado asked.

"Yes, the señora paid for their schooling...tuition and board. Señorita Chavez continues to do that, and we are grateful."

"John, are you the one who shot at me the night I was in the doorway with Isabella?"

"I never meant to harm you. I aimed the pistol well to the side, but you moved suddenly when you kissed the señorita."

"Isabella said you and Maria went to a movie and would not be home until quite late."

"We decided to have dinner on the wharf instead and returned earlier. After the shooting, Maria and I hid in the workshop until all was quiet."

"But why in hell did you shoot at me anyway?"

"I wanted only to discourage you from falling in love with her. I was afraid you would take her from us, and the estate would shut down. If that happened, I didn't know what I would do to support my family."

"Your thinking was all screwed up. You should have known that shooting near me or at me would make me more determined to find the shooter."

Gruenwald nodded. "I did not always reason clearly."

"Tell me what you did with the priest."

His brow wrinkled. "You mean that pig who called himself Father Julio Allende? That fraud wanted to go to the cemetery before the corpse of the señora was brought from the church. He insisted on preparing the sacraments for ascension of the soul and wanted everything in order at the mausoleum. His religious mumbo-jumbo chanting made no sense to me, but the thought of being alone with him excited me. My heart thumped wildly; I thought it would burst.

My vengeance was finally going to be satisfied. I felt for my razor-sharp hunting knife attached to my belt.

"At the cemetery office, I was told that the mausoleum door had been unlocked in preparation for receiving the señora's remains.

"While he knelt and prayed at the pre-burial sarcophagus, I brought in the tire iron and rope from the car's trunk and quietly placed them inside, near the door. With the clicking sound of the closing door, the priest stood up and turned to face me. Although he acted unconcerned, I knew he was frightened. He said, 'What is the matter, my son?'

"I brought my face next to his and told him to save his bullshit patronizing for those who were fooled by his charade. Even in the dim light from the slit windows above, I could see the pallor on his face and the fine beads of perspiration on his brow. The stink of his nervous sweating was further indication of his fear. I slapped him on one cheek, then the other and spat in his face. He pulled back and placed his hands over his face. I yanked his hands away and yelled, 'Look at me, you filthy pig!'

"He began to quiver and looked away, but I kept after him. 'Do you remember raping a mother and daughter, then killing them at Dachau?'

"He shook his head frantically and blurted out denials. I pulled out my wallet and forced him to look at photos of my wife and daughter. I warned him that if he denied raping and murdering them, I would cut his heart out then and there.

"He pleaded, 'No, no! I beg you. Please try to understand. I was under great pressure running that camp. I took pills and drank whisky to help me forget the horror and misery. I did not know what I was doing. We were brainwashed. We were told the inmates were enemies of the state. They were mere Jews—worthless *untermenschen*.'"

"I grabbed his amice and brought his face close to mine and shouted that those two worthless *untermenschen* you raped and murdered were my cherished loved ones: my whole world, my own flesh and blood, you miserable stinking *schwinehundt*. He backed away, pleading for me to spare his life. While moving backward toward the door, he caught his shoe in the hem of his cassock and fell down. Sprawled on the floor, he glanced about in desperation, saw the tire iron, and grabbed it. He swung it wildly at me but missed. I reached for my knife as he took another swipe at me. He scrambled to his feet, and I lunged at him with my knife. He struck my knife blade with an upward thrust that sheared off his nose.

"He screamed hysterically, dropped the tire iron and put his hands over his gushing nose or what was left of it. He passed out and fell to the floor. I thought he died. I grabbed the rope and tied his ankles, then brought the rope up to tie his wrists behind his back. His face, covered with blood, looked ghoulish.

"I dragged him to the plinth, placed him on his back while his head hung over the edge. I tore his cassock and under-clothes off. I carved a skin-deep crucifix from his neck down to his crotch and from nipple to nipple. Just as I finished, he regained consciousness and began screaming again, a terri-fied unholy sound. But no outsider could have heard him in that sound-proof death chamber. At that point I grabbed and pulled his penis, then cut it off at the base and jammed it in his mouth. I picked up the tire iron and smashed his skull to stop his yelling. He jiggered like a mackerel on a fish line, until he stopped."

"John, I understand your hatred, but sticking his cock in his mouth?"

"Any sonofabitch who misused his prick as he did, deserved to have it shoved down his throat."

"Yeah. No argument there."

Gruenwald continued, "I could not avoid the puddle of blood that formed below his head. I picked up his phylac-teries and clothes and wiped my knife and tire iron with them, then removed the rope. When I opened the door, I made sure I wasn't seen.

"Back at the estate, I burned my clothes and shoes, his clothes and the rope." Gruenwald grimaced, hesitated, then moaned, complaining of chest pain.

Amado said, "Did you paint the swastikas on that portrait of Franco and the señora?"

"Yes, and that was better than they deserved. That painting nauseated me every time I saw it."

"What was your reason for carving the cross on the priest's chest and belly?"

"Because he defiled it."

"And those men pretending to be Spanish detectives? Did you tamper with the steering apparatus and the brake lines on their car?"

A faint nod from the patient alerted Amado to listen carefully. "Why did you do that?"

Gruenwald answered slowly, softly. "I knew they suspected me since I was the last one to see the priest alive. As soon as I heard them talk, I knew Spanish was not their first language. They started asking Maria and me too many questions."

"Tell me about those two phony detectives," Amado persisted.

"I made some excuse for leaving them for a moment. With my hunting knife I jabbed the right front tire on their car. When I returned, I told them they had a flat tire, but I could repair it. They agreed. Once I jacked up the car, I loosened the steering gear and punctured the brake line."

"How did you know who they were?"

"On the front seat of their car, I saw airline tickets. They were return tickets to Buenos Aires. I knew that colonies of former Gestapo agents lived in Argentina and Brazil and formed a network with former Nazis living in Spain and elsewhere. I needed to get rid of them. I had to think of saving my life and keeping my family safe."

"What about the señora, did you kill her?"

Gruenwald looked at Amado, then at something behind him. An older nurse approached, a frown deepened the wrinkles of her weary countenance. "May I ask what is going on?" She walked toward Amado. "Who are you and why are you here?" She studied Amado's face, placed her hands on her hips and sighed, "Oh, for crying out loud! Freddie Amado! Are you playing doctor with that white coat? I swear, if I didn't see your picture and name in the newspaper, I'd never even know you're still alive. You don't come to the family picnics anymore—not even to the weddings, communions or funerals."

Amado blinked, hoping he could read the nurse's name badge without putting on his glasses. He stared at the name, *Bertha Mercado, Supervisor.* He smiled. "Bertha, it's so good seeing you again." They embraced and he kissed both her cheeks. "I'm guilty of playing hooky from family gatherings...it's my work." He was hoping to resume his questioning of Gruenwald when she hooked her arm around his and led him away from the bed.

"Look, cousin, you can break the rules elsewhere, but not in my hospital and not on my watch. You don't remember, but I changed your diaper and powdered your little butt. You were so cute then and well behaved."

"Bertha, I was about to get a confession from that guy. Please, I got to get back to him." Amado resisted her gentle pull until she jerked his arm forward.

"Come on, Freddie. This is not your turf. Behave. Don't make me call those security guards who can kick your *culo* into the next county." She stopped and watched him walk away, then called out, "Say hello to your mother, and leave that white coat where you found it."

Chapter 69

"I want a deputy posted outside his room twenty-four hours. That sonofabitch cost us more man hours than any other bastard in the past ten years," Rabino said to Amado who sat on the other side of Rabino's desk.

"He's not going anywhere," Amado said. "He's got a tube in his pecker and an IV in his arm, besides, he's too weak to..."

"Makes no difference," Rabino interrupted. "I want him under max security. That means no visitors. I want an hourly report...what he eats, when he sleeps, belches and farts, everything. By the way, what's with his wife?"

"Maria? The Mexican police finally located her. She should be arriving at the L.A. airport at 5:10 tonight with her kids. Do you want us to pick her up there?"

"Nah. She's not a suspect, but when she visits Gruenwald in the hospital, I want a deputy present. I don't want her slipping him a *pistola* concealed in a burrito."

"I'll be there. Mind if Miss Chavez, that is, Isabella, visits too?"

Rabino grimaced. "Why the hell do you constantly jazz up the rules? No visitors simply means no visitors, dammit." He looked out the window and gnawed the cigar stub in the corner of his mouth. He turned around. "All right, Casanova, but if she does anything to queer this case..."

"Thanks, Marv. I'll name my first-born son after you."

"Only if he's circumcised and observes the Sabbath."

"On second thought, maybe I won't."

Lobo sensed a generalized sadness as he trotted to accompany Amado to the door of the estate. In Lobo's world, the mistress of the house was unhappy and had only one arm with which to pet him. The chauffeur, his friend, and Maria who fed him, were both gone. Amado's familiar face was worthy of two throaty woofs. He accompanied Amado to the front door, then sat, swished his tail and watched with smiling anticipation as the lovers met and kissed.

At the door, Isabella placed her free arm around Amado's neck and cried. Amado reached for a handkerchief in his back pocket and dabbed her eyes. She took Amado's hand, pulled him inside toward the sofa.

"Oh, Fred, tell me this is all a nightmare and will disappear when I awaken." Even with eyes reddened and without makeup, Isabella's beauty was still stunning. Amado's hand brushed her hair, then he brought the back of his hand gently across her cheeks. He bent forward and kissed her lips lightly.

She shook her head and said, "My world has fallen apart. I'm so terribly sad—so unhappy. John was like a father to me. How could he have done...?"

"Try to understand, kitten, he still loves you as though you were his own daughter, a daughter snatched from him by a despicable monster. He fulfilled the needs of an aching heart when he wreaked a terrible vengeance on that animal. He inflicted punishment that was deserved and would never have been meted out if he hadn't acted." Amado held Isabella's hands and spoke gently. "When the laws couldn't be applied, he figured it was up to him to render justice as he saw fit."

Isabella nodded absently and said, "It all seems so unfair."

Amado continued, "This may sound pedantic, but Francis Bacon said that revenge is a kind of wild justice. I, for one, think he was right in this case. I can understand what Gruenwald did. Secretly, I admire him. Oh, I know what he did can't be condoned in a civilized society. But in the law of the jungle when one deals with wild beasts, what could be sweeter than tearing apart an evil enemy?... one that has robbed you of your loved ones?"

"Are you saying, John is a hero?"

"Look, sweetheart, you can argue all day about the cultural norms of a civilized society and sound clever, but remember, for all his trappings, man is still an animal. When he's stripped of his veneer of civility he reverts to his raw primal animal behavior." Amado knew he sounded preachy, but he felt the need to justify Grunewald's behavior to Isabella. "This kind of philosophical discussion could go on forever. I won't dwell on it longer, except to say that I think some vengeful acts might be justified."

"But Fred, we're taught that vengeance is the Lord's, alone."

"Yeah, well the Old Guy is too long in settling some scores."

"Would you defend John in a court of law?"

"I could attest to his character other than what he did to that priest. Of course, what he did to the priest is indefensible according to the law. Some clever defense lawyer might present a temporary insanity plea and get him off a Murder One charge, but what the hell's the use in guessing."

Amado, eager to change the subject, said, "Maria is coming in tonight from Mexico. I'm sure she'll want to go to the hospital to see Gruenwald."

"Does she know about John's confession?" Isabella asked.

"I'm sure she doesn't."

"Do you think I can go to the hospital with her, Fred?"

"Yeah, I cleared it with Rabino."

With a pleading look, Isabella peered into Amado's eyes. "When this is all settled, can we start making plans for our wedding?"

"As soon as the señora's murder is solved, we'll tie the knot, sail down to Baja, do some fishing—if I can stop loving you long enough—lie on the beach and drink tequila between episodes of lovemaking."

For the first time that evening, Isabella smiled. She

took her right arm out of the sling and brought her hands to Amado's face. With her eyes closed, she brought her open mouth to his. Their tongues met and played hungrily. Amado's hands reached her derriere and pressed her pelvis firmly against his.

"Better solve that murder soon, Amado. I'm thinking I'd like spending the whole day in bed with you."

"Would you like a trial run right now?"

"No thanks. Maria will be coming, and I...well I just wouldn't feel right."

"Hey, baby, I understand. I can hold off. It won't be easy, but I'll manage."

Isabella looked at her watch. "It's 6:55. Maria should be arriving soon. Excuse me, darling. I'm going upstairs to freshen up. Make yourself comfortable. Pour yourself a drink. There's a new issue of *Life* on the sofa. If Maria comes in before I finish, please send her up. I still have trouble holding my right hand up to do my hair."

Amado poured two fingers of Johnny Walker Black Label into a glass and added a drop of sparkling water. He mixed the drink with his finger, then took a long gulp. He removed his shoes and lay on the sofa with the issue of *Life*. His eyes grew heavy and the magazine fell across his chest.

The dog's barking, car doors slamming and children's yelling awakened him.

Maria emerged from the car and admonished the children to be quiet and go to their rooms. She ordered one of the caretakers to put the suitcases in her room, then stood in the driveway and looked up at the mansion before approaching the entrance.

Amado walked to the door and opened it just as Maria reached for the knob.

"Oh!" She put her hand to her mouth. "Detective Amado, I did not expect you. Quick, tell me about John. Is he going to be all right? When can I see him?"

"As soon as you settle in. We can take you there. Isabella

asked that you help her dress when you come in. Should I tell her you're here?"

"No, no, I will run upstairs and surprise her."

Amado, curious to watch the reunion, followed Maria up the winding staircase.

Maria ran into Isabella's room. Isabella was not there. Maria went toward the señora's room.

At the three-mirror dresser, Isabella sat in a sheer robe, brushing her hair as the señora had done three months before when she was murdered. Maria stopped at the door, looked at the figure brushing her hair. She screamed and collapsed.

Amado rushed to her side, picked her up and placed her on a settee.

Isabella rushed to Maria's side and grasped her cold hands. "Maria, are you all right? Talk to me."

Amado stood looking down at the ashen-faced Maria. Her eyelids fluttered, then opened, and she looked around, confused and frightened.

"What's the matter, Maria?" Amado asked. His voice had a flinty edge. "Overcome with *deja vu?* Did you think you were seeing the señora again?" He stared at her, then said, "That's right. The señora who you shot and killed?"

Maria closed her eyes, shook her head and sobbed with heaving shoulders, then held her head in her hands. "My soul has been tortured from the moment the señora died. I've cried every day and every night...perhaps not so much for the señora but for me and my family. I was fearful every time I saw you, Detective Amado. I suspected you knew. I worried about what would happen to my children and who would care for John?"

Amado glanced at Isabella and shook his head almost imperceptibly. He thought Maria's emotional condition too fragile to hear that her husband had already confessed to murdering the priest and would be held responsible in the deaths of the two Spanish hit men. He helped Maria stand and with Isabella's help guided her to a chair.

"Maria, why did you kill the señora?" Isabella, distraught and teary eyed said, "I thought your relationship with her was good. You never spoke ill of her."

In a voice barely above a whisper, Maria said, "I respected the señora until I found out she was forcing my husband to make love to her. I discovered that one night when John had a guilty look and his clothes smelled of her perfume. Her lipstick was on his collar, and once I found it on his shorts. When I confronted him, he did not—he could not deny his involvement. He swore he would have no more intimacies with her, and I believed him.

"Then one night he came home, and he was quiet like before when he was feeling guilty. We argued bitterly. I told him I would leave with the children if he did not stop. He said she forced him into having sex in the back of that old limousine. I became so mad, I confronted her that evening and told her I knew what she was doing with my husband. She laughed and said I was making too much of a small thing and that if I objected, she would throw John and me out along with the children. She angered me even more when she said John was in this country illegally, and she would report him.

"I went crazy. I ran to the colonel's den and took a gun out of the display case..." Maria's talking tapered off and her chin fell on her chest. She raised her head and started to talk again. "I don't even remember going back to her room, but as I got closer, I remember her saying, 'Is that you?' I cursed her, pulled the trigger and ran out of the room."

Amado said, "Did you tell John?"

"Yes, it was our secret. When I left with the children for Mexico, I thought I would never return. Word reached me about John's accident and his heart attack, and I thought I would die. I came back with the children as soon as I could."

"I'll have to take you in, Maria," Amado said.

The phone rang. Isabella picked it up and listened for a moment, then said, quietly, "Thank you." She slid the phone down her side slowly, then replaced it on the cradle. Her teary eyes looked at Maria, then at Amado and she began to cry openly.

"What is it, sweetheart?" Amado asked.

"That was the hospital. John died. Something about an embolus."

Maria collapsed into a chair and Isabella placed her right arm around Maria's shoulders and said, "I'm so sorry." Isabella leaned over, embraced Maria and both cried. Maria stood, dabbed her reddened, teary eyes and said. "I must say goodbye to the children—one last time."

"Sorry, that's against protocol," Amado said.

Isabella gave him a pleading look.

Amado looked at his watch. "Okay. Fifteen minutes, no more." He knew his decision was improper, but he couldn't resist Isabella's imploring look.

"Let me walk with you," Isabella said to Maria.

"No, no!" Maria touched Isabella's cheek, then kissed her. "Señorita, stay here with the detective. I will be fine. I want to be alone with the children."

Amado and Isabella watched as Maria walked down the staircase through the long living room, then out of sight.

"Fred, I should have gone with her. What will become of the children?"

"Don't worry. Maria has a large family in Santa Barbara. Placing the kids shouldn't be a problem. The problem will be with Maria. She's another case guilty of premeditated murder. A smart lawyer or a reasonable judge will see the depths of emotional conflict...we can only hope."

A popping sound interrupted the conversation. Amado sprung up. "Oh, jeezus!" He ran down the circular stairway, through the living room, the kitchen, then toward the servants' quarters. In the diminished light, he stumbled across something on the floor. It was Maria. A gun lay beside her. A bullet wound in the right temple. Her eyes staring in a lifeless face—a lifeless body and a small pool of blood at the exit wound on the left side of the head.

Isabella came running in, stopped suddenly at the sight of Maria's corpse. She bent over to look, to verify—to hope. "Oh, dear God," she moaned and collapsed into Amado's arms. He picked her up and placed her on a chair.

With a pained expression, Isabella looked up at Amado. "Fred, I've got to look in on the children."

"I'll go with you." Amado placed his arm around Isabella's waist. He opened the bedroom door, then whispered, "They're both sound asleep...slept right through the gunshot." Quietly, he closed the door.

Amado reached for the phone in the living room and called the deputy coroner's office, then Undersheriff Rabino's home.

"Marv, it's all over."

Epilogue

Amado and Isabella remained very much in love. They made their home on the Mesa in Santa Barbara overlooking the Pacific where they raised four children.

The old Montenegro mansion was donated to the county and converted to a museum for Spanish-American history.

The Amados' first child, Marvin Fernando was born seven months after the wedding, but he was in all respects a normal full-term newborn. The next three children were born after normal pregnancy periods. One daughter resembled Isabella with dark hair and turquoise eyes, the other was blonde and willowy like Amado's mother. The second male child, Alessandro, volunteered for the military and was killed in the Vietnam War. Both parents mourned his loss for the rest of their lives.

Fred Amado remained with the Santa Barbara Sheriff's Department for twenty-three years after his marriage and became the undersheriff when Marvin Rabino was forced to retire for health reasons.

Isabella assumed the role of *reina* in the Spanish-American community and headed the museum she donated to Montecito.

Marvin Fernando Amado, the elder son, at age forty-two became one of the youngest sheriffs of Santa Barbara County.

Undersheriff Rabino's son, Monte, became an art critic and taught in the fine arts department at UC Santa Barbara where he fell in love and married one of his students, Ariana

Amado, the dark-haired older daughter of the Amados.

Many of the paintings and art treasures in the Goleta warehouse and the Montecito mansion were sold; others were donated to the local museum. The proceeds of the sales were divided among the heirs of the Iberia-America Trading Co. and the heirs of the Montenegro estate.

About the Author

After serving in the Pacific Theatre during W.W.II as a field and hospital medic in the U.S. Army, Alvin J. Harris, M.D. F.A.C.S. graduated from the University of Illinois, College of Medicine. He completed an internship and residency in Orthopedic Surgery at the Cook County Hospital in Chicago, Illinois. There he instructed physicians as well as medical and nursing students in post-graduate courses.

 In Los Angeles, California, he served on the staff of the Children's Hospital, guiding residents in clinical and surgical techniques. While tending to his private practice, he served as chief of the orthopedic section at the Presbyterian Hospital in Van Nuys and the Holy Cross Hospital.

He practiced for twenty years in Washington State and founded the Sequim Orthopedic Center. As an expert witness, he has testified in cases of vehicular and industrial accidents, as well as physical abuse, and trauma.

When he isn't writing, Al attends lectures at the university or researches information for his novels. He occasionally squeezes in a game of golf or attends a concert with his wife Yetta.

Other Novels

Did you enjoy Farewell My Country? Be sure to pick up more A. J. Harris award winning novels at <u>amazon.com</u>.

Here's the direct link to all of the A. J. Harris novels: <u>amazon.com/author/ajharris</u>

Paperback and ebook formats are available.

A. J. is currently working on his seventh book.